Praise for the Dead-End Job mysteries
by Elaine Viets, winner of the Anthony Award and the
Agatha Award

"Elaine Viets is fabulous. I fell in love with her dead-on funny Dead-End Job mysteries, and so will you."
—Jerrilyn Farmer, author of *Desperately Seeking Sushi*

"Laugh-out-loud comedy with enough twists and turns to make it to the top of the mystery bestseller charts."
—*Florida Today*

"Fans of Janet Evanovich and Parnell Hall will appreciate Viets's humor." —*South Florida Sun-Sentinel*

"Elaine Viets knows how to turn minimum wage into maximum hilarity."
—Nancy Martin, author of *A Crazy Little Thing Called Death*

"Wit, murder, and sunshine . . . it must be Florida. I love this new series." —Nancy Pickard, author of *The Virgin of Small Plains*

"A heroine with a sense of humor and a gift for snappy dialogue." —Jane Heller, author of *Some Nerve*

"A stubborn and intelligent heroine, a wonderful South Florida setting, and a cast of more-or-less lethal bimbos. . . . I loved this book."
—Charlaine Harris, author of *Definitely Dead* and *Grave Surprise*

"Fresh, funny, and fiendishly constructed."
—Parnell Hall, author of The Puzzle Lady Mysteries

Murder Unleashed

A DEAD-END JOB MYSTERY

Elaine Viets

A SIGNET BOOK

SIGNET
Published by New American Library, a division of
Penguin Group (USA) Inc., 375 Hudson Street,
New York, New York 10014, USA
Penguin Group (Canada), 90 Eglinton Avenue East, Suite 700, Toronto,
Ontario M4P 2Y3, Canada (a division of Pearson Penguin Canada Inc.)
Penguin Books Ltd., 80 Strand, London WC2R 0RL, England
Penguin Ireland, 25 St. Stephen's Green, Dublin 2,
Ireland (a division of Penguin Books Ltd.)
Penguin Group (Australia), 250 Camberwell Road, Camberwell, Victoria 3124,
Australia (a division of Pearson Australia Group Pty. Ltd.)
Penguin Books India Pvt. Ltd., 11 Community Centre, Panchsheel Park,
New Delhi - 110 017, India
Penguin Group (NZ), 67 Apollo Drive, Rosedale, North Shore 0632,
New Zealand (a division of Pearson New Zealand Ltd.)
Penguin Books (South Africa) (Pty.) Ltd., 24 Sturdee Avenue,
Rosebank, Johannesburg 2196, South Africa

Penguin Books Ltd., Registered Offices:
80 Strand, London WC2R 0RL, England

Published by Signet, an imprint of New American Library, a division of Penguin
Group (USA) Inc. Previously published in a New American Library hardcover
edition.

First Signet Printing, May 2007
10 9 8 7 6 5 4

For my Pup

ACKNOWLEDGMENTS

I want to thank the Bone Appetít Dog Boutique and Posh Paws Grooming Salon in Fort Lauderdale. Keith Starling and Mark Tews were patient with my endless questions. Davi Souza makes the best doggie bone birthday cakes in South Florida.

But this is a work of fiction. The groomers Jonathon and Todd are figments of my imagination, along with Lucinda, Betty, and all the other customers in my novel. The real customers of Bone Appetít are law-abiding citizens and true animal lovers.

Only Lulu the dog is real. She is the store's supermodel. She has a bigger wardrobe than I do, she gets more massages and manicures, and men adore her big brown eyes. She also runs off to the Briny Irish Pub for seasoned fries and bacon cheeseburgers. For this novel, I've moved the Briny (now called The Wayward Sailor) from its real location at Oakland Park Boulevard and Federal Highway to Helen's neighborhood. That's the magic of fiction. I can move a whole bar and restaurant with the flick of a pen.

It takes more than a year to write and produce a novel. During that time, South Florida was slammed with some eight hurricanes, and I was without power for weeks. The hurricane depicted in this book is a minor one. I was able to work in the aftermath of the ferocious

Katrina and Wilma with help from my friends. Thanks to mystery author Barbara "Suspicion of Rage" Parker, who generously let me write at her home when my electricity was out. I'm grateful to Sibling's Coffee and Tea Store, who plied me with Dragon Well tea and sandwiches, and to Phyllis Littmann, who overnighted a big box of delicacies so I didn't have to live on those hurricane staples, canned tuna and peanut butter. I couldn't have made my deadlines without you.

This is my first hardcover mystery. Lots of bookstores helped take my series to the next step. I owe special thanks to Joanne Sinchuk, John Spera and the booksellers at Murder on the Beach, Mary Alice Gorman and Richard Goldman at Mystery Lovers Bookshop, Barbara Peters at Poisoned Pen, and Bonnie Claeson and Joe Guglielmelli at Black Orchid. My former boss at the Hollywood Barnes & Noble, Pam Marshall, has been a big supporter, and so has Susan Boyd in Plantation and Helen LaForge in Fort Lauderdale. Thanks also to Kim, Jamey, Jim, and the gang at Waldenbooks in Pompano Beach. Last but not least, there's Carole Wantz at the Barnes & Noble in Ladue, Missouri, who can sell tofu burgers at a cattlemen's convention. I know I've left many other names off this list, but I'd need another book to list you all.

Once again, I want to thank my husband, Don Crinklaw, who believes for better or worse includes answering questions about subjunctive clauses.

Thanks to my agent, David Hendin, who always has an answer.

Special thanks to Kara Cesare, who takes time she doesn't have to edit my books, and to her assistant, Rose Hilliard, and to the Signet copy editor and production staff.

Many people helped with this book. I hope I didn't leave anyone out.

Particular thanks to Detective RC White, Fort Lauderdale Police Department (retired), to Rick McMahan, ATF Special Agent, and to Anthony-award winning author and former police detective Robin Burcell. Any mistakes are mine, not theirs.

Thanks also to Susan Carlson, Valerie Cannata, Colby Cox, Jinny Gender, Karen Grace, Kay Gordy, Jack Klobnak, and Janet Smith. Bob Levine literally gave me the coat off his back when I was researching on a cold October day.

A tip of the hat to the librarians at the Broward County Library and the St. Louis Public Library who researched my questions. You can find a lot of information on the Internet, but only a good librarian knows if it is valid.

Special thanks to Librarian Anne Watts, who let me borrow her six-toed cat, Thumbs, for this series. Check out his picture on my Web site at www.elaineviets.com.

CHAPTER 1

"I want this party to be perfect," Tammie Grimsby said. "But I can't take any stress. No stress at all."

Oh, brother, Helen Hawthorne thought. The only stress in this woman's life was on her spandex.

Tammie's teeny white shorts showed the divide in her peachlike posterior. Her sports bra revealed considerable cleavage. Tammie's stupendous diaphragm development produced a disappointing little-girl voice. The effect was outrageously, ridiculously sexy.

Why do I always get the weird customers? Helen wondered. But she knew the answer to that question. She was working in a weird business.

"This is a birthday party, right?" Helen said. She took the party orders at Jeff and Ray's shop.

"For twenty guests." Tammie sighed, and her implants heaved like ships in a storm-tossed sea. "My little boy must be the star."

"What about a birthday cake?" Helen said. "Customers love our peanut-butter cakes."

"Peanut butter makes my baby boy sick," Tammie said.

"How about a nice garlic-chicken cake with yogurt icing?" Helen said.

"No cake, period," Tammie said. "With twenty guests, there will be fights. Besides, they're all on diets. I don't know why I did this to myself. It's too much stress."

Tammie had invited twenty tiny dogs to her Yorkie's birthday party. Helen guessed they would all be white fluff muffins, except the birthday boy. Malteses, bichon frises, and shih tzus, all yipping, yapping, sniffing, and shedding. Dust-mop dogs. The whole party wouldn't weigh as much as the well-toned Tammie.

Helen repeated the party line. "The Barker Brothers Pampered Pet Boutique in Fort Lauderdale prides itself on perfect pet parties," she said solemnly. "Your Prince will have the best birthday money can buy." If I can get his airhead owner to concentrate long enough, she thought.

Prince sat regally in the crook of Tammie's arm. The Yorkie had the calculating eyes of a con artist.

"My itty-bitty baby eats only the finest filet. I have to hand-feed him," Tammie said.

Right, Helen thought. I'd live on filet, too, if I could get away with it. On her pay, she was lucky she could afford hamburger.

The beady-eyed Yorkie stared at Helen, as if daring her to disagree. She didn't begrudge the dog its soft life. Prince paid a high price for his filet. Helen saw the intelligence in the dark eyes, and felt oddly sorry for the little Yorkie. Prince could manipulate the addlepated Tammie, but he knew he was stuck with her. Helen was glad Prince was a five-pound dog. If he had two legs, the Yorkie could run a drug ring—or the country.

Tammie picked up the little dog, kissed his nose, and baby-talked, "You're a particular puppy, aren't you? Oh, yes, you are."

At twenty, fluffy blond Tammie must have been endearing. At forty she was annoying. Rather like some of the Pampered Pet's pampered pets, Helen thought sadly. Cute didn't always age well.

"Those birthday cakes are ugly. Can't you do something more artistic?" Tammie said.

Helen didn't know how to answer her question. The cakes were bone-shaped, iced in white, and decorated with sugar roses. Could you make a sugared bone more artistic?

Helen needed the shop diplomat. She signaled Jeff,

one of the owners. Jeffrey Tennyson Barker looked like an elegant pedigreed pet himself, with his long nose, sensitive spaniel eyes, and thick brown hair.

The Pampered Pet was his baby. Jeff took a touching delight in his upscale boutique. He fussed endlessly over its racks of dresses and fake furs, jewelry showcases, and the glass cases of bonbons on lace doilies, all for dogs. The store also had a salon for grooming canine hair and nails. Jeff loved pleasing customers, even the impossible ones like Tammie.

"If you don't want a cake, may I suggest our doggie bags?" Jeff said.

He pulled out a small bag dotted with black paw prints. "We fill it with treats for your guests. Each treat is beautifully prepared."

They were, too. The display case's pastel bonbons were delicately iced and decorated. They were all canine treats: doggie doughnuts, Barkin-Robbins ice-cream cones, lady paws, and pupcakes—miniature cupcakes with sprinkles. Each doggie delicacy ran between one and three bucks.

"We'll put together a tasteful bag for your guests," Jeff said. "I'll have some doggie treats from the bin for flavor and others from the glass case for color."

Jeff lifted the lid on the bulk bin and picked out a cheese-and-bacon treat. His dog, Lulu, a beagle-dachshund mix, shot out of the back room like a guided missile. Her supersonic hearing could detect the opening of the bulk bin, although Helen's ears caught no sound. Lulu stared at Jeff with soulful, slightly popped eyes. She adored cheese and bacon.

Tammie looked at the plain brown treat doubtfully. It seemed homely after the dainty dog bonbons frosted in organic icing.

"My Prince won't eat that. He's too picky," Tammie said.

She set the Yorkie on the floor, reached into the bulk bin, and pelted him with cheese-and-bacon treats. Prince jumped back, surprised and confused. Lulu scarfed up the treats before the Yorkie could recover.

"See? He's picky," Tammie said.

Prince found a bit of turkey jerky Lulu had left on the floor and gnawed it happily.

"He seems to like that," Helen said, pointing to the double-dog-slobbered jerky.

But Tammie was pawing through the racks of dog clothes. "I need a special outfit for my doggie on his day. Ooooh, this is perfect."

She pulled out a blue sweatshirt embroidered with PRINCE. It had a matching bandanna with a silver crown. Tammie shoved the dog's head and front paws into the shirt. The outfit hung on him.

"Ooh. It's too big." Tammie stuck out her lower lip in a pout. She also stuck out her chest, giving Helen a look at more cleavage.

"It will have to be tailored," Jeff said.

"I can take it to Evie, the seamstress," she said. "The party's this evening, but if I pay extra, she'll fix it. But that's sooo stressful."

"How about a nice red shirt with 'Happy Birthday'?" Helen said.

That shirt was a better fit, but Tammie wasn't happy. "That color does nothing for his hair."

"A leather Harley vest?" Helen said.

"Too hot," Tammie said. "The blue will photograph best. Evie will just have to tailor it. The people at our country club are so snobby. They always ask, 'What are you wearing? Where did you buy that?' I don't care about those things. I just put this on." She indicated her exercise outfit with a flourish, like Vanna picking a letter. "I'm a very simple person."

"I can see," Helen said.

Jeff shot Helen a warning look. Tammie bent over to fish her cell phone out of her purse, and gave Helen another unwanted peek into her silicone valley. Tammie arranged an emergency tailoring session while Jeff rang up two hundred dollars' worth of treats for the dog's birthday.

"You'll decorate the doggie bags?" Tammie said when she snapped her phone shut.

"Certainly," Jeff said. "We'll put colored ribbons on the

bags. Does your party have a theme color, such as red or blue? Or would you prefer a rainbow assortment?"

"No rainbow," Tammie said. "I don't want anyone to think my dog is gay."

"My dog is a diesel dyke," Jeff said sweetly.

Lulu stared at him. The Yorkie piddled on the floor. Helen wiped it up.

"My Princey needs his hair done for the party," Tammie said. "How can I have him groomed if we have to go to the seamstress? I want this party perfect, but I can't take the stress. I just can't."

"We have a delivery service," Jeff said. "We can pick up your dog or take him home, or both. Do you want to leave him with us now for grooming? Helen will bring him back to your home for a small fee."

Actually, it was a stupendous fee. But the customers didn't seem to mind.

"No, silly, he has a fitting at the seamstress's, remember? It's ten o'clock now. Can your girl pick him up at noon? He has to be back home by four. The party is at six, and Prince needs a nap before his big night."

Jeff checked the date book. "No problem. Jonathon can take Prince."

Jeff pronounced the name with awe. Jonathon was the *prima donna assoluta* of the Lauderdale grooming world. He was famous for his towering rages, which made him suddenly pack up his case of supersharp scissors and move to yet another grooming salon. He'd been at Barker Brothers for six weeks now, and Jeff gloried in the groomer's full date book.

"Good," Tammie said. "I'll just go back and meet the groomer."

"No!" Panic smothered Jeff's pride. "Jonathon hates visitors." The star's contract guaranteed him no personal contact with salon customers, and he'd quit other grooming shops when it had been violated.

But Tammie the gym rat easily outdistanced the sedentary Jeff. There was a shriek and a yelp from the grooming room, followed by an anguished cry: "I am an artist. I cannot work like this."

His precious Jonathon was in distress. Jeff sped to his rescue. "Coming!" he shouted. Helen followed.

The star was majestic in his outrage—and his outfit. He wore a flaring royal-purple satin disco suit.

"Get this bitch out of here," Jonathon said. The gold medallion at his neck quivered with rage.

"Don't you dare call him that. Prince is an un-neutered male," Tammie screamed.

"I wasn't talking about the dog," Jonathon said. His face was an unfortunate puce, which clashed with his purple suit.

Jonathon's vintage seventies suit was outshone by his magnificent mane, streaked seven shades of blond. It was the envy of any woman who entered a beauty salon. Helen had never seen a hint of dark roots. She suspected Jonathon did his own hair at home with a complicated system of mirrors. Helen had no idea when Jonathon had the time. His own body rivaled Tammie's for gym-produced perfection. He had a cleft chin, a chiseled Roman nose, and the tiniest feet Helen had ever seen on a six-foot man. That was probably why his purple platform shoes didn't look like concrete blocks.

"You called me a . . . a . . ." Tammie's teeny brain balked at the enormity of the insult.

"Please," Jeff said. "It's an honor to have your dog done by Jonathon."

"Is it an honor to be insulted by that fruit?" she said.

"Every great artist has temperament," Jeff soothed. "Everyone at your party will recognize a Jonathon cut."

That did it. Tammie craved Jonathon's cachet. She swallowed the insult. Jonathon's complexion lapsed into a light lavender. The crisis was averted.

Todd, another groomer, came running out of the grooming room. In his simple jeans and T-shirt, he looked like a peasant boy next to the princely Jonathon. The effect was deceptively innocent.

"Tammie," Todd said, "I'm so sorry he said those things to you. Are you OK?"

"I'm fine," Tammie said, her voice saccharine sweet. "I know what he is, just like I know what you are. Dare

I say it in front of everyone? You're looking in the pink." She laughed. "And how are your dear parents? Mummy still famous for her entertaining in Okee-chobee? Daddy still in silver trading?"

Todd looked stung.

Jeff stepped between them. He gave Todd a diplomatic shove back into the grooming room, then gently guided Tammie and Prince toward the door. "Helen will stop by your home at noon to pick up Prince," he said.

"Tammie, where the hell are you?" A hulking figure darkened the grooming salon doorway. Helen couldn't make out the face, but the guy was built like Shrek. Too bad he wasn't as nice as the ogre.

"What's taking you so long?" he said. "Quit standing around yapping. You're worse than that damned dog."

"Coming, Kent, sweetie," she said. She scuttled out the door, Prince clutched protectively in her arms.

Jeff looked relieved. Helen wondered how long the ogre had been there, listening to Tammie and Jonathon scream at each other.

The boutique's bell rang.

"Helen, would you get that customer, please, while I talk to Jonathon?" Jeff said.

Two more birthday cakes and ten pounds of treats later, it was time to pick up Prince. Tammie and her husband, Kent Grimsby, lived about ten minutes from the Pampered Pet. Helen drove the shop's hot pink Cadillac, a florid gas guzzler from the seventies known as the Pupmobile. She didn't like pet pickups. The car was as long as a hook-and-ladder truck. Helen was driving with a fake license in another name. She was on the run from her ex and the court in St. Louis and had to stay out of government computers. Driving with a fake license in a huge hot-pink car in the crazed Florida traffic was no way to keep a low profile.

But she couldn't tell Jeff what was wrong. Instead, Helen drove as slowly as a seventy-year-old. The car felt unnatural at this funereal pace. Outraged SUVs honked and roared around her as she steered the house-sized pink Pupmobile down U.S. 1.

How did I ever get reduced to this? Helen thought.

But she knew the answer. Two years ago she'd been living in a St. Louis suburb, making six figures a year. She'd had a proper corporate job, a tasteful business wardrobe, and a silver Lexus. Helen worked long hours as the director of pensions and benefits. She had an expensively decorated minimansion in the right suburb, although she was hardly ever home to enjoy it.

Then she'd come home from work early and found her husband sleeping with their next-door neighbor, Sandy.

No, that was the problem. They weren't sleeping. They were on the back deck having the kind of acrobatic sex Helen had only dreamed about. Helen picked up a crowbar and started swinging. Those impulsive swings unleashed another, wilder woman, one who would never meekly carry a briefcase. Now Helen was on the run in South Florida, working cash-under-the-table jobs to stay out of the computers.

She pulled the Pupmobile up to the kiosk at the Stately Palms Country Club. The ancient white-haired guard napping inside didn't notice its long, lurid form. Helen tapped lightly on the horn, and the guard waved the Pupmobile through. She wondered why he was there. The old guy wasn't even ornamental.

The Grimsby mansion looked like a convention center constructed on cost overruns. Helen expected a marquee in the yard to say, APPEARING THIS WEEK . . .

She parked the Caddy in the circular drive and rang the doorbell. No one answered. Hmm. Must be out of order.

Helen knocked hard on the dark polished front door. It swung open.

Odd. Usually a maid or housekeeper did door duty in the posh homes. Some even had British butlers.

"Hello?" Helen stepped into the entrance hall. "Anyone home?"

The double living room was decorated like a Palm Beach funeral parlor. Huge gold mirrors reflected tapestries, taupe fabrics, tassels, and fringe. The gloomy urns could hold several loved ones.

The house was designed to show off the Grimsby dough. Helen could not imagine the owners really living in the place. She couldn't see Tammie eating popcorn and watching a movie, or Kent the ogre drinking a beer and barbecuing in the backyard. Did megamillionaires drink beer and watch movies?

"Hello?" Helen said, and tiptoed through the living room. Now she was in a dining room that seated twenty. The table looked like a mahogany runway. The candelabra could have lit up a castle. Over the sideboard was a painting of Tammie in evening dress. She looked like a nineteenth-century robber baron's wife. The painting was signed with a flourish—*Rax*.

"Hello?" A little louder this time. The last thing Helen wanted was to be arrested for breaking and entering.

The breakfast room was next. Helen was sure she'd seen it in an old *Architectural Digest*. She wondered what you ate for breakfast in a room liked this: a soufflé of nightingale tongues? Shirred eggs and lamb kidneys? Oats rolled on the thighs of Scottish virgins?

Helen grew more uneasy as she went through a country kitchen the size of a French province. The video room was bigger than the local multiplex.

"Anyone here?" The silence was unnatural. Did she have the right time?

Helen checked her watch. It was twelve-oh-two. Tammie may have acted like an airhead, but that party was important to her. She wouldn't forget Prince's noon hair appointment.

Maybe Tammie was taking a nap, recovering from the stress of party planning. Helen wandered through a labyrinth of halls hung with murky British landscapes until she found the master bedroom. The canopy bed looked like it slept six starlets. The miniature canopy bed next to it could hold one Yorkie. Both were empty. So was the master bath. The white terry robe on the door belonged in a hotel.

"Tammie? Prince?" she called. No one answered.

Now Helen was seriously worried. She eyed the bedroom phone. Maybe she should call Jeff. Maybe she should call 911. No, she couldn't bring in the police. They'd ask awkward questions.

Helen kept searching for signs of life.

The French doors in the master bedroom opened onto the pool, which was slightly smaller than Lake Okeechobee. Gaily striped awnings—no, wait, Tammie would never have anything gay—sheltered umbrella tables and teak lounges. Under a vast umbrella, Helen saw two tanned legs on a teak lounge, spread wide and unmoving. The toenails were bloodred.

The hair went up on the back of Helen's neck. "Tammie?" she said.

Her heart slammed against her ribs. Helen felt dizzy. She'd stumbled on a dead body before. She never wanted to see one again. Please, she prayed. Please let Tammie be OK. What if the woman had had a stroke or a heart attack? It happened to perfectly healthy granola chompers.

Helen looked at the splayed legs and winced. What if something worse had happened?

It wasn't natural for a woman to be so still. A fly crawled up one brown leg toward the knee. No manicured hand reached out to shoo it away.

Helen had to see the rest of the body, but she was too afraid to move.

"Tammie, please say you're OK," she begged.

No answer.

Helen unfroze one leg, then the other. She moved carefully around the umbrella table, alert for blood spatters or signs of a struggle. No furniture was broken or overturned, but the waxed legs on the lounge had a lifeless, rubbery look. The two tall glasses by the chaise were unbroken.

Then Helen saw the rest of the body and gave a little shriek.

"Oh, don't be such a prude," Tammie Grimsby said. "Haven't you ever seen a naked woman before?"

CHAPTER 2

Tammie Grimsby, lying in a sun- and alcohol-soaked stupor, didn't apologize for her nudity. She wouldn't deprive the world of a body like hers. Helen admitted it was imposing, but she wished Tammie would throw a towel over her nakedness.

"There's nothing wrong with sunbathing in your own backyard," Tammie said. She yawned and stretched until her massive mammaries arched upward. The big nipples were dark brown.

Is she coming on to me? Helen wondered. She wasn't sure. Tammie might be naked because she wanted to seduce Helen. But her natural state could also be contempt. Tammie simply couldn't bother dressing for a servant.

That was the problem with a dead-end job: Helen had no protection. She couldn't complain. It was her word against Tammie's, and the Yorkie's owner could say Helen made a pass at her. Her boss, Jeff, was a good guy, but Tammie had spent a lot of money at his store. Helen might find herself out of work.

"Most people wear clothes when I pick up their dogs," Helen said.

"I'm not most people," Tammie said, and stretched again.

Helen studied the sun umbrella and tried to look

bored. The woman was disturbingly sexual. In her work-out clothes she'd looked like an aging trophy wife. But stretched out on the chaise she was a lushly curved nude, an old master's model. Helen wanted out of there.

"I can't have tan lines." Tammie's voice was languid and slightly slurred. Helen caught the sweet, bitter whiff of alcohol.

"Does she have a body, or what?" The braying voice bounced off the pool deck. Kent Grimsby was ten years older and a foot shorter than his wife. He had the rolling walk of the overmuscled male. His arms were gnarly with muscle. His neck was thick as a palm tree trunk. Helen suspected he hit the steroids. This was the first time she had a clear view of the ogre's face. His nose, chin, and cheeks were thick lumps, shaded by black hairy eyebrows

Kent wasn't naked, but Helen thought nudity might be less obscene than his unlined Speedo. His equipment wobbled as he walked, reminding Helen of a rubber dog toy. She wondered if it would squeak if she squeezed it. She wondered if she could wash her mind out with soap.

"I tell her, with a body like that, you got nothing to be ashamed of," Kent said. "It's natural to go around with no clothes. You're born naked and you die that way." Wobble. Wobble. Kent and his rubber toy were getting too close for Helen's comfort.

"But in between, my mother told me to cover up," Helen said.

"Another waste," Kent said. "You look like you got a good body yourself. Nice high, pointy—"

"I've got to go," Helen interrupted.

Tammie thought so, too. She was still in the same languid pose, but her eyes were alert and hard. She didn't like Kent praising any body but hers.

"Me, too," Kent said. "I'm spending the afternoon test-driving Porsches. Vroooom. Vrooooom." He made car noises like a six-year-old. Wobble. Wobble. Helen didn't want to look at his stick shift.

Tammie wiggled her painted toes and waved a hand

vaguely toward the pool. "Prince is over there. Take him. This day has had too much stress. I need to relax."

Helen picked up the dog, who was docile and drowsy from the sun. "Does he have a pet carrier?" she said.

"Never!" Tammie said. "Prince has never been in a carrier."

First time for everything, Prince, old pal, Helen thought. She wasn't letting a dog loose in the Cadillac. Prince would head straight under the gas pedal. Helen kept a soft-sided carrier in the car.

"I'll make sure Prince is back by four," she said.

Tammie closed her eyes. Dismissed.

Helen hurried out, glad to be gone. She opened the hot-pink car door and plopped Prince in the carrier on the front seat. The little dog whined. She gave him a turkey jerky treat, and he slurped it quietly the rest of the trip.

Helen delivered Prince to the king of the groomers and went back to waiting on boutique customers.

That afternoon she sold a smuggling purse to Mrs. Delvecchio. The little widow wanted to sneak Samantha, her teacup poodle, into her high-rise apartment. The Pampered Pet was near the Galt Ocean Mile, a stretch of beach that looked like Manhattan with palm trees. Like Manhattan, its high-rises were thick with rich widows and divorcées.

When Helen saw the tiny woman in tailored black, she recited the New Yorker's prayer: "Oh, Lord, don't let me become a little woman with a little dog in a big high-rise."

Many high-rises banned pets. Cats were easy to hide, but a whole industry arose to help these women sneak in their dogs. Designer smuggling purses had special mesh airholes to safely conceal little dogs in their depths. Puppy training pads served the dogs' basic needs. Some animals never saw sunlight except when they went to the vet or the groomer.

"What do you do if your dog barks in the elevator?" Helen said, as she wrapped up the three-hundred-dollar doggie bag for Mrs. Delvecchio.

"I have a bad cough." The little widow made a horrible hacking noise.

"Clever," Helen said.

"Also, I tip the doorman well at Christmas. He knows to keep his mouth shut. Nobody comes between me and Samantha."

One look at the small, fierce woman and Helen could believe the stories that she'd helped the late Mr. Delvecchio make his money. He'd died of lead poisoning in a New Jersey clam house. Somebody put six bullets in his back.

A small, freckled woman stood shyly at the counter, waiting for Helen to finish with Mrs. Delvecchio. "I'm here to pick up my dog," she said. She was drab as a sparrow, except for her bright brown eyes.

"Mrs. Harrow," Helen said. "You have the little white shih tzu, Alexa."

"That's right. I'll pay now, before you get her. Was she good for Toddie?"

"Yes," Helen said. Actually, the spoiled Alexa yipped for three solid hours, but the salon always said the dogs were well behaved.

Helen raised her eyebrows when she saw the size of Todd's tip on Mrs. Harrow's credit-card slip. The handsome young groomer had made another conquest. Helen wondered how long it would be before the newly divorced Mrs. Harrow brought him blue Tiffany boxes wrapped in white ribbons.

Helen carried out the freshly groomed shih tzu, which smelled of flea shampoo and coconut cream rinse. Alexa quivered with joy when she was reunited with her owner. Dog and owner made small, excited cries.

They were barely out the door when Jonathon gave a howl of anguish. "I can't work with this moron. I can't take the distractions."

Helen and Jeff ran to the salon side. Jonathon had Todd, the other groomer, backed against the wall. Jonathon's ten-inch ice-tempered stainless-steel scissors were at Todd's throat. Todd was pale as Pottery Barn bedding.

"Is something wrong?" Jeff said mildly.

Helen nearly choked at his understatement.

"He kisses dogs," Jonathon said, twisting the scissors at Todd's neck. The pinioned groomer winced, but there was no blood on his tender skin.

"This raging idiot makes movements to deliberately distract me," Jonathon said, flinging his blond hair like a whip. "I am working on Toto. He knows she's skittish. I never drug my dogs, never. But I cannot have distractions. I need a private room. I must be away from this dog kisser."

"Of course I kiss Bruiser," Todd said. His voice came out a gargle with the scissors at his throat. He pointed to a chihuahua shivering on a grooming table. "I love her. Bruiser kisses me back."

The little dog licked Todd's hand on cue. "The hair dryer scares Bruiser. It's so noisy. I try to make her feel better by loving her."

"He's a dunce," Jonathon said, waving his scissors in the air.

Todd scooted out of range and stood behind Jeff, rubbing his neck. Both Helen and Jeff relaxed now that the razor-sharp blades were away from Todd's throat.

"I do not kiss dogs," Jonathon said. "I don't have to. They feel my power and hold still. They know I am in command. He is not master of his dogs. He uses short scissors."

It was the ultimate insult. Short scissors were for cutting human hair. Dog groomers used long scissors. In true male fashion, they measured themselves by the length. Jonathon went for ten inches of cold steel.

"Bruiser is a little dog," Todd said. He was twenty years younger than Jonathon and much prettier, with his smooth, unshaven skin and honey-blond hair. Both sexes drooled over the way Todd filled his white T-shirt and black jeans. Helen thought Jonathon was jealous of Todd's young good looks.

But Todd had good reason to resent Jonathon. Before the flamboyant star appeared on the scene, Todd had been the popular groomer at the Pampered Pet. Women loved to give him presents. A diamond-studded Cartier tank watch sparkled on his wrist. In his pocket was a gold cigarette case and a platinum lighter. Helen suspected Todd's women did not rely solely on their little doggies for companionship, but the groomer's social life was none of her business.

"I'll get the cage room ready," Jeff said. "Todd can work there."

"It's hot in there," Todd whined.

"I'll set up an extra fan," Jeff said.

"I will be back when my room is ready," Jonathon said. His rage was nearly as magnificent as his clothes. He stalked toward the door. Helen stepped out of his way. She respected Jonathon's skill with the scissors and the animals, but when he was in an operatic mood, she avoided him.

"Wait! You can't go, Jonathon. You have to groom Barkley," Jeff said. His brown spaniel eyes were pleading. "Barkley is coming at two. She needs you."

Barkley Barclay was the most valuable pup in Fort Lauderdale. The six-month-old chocolate labradoodle was part Labrador, part poodle, and all charm. She was the mascot of the nationwide Davis Family Dollar department stores, whose slogan was, "We Don't Doodle on Our Deals."

Labradoodles were "pedigreed" mutts. They were as cuddly as stuffed toys, with button eyes and curly hair. This one was owned by Francis Mortmain Barclay and Willoughby Barclay. Francis Mortmain was a CPA, about as colorful as a ream of typing paper. His wife, Willoughby, worked part-time at a boutique. Most of her paycheck went straight back to the store. She was addicted to cute things.

When people saw her drab spouse, they wondered why she married him. Francis wasn't cute. Willoughby had wanted a good provider. Francis could afford to buy her cute cars and tennis bracelets.

Willoughby, who knew how to accessorize, bought the pup because Barkley would look cute in the family Christmas-card photo. It was the smartest thing she ever did. She sent that photo in to the Davis department stores mascot search. Barkley beat more than ten thousand canine contenders.

Once the Davis department stores signed up the pup, both Barclays quit their jobs. Their dog made more money than both of them. Willoughby spent her share of the signing bonus on a mondo mansion that was cute as a sledgehammer. Willoughby wanted to hit everyone with her success.

The care of the profitable pup had assumed magical proportions. The Barclays believed only Jonathon could groom their dog. Each curly hair on her winsome body had to be washed and clipped by the master once a week.

"Jonathon, only you can groom that dog," Jeff said.

Helen sneaked a look at Todd to see how he took that slap. He had a fetching James Dean pout.

Jonathon flung his long hair about like a diva's cape. "All the more reason for me to have my own room. I will return when I can work without distraction," he said. "You have my cell phone. Call me after you take out the trash."

He shot Todd a venomous look and slammed the door.

CHAPTER 3

·······································

"**W**ho the hell was that?"
The woman in the door of the grooming salon was thin and tanned. She looked wonderfully normal in chinos and a pink polo shirt. A fat, friendly bichon waddled along beside her.

"That's Jonathon, our salon star," Helen said.

"I am lucky. I've finally seen the Howard Hughes of groomers," the woman said. "I'll be the talk of the country club now that I've seen him and his Technicolor rages. You sure he's not wanted for murder in Arizona?"

"Positive," Helen said. But she wasn't. She saw the way Jonathon had those scissors at Todd's throat. She tried a clumsy change of subject. "What country club do you belong to?"

"Most of them. But I do my serious golfing at Stately Palms."

"That's where Tammie Grimsby lives," Helen said. "She's giving a big party for her Yorkie."

"Tammie knows all about going to the dogs," the woman said. There was acid in her voice. "I've never seen anyone go so far on implants and raw nerve."

The word "raw" conjured up a perfect picture of the naked Tammie. Helen involuntarily moved her hand, as if brushing it away.

"She hit on you yet?" the woman said. "She and her

husband are swingers. Don't answer that. You don't
even know me. My name's Betty Reichs-Martin. You'll
see me in here a lot. Today I need a bag of food for Barney. And a pound of peanut-butter treats." Her voice
grew huskier. "I'm afraid the old boy isn't long for this
world. Might as well enjoy himself."

"Oh, I'm sorry," Helen said. She was, too. Betty would
seem incomplete without her dog.

"That's life," Betty said, and shrugged. "I can say that
now. When I have to take Barney to the vet to put him
down, I'll be a basket case."

Helen thought of her own cat, Thumbs, a six-toed
beauty with golden eyes. Would she have the courage to
do the kind thing if the time came? She hoped so, but
she didn't want to think about it.

"Hi, there, Lulu," Betty said, as the store's dog came
over to greet her. "Don't you look pretty?" Lulu was
working the room, modeling a yellow sundress and
matching yellow-painted nails.

"That dog gets more manicures than I do," Helen said.

Jeff came rushing out of the back room. "Betty!" he
said, and air-kissed her in a way that let Helen know the
woman was important.

"Betty is very generous to our favorite animal charities," Jeff oozed, "but she's not afraid to get her hands
dirty. She also cleans out the cages at the animal shelter
every Friday."

"I know how to shovel the shit," Betty said, with a
raucous laugh.

Todd came out of the grooming room. "I hate that
fan. It's too noisy," he said, like a spoiled child.

"I'll buy you a new one." Jeff sounded desperate.
"Helen, take special care of Betty for me while I get
Todd settled." He steered Todd back inside the grooming room. Helen could hear Jeff pleading over the barking dogs. "Please, Todd, just work the cage room for a
few days until Jonathon cools off."

"Do you have this dog bed in red corduroy?" Betty
asked.

"Let me check in the back," Helen said.

The dog beds were on the upper shelves, naturally. Helen was standing on a ladder in the back of the stockroom when she realized she wasn't alone. Todd had slipped in. He was by the door, with his back to her, punching in numbers on his cell phone. Helen froze. Should she tell him she was here? But Todd was talking on the phone. She couldn't hear what he was saying, but she didn't want to interrupt. Then Todd raised his voice. It had a hard, nasty edge Helen had never heard before.

"Listen," Todd said. "I don't care how you get the money, but I want it." He paused, but the air was electric with his silent anger. "That's your problem, not mine." Todd snapped his cell phone shut. He stomped out of the stockroom. Helen was relieved he hadn't seen her.

Well, well, Helen thought. Pretty Todd could be quite ugly. Did someone owe him money? Or was he shaking down one of the women who gave him those expensive presents? Or one of the men? It wasn't any of Helen's business. She shoved the dog beds back on the shelf and went out front to Betty.

"Sorry," Helen said. "Nothing in red."

Betty added the brown corduroy bed to her other purchases. Helen rang them up and helped her carry them out to the car. Barney the bichon wheezed along beside them. The parking lot was a long walk for his short legs.

Helen returned to find Jeff standing in his shop, wringing his hands. "I can't find Todd and I can't reach Jonathon on his cell phone. We have ten dogs waiting to be groomed, and Barkley is due in now."

Helen had never seen Jeff so upset. "They'll be back," she said. "It's good that the groomers took a break. They needed to cool off, both of them."

"I guess you're right," Jeff said. "You're friends with Jonathon. You know him."

Helen stopped herself before she said, "I'm not a friend, exactly." She'd never spoken to the star away from the store. Even there, she rarely exchanged more than a polite, "How are you today?" They didn't have much in common. Jonathon was wildly emotional. Helen was quiet and dull by his standards. But Jonathon didn't slam her with the seething contempt he saved for Todd. There seemed to be some unspoken bond between them.

Maybe it's because we have the same attitude toward animals, Helen thought. We like them, but we don't kiss them or do baby talk. They aren't furry children. The bell rang and more customers poured into the shop, demanding bags of food, stainless-steel bowls, treats, and toys. She was too busy to consider her relationship with Jonathon.

By three thirty the Pampered Pet was back to normal, if Helen could use that word to describe the Saturday chaos. Todd was in the cage room, kissing his dogs. Jonathon groomed his animals in solitary splendor. Six dogs were ready to go home. The others would be finished by closing, including the priceless Barkley.

When there was a lull, Helen said, "Is Jonathon OK?"

"Yes, thank goodness." Jeff leaned against the counter. He looked tired.

"He seems so . . . retro," Helen said.

"You mean he acts like an old queen," Jeff said.

Jeff was about as flamboyant as a button-down shirt. He loved khaki shorts, beer, pot roast—and a hunky interior decorator named Bill.

"The seventies queen act is a little dated, but that's how some groomers are," Jeff said. "They can be very emotional. The temperament goes with the talent. I know Jonathon won't stay here much longer. But I'll enjoy the income while I can. I can handle the problems he creates, including the jealousy. Todd has been snippy lately, and I'm not talking about his scissors."

"I have noticed his sulks."

"Todd will be OK," Jeff said. "He has his own following."

Helen wondered if Todd would take his customers to another salon. His ego was nearly as big as Jonathon's. She didn't envy Jeff the delicate task of dealing with temperamental groomers.

"Listen, Jeff, I was embarrassed when Tammie made

those remarks about rainbow ribbons," Helen said. "I'm really sorry. You shouldn't have to listen to that."

"And you shouldn't feel you have to apologize for rude straights—if that's what she is," Jeff said.

"What do you mean?"

"People who make nasty remarks about me being gay usually have problems trying to figure out which way they swing," Jeff said. "I wouldn't be surprised if she'd had a lesbian episode. Or maybe she and her husband are into threesomes."

Helen remembered Tammie's bare chest and her husband's wobbling Speedo. "That's what Betty told me. Tammie and her husband are swingers." The swingers scene was bigger, or at least more open, than in Helen's hometown of St. Louis. Swingers clubs took out bold ads in the alternative papers. One even promised a free salad bar, although Helen never found naked people and fat-free dressing a tantalizing mix.

"In Fort Lauderdale, anything is possible," Helen said. "But it's getting late. I'd better deliver Prince to Miss No Stress."

"How was Tammie at home?"

"Drunk and naked," Helen said.

Jeff raised one eyebrow. But before he could say more, the shop was invaded by an enormous shaggy brown dog.

"I need to guard the stock," he said. "It's Willis."

Willis was a lovable old bear of a dog who slyly helped himself to treats and toys. He knew how to nose open the bins to sneak bacon-and-cheese treats. He took toys from the rack and hid them in his neck fur. The shaggy shoplifter had to be watched every minute.

Helen went back to the grooming room to collect Prince, the party animal. Jonathon had done wonders with the Yorkie's thin, flyaway hair. Now Prince had a regal coat. He was crowned with a jaunty blue bow.

"Looking good, big boy," Helen said.

She put Prince in the soft-sided carrier with more turkey jerky. The Yorkie settled happily on the seat of the hot-pink Pupmobile. He was a sensible little animal.

He deserved a better owner. Helen hoped she'd find the stressed-out Tammie sober and dressed. Or better yet, soberly dressed.

As they approached the country club, Helen looked down at her black pants. They seemed different. More like a tweed blend. She was covered in dog hair. Terrific. Well, if Helen had to look at Tammie's hide, Tammie could put up with Helen's hair.

At the country club, the somnolent security guard woke up long enough to wave Helen through. Helen thought she saw Betty the animal lover leaving, golf clubs in her car. But when Helen waved, the woman looked right through her. Helen decided she must be wrong. A lot of women in Florida looked like Betty.

Helen rang the doorbell to the Grimsby mansion. No one answered. She knocked on the front door. It swung open.

"Hello?" Helen said.

Silence.

The little dog whimpered.

Enough, Helen thought. I am not going through this again.

She stood in the vast foyer and yelled, "Tammie, are you home?" The sound echoed off the marble.

That should be loud enough to get Tammie out of a drunken stupor, Helen thought. She waited five minutes, but there was no answer. The room was cold and dark as a mausoleum. Prince shivered. It felt like sun-warmed leaves moving in the breeze. The little dog seemed frightened. Helen wondered if he didn't want to go home to his drunken owner.

Well, she couldn't stay here all afternoon. She gave Prince a reassuring pat. Then Helen marched through the living room and straight down the hall to the master bedroom. She stopped in the bath and took the terry robe off the hook. She was not going to deal with a naked Tammie twice in one day.

On the pool deck, Helen blinked in the bright afternoon sun.

"Hello? Tammie?"

No answer. The naked legs with the bloody toes were again roasting in the sun. More flies crawled on the waxed limbs, but Tammie still didn't shoo them away. She must be out cold, Helen thought.

Prince whimpered again and hid his head in her armpit. Could his sensitive nose pick up his owner's alcohol? Poor little fellow. Helen wondered if the drunken Tammie had ever hurt Prince.

"It's OK," she said, and scratched his ears.

Helen walked around the umbrella table and saw three more drinks lined up next to the first glass. All were empty. Tammie's head had fallen forward on her massive chest. Sure enough, she was naked. Helen was grateful that Tammie's long blond hair covered her bare chest.

One look at that slumped figure, and Helen knew it would take gallons of strong black coffee to revive the hostess before Prince's party. Well, it wasn't her problem. She just had to deliver the dog.

"Tammie," Helen said, and shook her. She needed Tammie's signature on the delivery form. The alcohol odor nearly knocked Helen flat. Prince's owner was dead drunk.

Then Tammie's blond head lolled to one side.

Helen saw the ten-inch ice-tempered stainless-steel scissors sticking out of Tammie's chest.

CHAPTER 4

・・・・・・・・・・・・・・・・・・・・・・・・・・・・・・

H elen dropped the dog.
   She didn't mean to. But those grooming scis-
sors were driven into her mind as well as Tam-
mie's naked chest. The dead woman looked more than
ever like an artist's model. Now she was *Still Life with
Death*. Her voluptuous body was a delicate gray-green.
A dark trail of blood ran down her unnatural breasts.
Tammie was frighteningly beautiful.

Helen literally lost her grip at the sight, and Prince
went into a free fall.

She caught the Yorkie like a fumbled football before
he hit the pool deck. Helen held him contritely to her
chest and tried to soothe him. "Prince, I'm sorry. I'm so
sorry," she said.

Prince made a small mewing sound, more like a cat
than a dog. Then he raised his head and gave a single
high-pitched howl. It was a cry of mourning. His loss
hung in the air like a dark veil. Helen had no idea the
pampered little animal could feel primal grief.

Helen's own senses seemed supersharp. Everything
was extra bright. She saw the sun glinting off the grooming shears in Tammie's chest, heard the frantic buzzing
flies, felt a slight breeze bring the first noxious death
smells.

She saw Tammie's long, strong hands hanging over

the sides of the chaise. She was a muscular woman who could have fought death. But there were no cuts on her palms or arms. Tammie had not tried to defend herself. Death came as a surprise. She'd been stabbed by someone she did not fear and almost certainly knew. Who was it? Her husband? A friend? A lover?

Tammie's killer had plunged the scissors through the skin and muscle just above her breasts with a single thrust. That was pure rage.

Helen was gripped with a less noble emotion than Prince. She felt raw panic. She had to get out of this death house. Tammie's killer could still be inside.

She had to get away for another reason: She could not be involved in a murder. She could not have the police asking awkward questions. If they looked into her past, they'd find out she had attacked a naked woman in St. Louis. Helen could see Sandy now, fleeing from Helen's wrath, searching for her cell phone in her pile of clothes. Helen had had a good reason for going after her, and Sandy had never filed charges. But she had called the police, and they had made a report. The detectives investigating Tammie's homicide might believe that this time Helen had killed a woman. They'd see the motive for the attack was the same: sex.

Jeff had seen Tammie coming on to her at the store. Helen had complained that Tammie was drunk and naked. The cops would find out she was a swinger soon enough. Unwanted advances could be a powerful motive for murder.

And the weapon? It was a natural for Helen, too. She could have taken the grooming scissors from the Pampered Pet, where she worked. Where Jonathon worked. The star groomer used ten-inch scissors.

If I'm not the killer, then I'm working with one—or for one, she thought.

Helen would worry about that later. She had to get away first. She tried to remember if she'd touched anything in Tammie's house.

Yes! Her fingerprints were all over the front door. What could she use to wipe them off? She looked frantically around the pool deck. Nothing. Tammie didn't have a towel or a swimsuit cover-up. Helen was afraid to rummage for one in the bathroom and leave more traces of herself.

For one wicked moment she eyed Prince's long fur, and considered him as a canine handy wipe. Then she caught his sad brown eyes under his ridiculous blue bow and felt ashamed. He'd suffered enough indignities. Besides, she finally noticed the terry robe she'd brought to cover Tammie. It was dropped at her feet.

Prince was shivering now, even in the afternoon sun. He must be in shock. Helen tucked him tenderly into the folds of the robe, feeling guilty. How could she even think of using that poor dog to wipe away the evidence of his mistress's death? Helen carried him through the cavernous house to the front door. She held him tightly while she rubbed the robe's sleeve over the front door panels, frame, knob, and bell. She pushed in the lock button, then wiped it down again.

If the killer's prints were on that door, I'm destroying evidence, she thought. But killers wore gloves, didn't they? Not always, said a little voice. Sometimes they made stupid mistakes. Especially when they killed in an unplanned frenzy. You could be helping a murderer go free.

Something small and twisted slithered into her soul, a guilty imp who would torment her during the long nights. Helen didn't have time to indulge it right now. She wiped down the front door once more. Holding the robe, she slammed it shut, then ran to the pink Pupmobile. Could she drive anything more conspicuous?

Prince whimpered as she put him in the pet caddy. She gave him another pat, but he couldn't stop shivering. Even turkey jerky didn't calm him.

Poor Prince. She wondered if Tammie deserved such loyalty. Helen scratched the dog's ears until he stopped shaking. She felt shaky herself, but she had to get back to the shop. Prince would be OK there. Jeff would protect him until Tammie's husband took the little dog home. The shop owner had a soft heart.

The security guard was snoring in his kiosk when Helen left the country club. He didn't even wake up to wave her through the gate. Good. As the Pupmobile idled noisily in the Saturday afternoon traffic, Helen concocted her story for Jeff. She'd tell her boss that Tammie didn't answer when she rang the doorbell. Helen had knocked and beat on the door, but nobody opened it. Finally she'd left.

Helen never went inside Tammie's house, never saw her dead body, never heard the buzzing flies or saw the sun shining on the groomer's scissors. She looked at her face in the mirror. How was she going to pretend she was fine when her skin was flour-white and her eyes were wide with fear?

I'll paint on some color, she thought, and reached for her purse. That's when she saw the white robe on the car seat. Ohmigod! She'd brought Tammie's robe with her. How stupid was that?

Helen had to get rid of it. She pulled into a strip mall, then realized she was driving a block-long pink Cadillac. Someone was sure to see her poking around in the Dumpster.

A bigger mall half a block away had an Old Navy, a Marshalls, a Target store, a bagel shop, and a bank, like every other shopping center. She parked the Pupmobile and picked up Prince. It was too hot to leave him in the car. She tucked him into the crook of her arm. Now she was just another shopper carrying her little dog—and a big fluffy white bathrobe.

Helen hiked two blocks to a depressing string of doctors' offices, a nail salon, and a Chinese restaurant. It was so anonymous, Helen doubted she could even find it again. She threw the robe in a Dumpster behind the building. Prince yipped.

Flies crawled over the Dumpster, just like they were crawling over Tammie's body. Prince's owner was lying dead by her pool. Helen remembered Tammie's blank eyes and gray-green skin. What if some innocent partygoer found Tammie's body and had a heart attack? What if her husband, Kent, wasn't the killer? He didn't deserve to stumble on that dreadful scene. His last memory of his wife would be of a flyblown corpse. A maid, a neighbor, a child who lost her ball—any of them could find Tammie and have nightmares forever.

Helen had to call the police. She knew it was risky, but she couldn't live with herself if she didn't.

A pay phone rose like a mirage in front of her. Then she saw that the phone had been vandalized. The cord dangled without a receiver.

Was that a sign not to call?

Nope, it was a sign she was in a rough area of Lauderdale. The next phone worked. She dialed the police nonemergency number.

"I want to report a murder," Helen said quickly. The officer who answered tried to interrupt, but she bull-dozed ahead. "It's at the Grimsby house. Stately Palms Country Club. There's a dead woman by the pool."

Helen hung up. She hadn't tried to disguise her voice. She wondered if the call was being taped. She ran back to the car and drove the six blocks to the Pampered Pet.

Her heart was slamming in her chest and her hands shook so hard she had trouble locking the Pupmobile. She plastered a smile on her face and walked into the shop holding the whimpering Prince. Jeff was in the back room eating a pot-roast sandwich and drinking an orange soda. Helen realized she hadn't had any lunch.

"Well, you took long enough," Jeff said. "Traffic bad this afternoon?"

"The worst," Helen said. "Plus I got stopped for a drawbridge over the Intracoastal and a train on the Dixie Highway."

Helen was amazed how easily she could lie.

"All that, and I couldn't deliver Prince. Tammie didn't answer her door. I rang the doorbell and knocked until my knuckles were raw."

"She was probably passed out drunk," Jeff said, and shrugged. "Unless she forgot. That woman is such an airhead. Don't worry. I'll charge her a boarding fee for Prince. What was she thinking, abandoning that poor dog? Listen how upset he is."

Jeff peeked inside the carrier and said, "Don't you worry, guy. We'll take care of you." He fed the Yorkie pot roast from his sandwich. Prince licked Jeff's fingers greedily. Helen looked hungrily at the remains of the sandwich, but Jeff didn't notice.

The phone rang. Jeff set his sandwich next to a pile of lamb-lung treats. Helen lost all taste for pot roast.

"Francis," he said, smiling into the phone. "Yes, Barkley is ready. Of course you can pick her up early. You'll be right over? Terrific."

Helen went back to the cage room to get Barkley. The little labradoodle was irresistible. Her chocolate-brown eyes melted with love. Her tail wagged with delight. No wonder she'd snagged the Davis department stores contract. Helen wanted to pick up the pup and hug her.

Her master, Francis Barclay, was at the grooming shop in two shakes of a Rolex. Jeff was busy with customers on the boutique side when the most anonymous man Helen had ever seen came into the shop.

"Francis Barclay," he said. He gave her a thin smile. There was something dislikeable about it. "Here for the dog."

Francis's hair was the color of dead grass. He had a small, straight nose, thin lips, and beige eyes. Helen couldn't remember if she'd met him before or not. There was nothing about him to remember, except maybe his knobby knees. Some men shouldn't wear shorts.

While Francis paid for Barkley's grooming visit, Helen tried to talk to him.

"Barkley is irresistible," she said. "No wonder she has that big contract. I've never seen such a lovable dog."

Francis grunted.

"Would she like a treat?" Helen asked.

"Is it free?" Francis said.

What a cheapskate. "Of course," Helen said. She stepped out from behind the counter to get a cheese-and-bacon biscuit. As she bent over the bin, she felt a hand brush her bottom. Was the touch accidental? Now the fingers cupped her rump. Yuck. The knobby-kneed nonentity was feeling her up.

"Sorry," he said, and looked her right in the eye.

Helen stepped back, stomping hard on Francis's foot. "Oops," she said. "You startled me. I didn't mean to do that, any more than you meant to touch me."

"Of course," he said with the same insincerity. He was still standing too close. She could feel his hot, damp breath.

Helen backed farther away. How could any woman marry this creep? she thought. He couldn't even hit on her like an adult. He almost wasn't there, except for his knobby knees and roving hands. Even his clothes were anonymous. He wore khaki shorts and a blue polo shirt. He looked like someone she'd just seen.

But Francis was special to Barkley. The curly-haired pup gave a joyful bark when she saw her owner and licked his chin. Francis didn't even give her a pat.

Some dogs don't deserve their people, Helen thought.

Francis was out the door without a good-bye, Barkley slung under his arm like a sack of laundry.

Jonathon stuck his head out the grooming room door. "Any customers?" he asked. "I want a soda." Jonathon didn't like to be in the store when there were shoppers. Helen thought it was part of his mystique. She could see Todd peeking out behind him, still sulky. If the boy groomer was smart, he wouldn't get too close to Jonathon.

"The coast is clear, but I can't promise for how long on a Saturday," she said.

Jonathon zipped into the back room and came out with a frosty bottle. "What's the matter, Helen? You look upset."

"That creepy Francis Barclay felt me up," Helen said.

"Want me to neuter him next time he's in?" Jonathon said.

"Thanks, but I 'accidentally' stepped on his foot. He got the message," Helen said.

Jonathon laughed and slipped into the grooming room just as the doorbell rang. Todd was nowhere to be seen.

Ten minutes later, Willoughby Barclay trotted into

the Pampered Pet. She was almost as cute and curly as her dog. Even her shoes were lovable. Helen wished she could wear flowered flip-flops and not look like she was heading for the shower at summer camp.

"Hi," Willoughby said, all smiles. "I'm here to pick up Barkley."

"Your husband just got him," Helen said.

Willoughby turned white as a dog bone. "What? Francis was here? And you gave him my dog?"

"Is something wrong?" Helen said.

"Everything's wrong," Willoughby wailed. "I'm divorcing that jerk. We're separated. I have temporary custody of Barkley."

"Divorce?" Jeff was there now, his face anxious. "You didn't tell us you were divorcing, Mrs. Barclay."

"Yes, I did," she said. "I called here today and talked with you. I said this was a sensitive subject and I didn't want my personal life discussed in public and I wouldn't mention it when I came in. You said you understood and you'd put the information in your computer."

"I'm sorry, but I didn't get a call like that," Jeff said. "I would have remembered."

"Are you calling me a liar?" Willoughby said. She looked like she might bite.

"There has to be some mistake," Jeff said. "Are you sure you talked with me?"

"Yes. Absolutely. Francis has violated a court order. He's kidnapped my dog. Call the police."

"The police?" Helen said. She felt the floor fall out from under her, and grabbed onto the counter.

"Do you know what that dog is worth?" Willoughby said. "You gave him my dog. You're an idiot. I'll sue. I'll haul you into court. I can't believe you were so careless. I—"

Willoughby kept raging, but the words no longer registered with Helen. She wanted to run. She wanted to hide. She wanted to rip off her face and find a new one. She was mixed up in kidnapping and murder. There was no way she could escape the police now. She was doomed.

Willoughby had stopped yelling at Helen. Jeff was hovering nearby, looking like a concerned canine in a polo shirt. "Please, let's talk this over."

He tried to calm her, but Willoughby ignored him, whipped out her cell phone, and called 911. Soon Helen could hear the police sirens.

The dogs in the grooming room began to howl. Helen wanted to join them.

CHAPTER 5

·······································

Helen hated Detective Ted Brogers. She didn't like most police on principle. But this was personal.

Detective Brogers had a gold shield, but his real job was public relations. He had to please the rich residents of Wakefield Manor, a town grafted onto the north side of Fort Lauderdale. Wakefield Manor had historic charm by Florida standards. Real estate agents bragged that its houses were half a century old.

So was Ted Brogers, but Helen found him short on charm. He should have been handsome with his gray-blue eyes and thick snow-white hair. He swaggered into the Pampered Pet gut-first. Helen decided it was a beer belly, not a doughnut gut. She bet he got it drinking in a bar that had a man's name: Johnny's, Bob's, or Bill's Hideaway.

A bit of white dog fluff wafting on the air landed on his navy suit. Helen had to restrain herself to keep from picking it off. The detective's suit was well cut, but it didn't quite fit him. The pants were a smidgen too short and the sleeves were a fraction too long. Helen wondered if he'd bought it at a resale shop. Brogers probably couldn't afford custom tailoring on his salary, but he was shrewd enough to know rich people were offended by cheap suits. He knew everything that might upset the wealthy of Wakefield.

The rich were temperamental as racehorses. They expected special treatment. A bigger city might send a uniformed officer for Willoughby's call. Wakefield Manor sent a detective to hold the victim's hand.

Willoughby presented Detective Brogers with a dainty paw and smiled bravely. She was going to play the victim to the hilt. She was a man-pleasing combination of pink, pearls, and blond curls. Helen could see the detective calculating the price of Willoughby's Kate Spade purse, designer clothes, and salon cut. Definitely someone to placate.

"What seems to be the problem here?" the detective said. His face was broad and red as a slab of rare roast beef.

"This person let my husband—my ex-husband, almost, we're divorcing—steal my dog."

"I didn't—" Helen said.

"Let her finish," Brogers said. Judging by his sharp tone, the detective had also added up the cost of Helen's worn wardrobe and resoled shoes.

"She gave my dog to Francis," Willoughby said, pointing dramatically at Helen. "He's my husband. She gave Barkley away without telling me. It's so awful." A tear glittered like a diamond in the corner of her eye. Helen wondered how Willoughby had mastered the art of ornamental crying. Helen's nose always turned red and dripped.

"It's a very valuable dog, Detective Brogers, sir," Willoughby said.

Detective, sir? Oh, barf. Surely the detective was smart enough not to fall for that.

Brogers's chest swelled at this show of respect, and he gave Willoughby some of his vast worldly experience. "This happens a lot, mostly with cars and animals, when a couple is in the process of divorcing," he said. "But unless a court has awarded you custody, then the dog is your hubby's, too."

Hubby. Married to the little woman.

"But I do have temporary custody," Willoughby said. She looked up at him. "You're the only one I can depend on, Detective. I certainly can't count on her." She glared at Helen.

"I—" Helen said.

Brogers ignored her.

"What I can do is write out a civil complaint for you, Miss . . ." He paused.

"Barclay," she said. "Willoughby Barclay. I live in Wakefield Manor." She sweetly let him know who paid his salary.

"And I'm a Wakefield Manor businessperson," Jeff spoke for the first time. "I'm terribly sorry this has happened, but we're not responsible—"

"You're certainly not," Willoughby said. "A responsible person would have never given my dog to Francis."

"Your husband often picks up the dog," Jeff said.

"Not since I threw that asshole out," Willoughby said, forgetting she was supposed to be sweet and helpless. "I called you and told you we split."

"I never received such a call," Jeff said.

"OK, OK," Brogers said. "Let's settle down and talk one at a time."

The boutique doorbell rang. "Can I wait on my customers?" Jeff asked.

Brogers waved him away. A manly detective had no interest in someone like Jeff.

Jeff rushed to the boutique side, desperate to keep the customers away from the grooming room. A dog had disappeared while under his care. Helen knew Jeff must be frantic to keep this scandal quiet, but she still wished he hadn't abandoned her. She hoped the new customers couldn't hear what was going on. Industrial hair dryers were roaring. Water splashed in the washing tub. Bored caged dogs were barking themselves into frenzies, demanding their masters. Willoughby was weeping prettily.

"Now," Brogers said. "What happened, Mrs. Barclay?"

"Call me Willoughby," she said. She batted her tear-bright eyes. Helen noticed that Willoughby's eyeliner didn't run. How did she do that?

"I took my dog Barkley in for her regular Saturday grooming with Jonathon. I always take her in about two. I was supposed to pick her up at five. But when I got here, this person had already given my dog to my husband."

"But—" Helen said.

"I said, let her talk," Brogers said.

"You must help me." Willoughby raised her eyes to the detective, like a Victorian maiden pleading for protection. "My dog is supposed to have a photo shoot in Miami tomorrow at ten. She's the Davis department stores mascot. She can't miss that shoot. They'll cancel her contract. Do you know how much money I'll lose? Thousands. Absolute thousands." Helen thought she sounded more worried about her money than her dog.

"Do you think your husband will take the dog to Miami himself?" Detective Brogers said.

"No. Not now," Willoughby said. "Not since I got temporary custody. He's trying to ruin me. He's been acting crazy ever since I filed for divorce. He'll keep Barkley locked up somewhere. He could hurt my dog. He'll do anything to get even with me."

Helen thought it would take a heartless human to harm Barkley. But Francis seemed colder than a Canadian winter. Barkley had begged for his attention, and he wouldn't even give her a pat.

"Are you sure it was your husband who took the dog and not someone else? A kidnapper maybe?" Detective Brogers said.

"I'm positive," Willoughby said firmly.

Helen wasn't. She'd only seen Francis once before, when he was with the charismatic Barkley. There was no other reason to notice the man. All she could say was he had roving hands. And he'd mumbled his name, like he wasn't sure how to pronounce it. Helen had a sudden horrible thought. Maybe the detective was right, and a kidnapper had taken Barkley for ransom. Oh, God. Would he cut off the pup's ear to show he meant business? Helen had a vision of a bloody pup ear in an envelope. Her stomach lurched. The little curly-haired pup had looked at her so trustingly, and Helen had care-lessly betrayed that trust.

"Are you going to take fingerprints?" Willoughby asked. She added five more to the grooming counter by putting her hand on it.

Helen had wiped down the counter that morning, but since then thirty dog owners had left their prints on it, and thirty dogs had walked, shed, drooled, or, in the case of one elderly chihuahua, peed on the counter.

"What's to fingerprint?" Detective Brogers asked. Good point.

"Someone on this staff knows something," Willoughby said, staring at Helen. "I made that call, no matter what that Jeff person said. I told them not to give my dog to Francis, and she deliberately gave it away. He bribed her. I know he did."

"He did not!" Helen was furious. But Willoughby's anger seemed righteous. Helen was sure the woman had called the store. A man answered the store's phone and—either by accident or on purpose—did not enter the vital information in the computer. It couldn't be Jeff. He'd never jeopardize his business. It had to be Todd or Jonathon. Did they forget the call in the drama of the morning? Or did someone want to punish Jeff by driving away his most important client?

"You need to get to the bottom of this," Willoughby said. At the word "bottom," Helen felt Francis's hand again, groping her.

"I'll tell you what. I'll interrogate the staff," Detective Brogers said. He pointed to Helen. "We'll start with you. Step into the back room." Brogers wasn't wasting any charm on a poor nonresident of Wakefield Manor. "Please wait here, Willoughby," he said, and gave her a toothy smile.

Todd was at the bathtub cleaning a poodle's anal glands when Brogers walked through the grooming-room curtains. The detective turned slightly green and made a U-turn back into the shop. "And I thought crime scenes were bad," he said.

"Groomers earn their money," Helen said. "We can

talk in the stockroom. It's quiet there." She'd keep him away from the lamb lungs.

In the stockroom, Brogers took the only seat, the tall stool next to Jeff's pot-roast sandwich. Helen dropped a towel over the lamb lungs. Lulu strolled in after them. Now she was wearing a rhinestone collar and a hot-pink feather boa. Her nails were fuchsia. On anyone else the outfit would have been overdone, but Lulu looked like a countess.

"Whose little girl are you?" Brogers asked, and bent down to scratch her ears. The detective toadied to any resident of Wakefield, even the ones who weren't human. Lulu wagged her tail and stared soulfully at Brogers. She could teach Willoughby a few lessons when it came to flirting.

The detective wasn't nearly as kind to Helen. He hit her with rapid-fire questions: "Who brought the dog in?"

"Willoughby," Helen said. "Mrs. Barclay."

"And the husband picked it up?"

"Yes," Helen said.

"Is that normal?" Brogers said.

"I don't know if it's normal, but he's done it before."

"How often?" he asked.

"I don't know," Helen said. "Often enough that Jeff knew the man's voice."

"And the wife never complained before when her husband picked up the dog?"

"No," Helen said. She kept her answers short. The less she said, the less chance she had to trip herself up.

"Do you know the husband?" Brogers said.

"Not really," Helen said. "I've only seen him once before."

"Did you talk to him on the phone today when he wanted to pick up the dog?"

"No, my boss did. Francis called Jeff about four thirty and asked if the dog was ready. Jeff said he could pick up Barkley anytime. Francis was in the store two minutes later. He paid and left."

"Anything unusual about that?"

"No," Helen said. "People often call to see if their dogs are ready."

"Were you at the store all afternoon?" Detective Brogers said.

"Most of it," Helen said. "I had to go out for a dog pickup and return."

"Where was that?"

"The Grimsby home in Stately Palms."

The house with the dead body, Helen thought. She wished Brogers would stop. She was too frightened to think straight.

"When did you return?" he asked.

"About four thirty." After I found the murdered woman, destroyed evidence, and left the scene of the crime, she thought. Helen could feel herself flushing.

"Did you ask for any ID when the husband picked up the dog?"

"Why would I? He was the dog's owner."

"You didn't check the computer for Mrs. Barclay's message?"

"There was no message," Helen said. "It would have popped up on the screen when I rang up the grooming fee."

"Unless you erased it," Ted Brogers said. His eyes grew suddenly hard. "How much do you make an hour, Miz Haggard?"

Helen didn't tell him that her name was Hawthorne. "Six dollars and seventy cents," she said.

"Francis didn't offer you a little bonus to keep the dog in a safe place, maybe give the wife a scare?"

"I would never do that," she said.

"Then you should be more careful who you give your dogs to."

"I—" Helen started to say, then stopped herself. She couldn't afford to argue with Brogers. "I will," she finished. She was furious and frightened.

Helen hung around outside the stockroom while Brogers questioned Todd and Jonathon. A curtain divided the room from the boutique, and she could hear everything. The two groomers knew nothing about

Barkley's disappearance. They'd been working on the dogs in the back room. They both denied taking any call from Willoughby instructing the shop not to give the dog to her husband. Brogers gave them both his card and said, "Call me if you remember anything useful."

Jeff trotted in next, running his fingers through his thick brown hair. He looked so worried, Helen was afraid he might tear it out. Helen knew he blamed himself for Barkley's disappearance.

At first Brogers sounded as if he couldn't decide whether to treat Jeff as a Wakefield business owner or a potential dognapping conspirator. But Brogers knew who stuffed his pay envelope. He turned on the charm for Jeff. "Francis called and asked me if he could pick up the dog early. But that's not unusual," Jeff said.

"Of course not," Brogers said. The detective even slapped Jeff on the back as they walked out to the front of the store, where Willoughby was waiting.

"This sounds like a marital misunderstanding," the detective told Willoughby. "Don't you worry now. I'll drop by Francis's place and have a little talk with him."

Willoughby gave him another grateful smile and Helen another glare. Detective Brogers escorted Barkley's owner to her car, as if he expected attackers to be lurking in the lot. Helen and Jeff watched Willoughby walk across the parking lot, her pink purse swinging at her side.

"She's going to sue," Jeff said.

"How can she?" Helen said. "You didn't know she was in a custody fight with Francis. She should have given you the instructions about her dog in writing."

"It won't make any difference," Jeff said. "This has been my nightmare. I've been afraid something like this would happen, and now it has—and with our most high-profile pup. Willoughby will sue. Her kind always do. The publicity will kill my store. I'll lose everything I worked for."

Publicity? Oh, Lord, Jeff was right. This story was made for the media. Hour after hour, they would run clips from Barkley's commercials. Helen's name would be all over the TV. She was the idiot who'd handed over the priceless pup.

That would be the end of her life in Florida. Helen's ex-husband would find her, and so would the court. She could see herself in handcuffs, heading for St. Louis. She hoped the police would cuff her hands in front, not in back. The trip would be more comfortable that way.

There had to be some way to hold back the flood of publicity, before they all drowned.

"Why don't you talk to Willoughby? Tell her you need time to find the dog. Ask her for mercy," Helen said.

"There is no mercy in that woman," Jeff said.

CHAPTER 6

Friends help you move. Real friends help you move the body.

Helen had seen that on a T-shirt once. She wasn't sure if Margery Flax would help her hide a body. But Helen could tell her landlady that she'd found a dead woman.

Still, it took two glasses of wine before Helen got up the nerve—and it took nerve to drink that much box wine. Margery bought the stuff at the Winn-Dixie supermarket. The wine didn't have a vintage year. It had an expiration date. It didn't claim any connection to a grape. WHITE WINE was all the cardboard box said. It had a spigot for easy guzzling. But it was cold, wet, and had alcohol in it, and right now that was what she needed.

By the second glass, Helen was nicely numb. She and Margery were sitting out by the pool at the Coronado Tropic Apartments on a warm September evening. The two-story white stucco building rose like an iceberg above a sea of palm trees. The window air conditioners rattled their night song. The sunset-streaked pool glowed pink, like the inside of a seashell. Usually Helen found that romantic. Tonight it gave her the creeps. She kept seeing Tammie's pool and her dead body.

"So you found the Yorkie's owner out by the pool," Margery said, "and she was definitely naked and dead."

"Real dead." Helen took a gulp of wine and waited for its woozy warmth before she continued. "There were flies crawling on her legs. The scissors were driven deep into her chest. It was awful, even if there wasn't much blood."

"The scissors probably plugged it up," Margery said. "Must have been a shock finding her like that. Did you have to sit down before you called the police?"

"I didn't sit. I ran. I took Tammie's bathrobe, wiped down the door with it, picked up the Yorkie, and took off."

"That was dumb," Margery said. "Cops are like dogs. They chase whatever runs."

It's true, Helen thought. They came after me when I fled St. Louis. My sister said the police questioned her about where I might go, but Kathy didn't know. How could she? I didn't know, either, until I got here.

For months Helen had zigzagged wildly around the country before she ended up in South Florida. Helen had never wanted to live in Fort Lauderdale. She didn't have the fond memories of childhood vacations that lured so many people to settle in Florida. But it turned out to be the perfect place for her. Florida accepted everyone from snowbirds to serial killers. Local etiquette said you never asked anyone where they were from and you never questioned anything they said about their past. Maybe the old guy with the six grandchildren and the marinara sauce bubbling on his stove really had been an accountant up in New Jersey, just like he said. It wasn't polite—or healthy—to pry.

Helen wondered how Margery got her view of the police. Her landlady didn't look like the seventy-six-year-olds Helen knew in St. Louis—not in her tie-dyed shorts and gauzy purple top. Helen wished she had Margery's straw huaraches. Her face was wrinkled as a flophouse sheet, but Margery had style. She lit a Marlboro and puffed on it like an actress in a forties movie, while she considered Helen's dilemma.

"You panicked and ran. It's understandable, but the police are going to find you," Margery said. Smoke curled around her like wisps from a sacrifice. She looked like an ancient priestess predicting the future. In Helen's case, the news was bad.

"I don't think so," Helen said. "I was careful. I wiped everything down. Anyway, no one notices me. I'm a servant."

"Are you kidding? How did you get to Tammie's house? You don't have a car."

Helen couldn't afford one with the money she made in her dead-end job. Somewhere in Kansas, she'd traded in her nearly new Lexus for what turned out to be a junker in disguise. If Helen ever got back that way, she'd pay that used-car salesman a little visit. She'd like to give him a free alignment. Or maybe not. When the heap died in Fort Lauderdale, she'd found Margery and the Coronado. The crook did her a favor.

"Were you driving that pink pimpmobile?" Margery said.

"It's the Pupmobile," Helen said.

"I was right the first time. Even a blind man can see that thing." Margery tapped her cigarette on the edge of the chaise. Helen watched the glowing embers blow in the breeze like tiny fireflies.

"Someone had to see you at Tammie's house, and that someone will tell the cops. Make it easy on yourself. Call the police right now. I haven't seen the story on the TV news yet. You've still got a chance. If you let them know before they find it out from somewhere else, it will look a lot better. Tell them you were afraid and you ran. They'll give you a lecture and let you go."

"I don't like talking to the police," Helen said. What if her picture was on some yellowing "Be on the lookout for" bulletin at the station? She didn't think she was important enough for a national search, but she didn't know and she didn't want to take the chance. Cops had sharp eyes and long memories.

"Who does?" Margery said. "I don't like talking to the cops, either."

Seventy-six-year-old women never said that in St. Louis, Helen thought.

"Listen, I know a criminal lawyer—there's a redundancy for you—named Colby Cox." Margery took a lung-busting pull on her cigarette. "Colby's a good old girl, and she owes me a favor. I'll get her to go with you when you talk to the police."

Does your lawyer friend know anything about extra-dition to another state? Helen wanted to ask, but she didn't have the courage. Margery didn't know her whole story. No one did but her sister, Kathy. Even Helen's mother didn't know where she lived now. Helen couldn't trust Dolores not to rat out her own daughter to Rob, her ex-husband.

Margery knew Helen was avoiding her ex. Helen had given her the impression, without actually saying it, that Rob had beaten her and she'd run from him. She'd never mentioned the part about the court being after her. Helen didn't know how much her landlady had fig-ured out.

"I'll be fine, Margery," Helen said. "I had a reason to be at Tammie's house. I was delivering a dog, re-member?"

"How long were you there?" Margery asked.

"I don't know, maybe five or ten minutes," Helen said. Margery's questions made her uneasy. She took another sip of wine. This time it brought her no comfort, no welcome rush of warmth. She had a sick, sour feeling in her stomach.

"It only takes a few seconds to stick scissors in Tam-mie's chest," Margery said. She was relentless. If her land-lady interrogated her like this, what would the police be like? Helen knew she'd fold and confess everything.

"Why would I kill her?" Helen said.

"The cops will find a reason," Margery said. "They'll go after you for sure. If they catch you lying, they'll be really pissed. They'll throw you in jail for the hell of it. You need help. If you won't use Colby, why don't you call Phil? He's a trained investigator."

Phil. The man next door had turned into Helen's dream lover. She felt a warm rush when she thought of him, and it wasn't from the wine. She'd seen Phil three nights ago. All night.

"He's in Washington," Helen said.

"Is he working undercover again?" Margery asked.

Helen remembered what they'd done between his black silk sheets and blushed. She hoped Margery couldn't see her face in the gathering dusk.

"No," Helen said. "It's a business trip."

"Then you need to call him. He has the law-enforcement contacts. He can help you."

"I can help myself," Helen said. She had her pride. She wasn't going to run whining to Phil. "I'm not one of those weak women who has to ask a man for help."

"Strong women know their limitations," Margery said. She stubbed out the cigarette, grinding it into the ashtray, but said nothing more. Her silence sounded like an accusation.

Helen was glad when she heard a rustling near the bougainvillea. Another Coronado resident was walking toward them. It was Peggy, with Pete the parrot on her shoulder. Peggy was as slender and elegant as a wading bird, with a splendid beak of a nose and a crest of red hair. Pete, her green Quaker parrot, was a tad on the tubby side. Peggy had him on a diet. Instead of the cashews he craved, the little bird sat on Peggy's shoulder and resentfully crunched a celery stick. Margery had a no-pets policy, so Helen politely ignored Pete.

"Did you see the news?" Peggy said. "There's a category-three hurricane due to land in two days. It's supposed to be headed straight for South Florida. They think it might hit Lauderdale hard this time."

The evening sky was a glorious show of peach and hot pink. It looked peaceful as a painting. A light breeze stirred the palm trees.

"I can't believe a major storm is coming," Helen said. "It's so quiet."

"Hear that?" Peggy said. "Someone believes the weathercasters." The ominous sound carried on the evening air—hammers pounding on plywood. Floridians had started boarding up their homes.

"I know there's a hurricane coming," Margery said. "I

can see it in my dancing tree. It's my storm indicator. Look at it, over by the pool gate."

All the Coronado trees were bending in the breeze. But one palm tree was whipping around in weird circles.

"That circular movement is the first sign of a hurricane," Margery said. "It will get worse as the storm gets closer, until that tree is doing the shimmy and the others are bent flat. I'd better clip those coconuts tomorrow. They go through windows like cannonballs."

There was another uncomfortable silence while everyone imagined what the Coronado would look like after a hurricane. Pete the parrot moved restlessly along Peggy's shoulder, mumbling to himself. Helen wondered if he hated his diet, or if he could feel the approaching storm. Peggy petted him with one finger until he settled down.

Margery lit another cigarette, then said, "I've rented apartment 2C."

"Awwk!" Pete said. Peggy and Helen groaned.

"Which crook do you have in there now?" Peggy said.

The apartment was notorious for attracting scam artists. No matter how much Margery checked out the tenants, they were always involved in something shady.

"They're not crooks," she said. "I have two women. Grown-ups, in their fifties. Good, responsible tenants with references. They clean houses free for older people. They work for a foundation that benefits seniors."

"Oh, no, not more do-gooders," Helen said. They'd lived with a sanctimonious couple who turned out to scam mom-and-pop businesses.

"No, these two are legit," Margery said. "I even called their organization and talked with the director. They're paid by the foundation to clean homes for seniors. Keeps older people independent and out of the institutions."

"Are they going to clean your house?" Helen said.

Margery bristled. "I'm not that old. I can take care of myself."

Oops, Helen thought. I've stepped in it this time.

"Do they drink?" Peggy said quickly. A previous pair of teetotalers in 2C had been a real pain.

"Yes. I made sure. They like booze. They also smoke," Margery said. "They're not on bizarre diets and don't belong to any cults. They dress like normal people."

"That will make them weird down here," Helen said.

"I mean normal for South Florida. They wear shorts to everything but funerals."

"Sounds like you've finally picked some winners," Peggy said, and Pete squawked his approval.

"I've got a good feeling about this pair," Margery said. Her cell phone rang. She snapped it open and answered it.

"I should have known," she said, smiling. "No, no problem, Phil. I don't mind being Helen's answering service if I get to talk to you."

Margery grinned wickedly, and handed the phone to Helen. She strolled into the far reaches of the yard, away from her flirtatious landlady.

"Hi," Phil said. His voice was flat.

"You sound tired," Helen said.

"I am," Phil said. "I was in meetings all day. I have to be up at four thirty tomorrow morning. I wanted to crash, but I couldn't sleep until I told you good night."

Helen wished he were there with her. She could feel his slightly scratchy beard on her skin, and that small tender spot at the base of his neck, and his long, soft hair. Rock-star hair, shoulder length and stark white, worn in a ponytail. It set off his startling blue eyes.

"I miss you already," Helen said. This was no time to mention Tammie's murder, she told herself. The man was dead tired. It would be selfish to dump her problems on him tonight.

"I love you," Phil said.

"And I love you," Helen said.

When he hung up, Helen was filled with regret. She should have said something. She should have told him about Tammie. She could argue that she kept quiet for Phil's sake, but she knew better.

Her omission felt like a lie.

CHAPTER 7

●●●●●●●●●●●●●●●●●●●●●●●●●●●●

Helen hated it when she got a hangover before she went to bed. She'd had two glasses of box wine on an empty stomach. Now demons pounded her head with pointed hammers and ran through her stomach in iron shoes. Her skin felt coated with chicken fat.

A mosquito stung her as Helen made her way back through the wind-shifting shrubbery to the pool, where Margery and Peggy were sitting.

Maybe she didn't have the wine flu, she thought, as she rubbed at her bitten arm. Maybe she felt this way because she'd found a dead woman. Or she'd been dragged into a dog custody fight.

Maybe, whispered one of those iron-shod demons, it's because you lied to the man you love.

I didn't lie, Helen nearly shouted to no one.

Deliberately misled, whispered the little demon, and kicked her in the gut.

"Thanks for letting me talk to Phil," Helen said, as she handed Margery her phone. "That's the only good thing that's happened to me today."

"You look like forty miles of bad road. You need some food," Margery said. "Let me fix you a sandwich."

"I'm not hungry," Helen said. "It's only seven thirty, but I think I'll crash. I'm declaring this rotten day officially over."

But the day wasn't finished with her. There was a screech of brakes in the parking lot and the sound of slamming doors. Margery peered through the palm trees. "There's a big Crown Victoria blocking in all our cars. Looks like we've got plainclothes cops."

"Awk!" Pete said, and flapped his wings. Green feathers flew on the wind.

Peggy's porcelain skin lost all its color. A few months ago she'd been taken away from the Coronado in handcuffs. The memory of that night still left her shaken. Peggy hid her fear with a bad joke. "Are the cops coming to arrest the tenants in 2C already?" she said.

No one laughed. Helen knew who they were after.

Two men in dark suits moved swiftly down the Coronado's cracked sidewalk to the pool. One was tall and skinny, with a red, acne-scarred face. His arms and legs were loose and too long, as if the factory-installed models weren't available. He seemed in constant motion. His suit flapped, his Adam's apple bobbed, and his no-color hair stuck straight up. He should have looked like a comical country boy. Instead he seemed full of menace.

The other man was short, solid, and very still. He was built like a Russian nesting doll, with a shiny bald head, no neck, and feral yellow-brown eyes. He kept them trained on Helen as he flashed a badge.

"Helen Hawthorne," he said. It was a demand. "Detective Jim Crayton." He didn't wait for her to answer.

He knows who I am, Helen thought.

"This is my partner, Detective Skip McGoogan. We're Stately Palms homicide. We'd like to talk to you."

"About what?" Helen said, although she already knew. The demons were swinging their hammers relentlessly in her head. Her mouth was dry. This wasn't a hangover. It was fear. Over by the pool gate, the dancing palm tree was doing the hurricane hula. It told Helen what she already knew: Bad things were coming.

"I'll stay with you, Helen," Margery said. She was no longer the languid Marlboro smoker. She'd turned into a purple crusader. Peggy stood beside her, arms crossed, ready to defend her friend despite her own fear. Pete patrolled Peggy's shoulder, his celery stick abandoned on the pool deck.

Helen didn't want any of them there, especially Margery. Her landlady might tell the police that Helen had discovered Tammie's body. Margery would do it for Helen's own good. She couldn't risk that.

"No, you go on inside," Helen said. "I'll be fine."

"You're sure?" Margery asked.

Helen nodded.

"In that case," Margery said, "I'll put on my bathrobe and get comfortable."

That was her landlady's unsubtle way of telling Helen she should confess. Now Helen was sure she'd made the right decision. Margery liked to meddle.

When her landlady and Peggy had disappeared into the darkness, Helen chose a chair from the poolside umbrella table. Reclining in a chaise would make Helen feel vulnerable. The brightly striped umbrella, made for sunnier times, seemed to mock this occasion. Crayton, the Russian-doll detective, pulled out a chair, too. The screech of metal legs on concrete made Helen wince.

Detective McGoogan sat next to him, leaving Helen isolated on her side of the table. Even sitting down, the detective was in perpetual motion. McGoogan scratched his scalp, which explained why his hair stuck straight up, then ran his huge hand across his pitted face, rubbed his nose, and drummed his fingers on the table.

Helen itched just watching him.

"What time did you go to Tammie Grimsby's house today?" Detective Crayton, the Russian doll, asked. McGoogan fiddled with his cuff link.

"I picked up her dog, Prince, at noon for a grooming appointment," Helen said. "I tried to return him about four o'clock, but Tammie never answered her door. Why? Is there a problem?"

"You could say that," Crayton said. "She's dead."

"No," Helen said. She sounded like a ham actor. "What happened?"

"She was murdered," Detective Crayton said. McGoogan straightened his tie and scratched his wrist.

"No," Helen said.

"Yes," Crayton said. "You're sure no one was at home? You didn't hear anyone in the house?" Mc-Googan twisted his shirt button.

"No," Helen said. Did she know any other word? "I knocked and rang the bell. No one answered. Then I left."

"Give us a detailed account of your whereabouts from the time you left the store until you returned."

Helen did. She only left out the part where she found Tammie, wiped down the door, dropped the dead woman's robe in the Dumpster, and phoned the police. She tried to remember everything she said, because she knew the detectives would ask her again and again, trying to trip her up. It was hard to concentrate when Mc-Googan was rubbing his neck and pulling on his earlobe.

"Tell us about the argument the victim had with the groomer, Jonathon," Crayton said.

So Todd had talked about the fight with Tammie, Helen thought. He wouldn't miss a chance to stick it to his rival. Helen liked Jonathon and his theatrical style, but no matter how much she wanted to, she could not deny that this incident had happened. She tried to downplay it.

"Jonathon is a little temperamental," she said. "He doesn't like to be disturbed when he's grooming the dogs, and Tammie barged in on him. He asked her to leave. It wasn't a big deal."

"I heard he called the victim a bitch," Detective Crayton said. "They had a screaming battle in the store. Then later that same day, he threatened the groomer Todd with ten-inch scissors. I guess that didn't mean anything, either."

Todd got his revenge for being shoved into the cage room, Helen thought.

"Jonathon was a little annoyed with Todd," Helen said.

"He cut Todd's throat with those scissors," Crayton said. "I saw a two-inch-long wound on the man's neck. That's assault."

"A cut?" Helen couldn't hide her surprise. "I didn't see any cut. I was there when it happened."

Did Todd cut himself so he'd have something to show the police?

"How long have you known the victim, Tammie Grimsby?" Crayton said. McGoogan flicked something off his nails.

"Today was the first time I saw her," Helen said. "She wanted help with a birthday party for her Yorkie, Prince. She also wanted to have him groomed. She didn't have time to bring the dog back to the shop for his appointment, so Jeff arranged a pickup. It was the first time I'd ever done a pickup at her house."

"You've had no prior dealings with the victim outside of the store?" Detective Crayton said. "You never went to any parties at her house, for instance?"

They know Tammie and Kent are swingers, Helen thought.

"Never," she said. "Today was the first time I was ever at her house, and that was to get her dog."

Now the other detective, McGoogan, stopped picking, flicking, and scratching. His cop's eyes bored in on Helen. "And how was the victim dressed?" he said.

"Dressed?" Helen said.

"Is there an echo in here?" McGoogan said. "What was she wearing?"

Something *shear,* Helen wanted to say, as she pictured those scissors in Tammie's chest.

"Nothing," Helen said. "She was on her chaise longue and she wasn't dressed at all."

"Did she throw a towel over herself or anything?"

"No," Helen said.

"And how did you react?" Crayton was back asking the questions again. McGoogan was scratching his elbow.

"I ignored it," Helen said. "I picked up her dog and left."

"You weren't offended by her nudity?" he said. McGoogan pulled on his shirt collar.

"Rich people are eccentric," Helen said.

"Anyone else in the Grimsby house while you were getting the dog?" Crayton said.

"Her husband, Kent."

"And what was he wearing?"

"A Speedo," Helen said. "He came out by the pool to talk to us."

"About what?" Crayton said.

"He was going to test-drive a new car. A Porsche or a Ferrari, something fast." Helen left out the part where Kent talked about his wife's body—and hers.

"Did the victim get up off the chaise longue while you were there? Did she walk you to the door?"

"No," Helen said. "She just laid there." Or was it lay? She never got that straight. In Tammie's case, either one was probably correct.

"So at the time that you left the house, the victim was on the chaise longue and her husband was by the pool. There was no one else in the home. No servants or guests?"

"No one," Helen said. "No housekeeper came to the door. Kent said he had to get dressed for the test drive. Tammie pointed to the dog. Prince was sleeping in the sun. I picked him up and let myself out."

"And what happened when you returned to the Grimsby home with the dog?"

How many times was she going to have to repeat this? "I knocked on the door. I rang the bell and shouted her name, but Tammie never came out. When I couldn't get any answer, I drove Prince back to the shop."

"Did you drive straight back?"

"Yes," Helen lied. She watched McGoogan pick at a crater on his red face.

"We'd like to have a tech take your fingerprints," Detective Crayton said.

"Mine? Why?"

"For elimination purposes. We should find them on the door and the bell."

Helen had a sick feeling. "Uh, sure," she said.

"And Miss Hawthorne," Detective Crayton said.

"We'd like you to remain available for future questioning."

Remain available for future questioning. It sounded like a curse. Remain available. Remain available. The words echoed in her dreams. That night Helen slept poorly, sick with worry and cheap wine.

When she got to the shop in the morning, Jeff looked like he'd had the same kind of night as Helen. His hair was flat and oily and his face was baggy as an old hound's. His yellow polo shirt looked like he'd picked it up off the floor. Jeff hadn't bothered dressing Lulu that morning. The store's top model looked oddly naked in her own fur coat.

Jeff sat at the counter with his head in his hands, an extra-large coffee beside him. Helen said good morning. He grunted. She didn't ask if the police had talked to him about Tammie. She knew that answer.

Only Todd looked sleek and cheerful. He came out of the back room carrying bags of dog food, his chest and arm muscles bulging against his white T-shirt. He had a bandage on his neck. Was this the site of Jonathon's alleged attack?

"Did you hear the news, Helen?" Todd said. "Jonathon is at the police station. The detectives are questioning him about Tammie's murder."

"This is a disaster, personally and professionally," Jeff said. "Jonathon is my top groomer."

She could see Todd grip the dog-food bags until they crackled in protest. Jeff must be upset if he didn't try to soothe Todd's feelings. He was always so diplomatic.

"The police say he killed her with his grooming scissors," Todd said.

"They didn't say anything like that," Jeff snapped. "The detectives asked a lot of questions about some grooming scissors. I think they were found at the scene."

"Any fingerprints on the scissors?" Helen asked.

"They won't say," Jeff said.

"But they did say Jonathon was missing a pair of ten-inch scissors from his case," Todd said. This time he didn't hide the sly smile.

"Anyone could have swiped them," Jeff said. "This place was a zoo Saturday."

"Well, there you are," Helen said. "Besides, Jonathon doesn't have a history of violence, does he?"

She waited for Jeff to say no. Instead there was silence.

"Jeff?" Helen said.

Jeff talked into his coffee cup. "I've heard rumors that Jonathon killed a man in self-defense. This was twenty years ago, when he was first starting out. The way I heard it, Jonathon was walking home from a grooming salon in Miami, and a couple of men decided to amuse themselves by rolling queers. They attacked him and beat him up pretty badly. But Jonathon knew how to defend himself. He killed one attacker and the other ran away. No charges were filed."

"Jonathon actually beat a man to death?" Helen said.

"No," Jeff said. "They say Jonathon stabbed him. With grooming scissors."

CHAPTER 8

An anguished cry came from the grooming-room cages. This wasn't some spoiled poodle demanding a pat. It was the sound of heartbreak. Helen recognized it.

"That's Prince," she said. "Tammie's Yorkie. He's crying for his mistress."

The little dog with the shrewd eyes and the silly bow had howled out his grief all morning.

"I'm sure Tammie's husband has forgotten about him," Jeff said. "Lord knows that poor man has enough on his mind. I'll give Kent a call on his cell phone and find out when we can deliver the Yorkie. Helen, why don't you get on the extension? You're doing the driving. He may have special instructions."

This was a phone call Helen didn't want to miss. She wondered if Kent knew that the Yorkie's groomer was a suspect in his wife's murder. She had to hear how Jeff the diplomat would handle this situation.

Kent Grimsby answered on the second ring. "I'm so sorry about Tammie," Jeff said.

"Yeah," Kent said. "That fingerprint powder leaves a real mess. It's everywhere. The cops still have the whole place sealed off as a crime scene. I couldn't spend the night in my own freakin' house. I had to sleep in a hotel. I couldn't use my pool this morning.

They won't even let me get my own clothes. I called my lawyer and he chewed the chief's ass. Now they're saying I can get back in tomorrow. Can you believe it?"

The selfish twit. He never mentioned his dead wife, Helen thought.

"It must be horrible," Jeff said. "I'm sure you've forgotten in the confusion"—he was too tactful to mention the word "murder"—"but your Yorkie, Prince, is staying with us. We can keep him until you're back home. The delivery will be free of charge and we won't bill you for the boarding, but Prince needs to go home. He's very distressed. We hope he'll be less upset when he's back in familiar surroundings. When would you like Helen to bring him home?"

"Never," Kent said. "That thing's not mine. It's hers. I hate it. It's nothing but a long-haired rat."

"But, sir, what am I going to do with—"

Kent cut him off. "You can put it to sleep for all I care. I never want to see that useless little bastard again. All it ever did was bark and piss."

"But—" Jeff said.

"Don't try to bring that nasty yapper here. I'll wring its neck right in front of you. Got that?"

Kent slammed down the phone.

Helen's ears rang from Kent's phone slam. She shook her head to clear it. That was a bad idea. Her head clanged and wobbled. She was still rocky from last night's wine, but her anger at Kent's cruelty was burning away her hangover.

"That creep," she said. "I can't believe Kent would do that. Prince is a terrific dog. He's loyal and smart—everything Kent isn't. I'd love to beat some sense into that gym-sculpted hunk of lard."

"You'll never get any sense into Kent's rock head," Jeff said. His long spaniel face was paler than usual. He was shaken by Kent's threats to kill Prince.

"How can he threaten that harmless little animal?" Helen said. "Prince is the only living reminder of his murdered wife."

"I think you just answered your question," Jeff said.

"Does he hate Tammie that much?" Helen said. "Do you think he hated his wife enough to kill her?"

"He certainly doesn't sound like a grieving husband," Jeff said. "Prince is more upset over Tammie's death than he is."

"How are we going to make Kent take care of that dog?" Helen said.

"We aren't," Jeff said. "I won't turn Prince over to that heartless maniac. I'll find him a decent home."

Jeff had an amazing ability to find homes for stray kittens, lost dogs, and other abandoned animals. He knew whose dog or cat had died and when his customers were ready to adopt another pet.

"If you could find a home for that Jack Russell, you should be able to place a two-year-old Yorkie," Helen said.

"Gizmo was my greatest triumph," Jeff said.

The old, white-muzzled Jack Russell terrier was brought in by a weeping blonde who hobbled in on needle-nosed Prada slingbacks. "We're moving to a condo that won't allow animals, and my husband says I have to get rid of Gizmo," she said. "My husband says Gizmo's too old and I should put him to sleep. But I can't. There's nothing wrong with him. I've had him for ten years. You have to help me.

"Here." She'd handed Jeff the dignified old dog, who studied him with trusting eyes. The woman's tears stained Jeff's counter. She wasn't a regular customer, but Jeff promised to find Gizmo a home.

"Personally, I'd get rid of the husband," Helen said when the weeping woman left.

"Gizmo won't keep her in Prada," Jeff said. "She's made her choice and she has to live with it—and herself."

At ten years old, Gizmo was hardly an ideal age for adoption. But thirty phone calls later, Jeff found the dog a home. A man was looking for a four-legged fishing buddy, and he enjoyed older dogs. Like most Jack Russells, Gizmo loved the water. The man and his old dog now spent many hours fishing together, eating ham sandwiches, and drinking beer.

A mournful yowl reminded Jeff of his current duty.

"I hope I do half as well finding a home for Prince." Jeff flexed his dialing finger and said, "Now the magic begins."

While Jeff made his calls, Helen waited on customers and Todd gave Lulu a bath, a massage, and a manicure. Wish I could have a day of beauty, Helen thought. No wonder Lulu looks like a million bucks and I look like a dog.

But Helen knew she needed more than pampering to feel better. She was weighted down with dread. Margery was right: Helen should have told the police about finding Tammie's body. She should have never destroyed that evidence. Tammie's killer was getting away with murder, and Helen had helped him. She was sure it was a man—Tammie's husband, Kent. She remembered his hulking form filling the grooming-room door. He was at the salon that day. He could have stolen Jonathon's scissors.

Four aspirins later, Helen's headache was still pounding. Helen had to grit her teeth to wait on a twenty-something blonde with fake boobs and a belly shirt that showed her flat stomach. On her finger was a diamond the size of a Chicken McNugget. On her arm was a white fluff muffin. At her side was a fifty-something man, barking orders.

A trophy wife, Helen decided, with a demanding husband. He was a generic businessman with a seventy-dollar haircut, a gray suit, and bulldog jowls.

"Come on," the man said. "Let's go. How much more of my money can you spend in here?"

Mr. Charm, Helen thought. He'd just reminded his wife who had the bucks.

"Now, sweetie, remember what you promised," Mrs. Trophy said softly, as she covered the counter with five hundred dollars' worth of dog statues, Christmas ornaments, and needlepoint pillows, all immortalizing her silent white bichon.

"And remember what you promised," the husband said. "You better get that ass into bed as soon as we get home."

The guy wasn't housebroken, Helen thought.

"This dog saved my life, you know what I mean?" the woman whispered to Helen, as she hugged the fluffy little bichon. "He's a great dog. He goes where I want and never says anything."

"Come on," her husband barked. "I want to go. Now."

"Just let me buy this leash," Mrs. Trophy said. "It's for special occasions." She quickly piled a rhinestone leash, a candy-striped pet caddy, and two designer food bowls with a matching stand on the counter. Another five hundred dollars in a single sweep.

Was the money worth it? Helen wondered as she rang up the woman's purchases. In my old St. Louis life, I could have spent a thousand dollars on trifles, just like Mrs. Trophy. All I had to do was shut my eyes to my unfaithful husband. But I couldn't.

Helen studied the stress lines around the woman's frantic eyes and frightened mouth. I worry about paying my rent, but I still don't think I'd trade places with you, she thought.

Her husband stood at the store door. "Get your ass out here. Now," he said. He stalked outside, slamming the door. The bell jangled. The blonde grabbed her shopping bags and trotted after her man, clutching her white dog. The black-eyed bichon was silent as a ghost.

Helen wiped down the door after she left, as if she could erase the woman's desperation.

"What is it about useless little women and their useless little dogs?" Helen said.

"You're in a mood today," Jeff said. "You need to understand the difference between little-dog and big-dog people. Little dogs are babies. Big dogs are adults. They're buddies. You can have a beer and watch a movie with a big dog.

"Little dogs stay babies twelve or fourteen years. You can pick them up and carry them. You can hold them in your arms. They won't grow up and turn into teenagers. They don't go off to college. They stay babies until the day they die—and then you carry them to the vet for the final time."

Helen shuddered. "What about us cat people?"

"You are another breed altogether." Jeff, tactful as ever, would say no more.

Shortly before noon, a small woman in a smart black suit clattered in on Gucci heels. She was about sixty, with the delicate bones of the overdieted. She carried a matching Gucci pet caddy.

"I'm Mrs. Mellman," she said. "Jeff called me about the abandoned Yorkie. I said it was too soon for me to adopt another dog. My Yorkie, Gucci, has only been dead two months. But Jeff said my Prince had come, and I couldn't be in mourning when another doggie needed me."

"He does, Mrs. Mellman," Helen said. "Can you hear him?"

Prince let loose another heartrending howl.

"He's so sad," Mrs. Mellman said.

"Not for long," Helen said. "I'll get him for you."

Todd had brushed the Yorkie's coat and put in a fresh blue bow. "Now he's ready for his new home," the handsome young groomer said. He gave the dog a kiss on the nose.

Helen thanked him. She noticed that Todd had reclaimed his prized spot in the grooming room. There was no sign of the temperamental star, Jonathon.

"OK, Prince, this is your chance," she whispered. "Play it right, old boy, and you'll never see Kent again. I'll make sure you live on filet forever."

Helen thought the Yorkie might actually understand what she was saying. He still looked sorrowful, but he held his head a little higher. Helen carried him out to the counter.

"Oh, you are a Prince indeed," Mrs. Mellman said. The little dog managed a weak tail wag and a whimper. Mrs. Mellman reached for him. Prince settled regally into the crook of her arm. She patted his well-groomed coat.

"He only eats filet, and he has to be hand-fed," Helen said. Mrs. Mellman nodded. She would glory in Prince's demands.

"It's love at first sight," Jeff said. "See, I was right, Mrs. Mellman. Your Gucci wouldn't want you to wall yourself away. You have too much love to give, and Prince needs you. Here are a few gifts for your new baby." Jeff handed her a beribboned bag of toys and bonbons.

Helen threw in a package of turkey jerky. "This is his favorite treat," she said. "He needs at least one a day."

Prince stared at her with knowing eyes, but said nothing. Gratitude was for lesser animals. He was royalty.

CHAPTER 9

The woman wore her boredom like an expensive perfume. She seemed to issue a challenge when she walked into the Pampered Pet: Amuse me. But I know you'll fail.

She looked like Paris Hilton thirty years later. Her blond hair was long and dyed. Her lips were puffed with collagen. Her fake breasts bulged out of an underwire bra. Her eyes had been done and her forehead Botoxed, but nothing could remove her world-weary expression.

Jeff pushed Helen out on the floor. "That's Lucinda," he said. "Go wait on her. She's a trip." Helen didn't like the sly grin on his face.

"Hi," Helen said. "May I help you?"

Lucinda's eyes flicked over Helen, but she said nothing. She didn't need to. Her clothes shrieked money. Her skimpy sundress cost more per square inch than waterfront real estate. Helen saw no sign of a rich husband, not even a wedding ring. Lucinda was escorted by a respectful young man with innocent eyes and a peach-fuzz complexion.

That's nice, Helen thought. Her son is home from college.

Lucinda rummaged silently through the racks of dog

collars. She picked out one suitable for a junkyard dog. It was wide black leather with metal studs.

At last Lucinda spoke. "I want a dog collar. For him." She pointed to the young man.

So much for sonny boy's innocent eyes. Helen didn't know what to say. She'd never sold a dog collar for a human. She didn't know what size the guy wore. Dog collars were measured in inches, and she wasn't about to ask how many inches he was.

Jeff took over from the flummoxed Helen. "No, no, Lucinda," he said. "Everyone buys that. You want this one." Jeff picked out a black leather collar with chrome disks. Lucinda bought it and left without another word, her boy toy obediently loping alongside her.

"What was that?" Helen said.

"Lucinda is richer than God and wicked as the devil," Jeff said. "She's an education."

"Do I want to know these things?" Helen said.

"They could come in handy." Jeff's words would prove prophetic, but Helen didn't listen to him.

After a rocky morning, the store was nearly back to normal. Jeff had jangled his nerves with three monster mugs of coffee. Now he was eating comfort food: a giant pot-roast sandwich, which he hid behind the cash register when customers came in. People didn't see it, but their dogs sniffed it out and headed straight for the counter, tails wagging. Jeff had to buy them off with cheese-and-bacon treats.

Lulu was dressed and working the room. She sauntered through the store modeling a fake-fur coat in hot pink. Her nails were painted rose. Helen's own winter coat was a sensible black and five years old. Her nails were chipped.

I wish I had a dog's life, she thought.

Todd was in the back room, grooming and kissing his dogs. Only Jonathon was missing. Jeff had to call and cancel the star's grooming sessions for the day. He offered to reschedule their dogs with Todd, but most of the regulars said no. They wanted Jonathon or nobody.

"Is Jonathon OK?" Helen said.

"He's recovering," Jeff said. "The police questioned him for hours yesterday. He was too exhausted to come into work. I told him to take the day off."

Helen was gripped with guilt and fear. The cops had grilled Jonathon like a backyard barbecue. What would they do if they found out she'd lied? They won't, she told herself. They were too busy questioning the wrong people, like Jonathon. She was safe. So why didn't she feel safe?

"How can the police go after Jonathon? Tammie's husband killed her," Helen said. "It's obvious. You heard Kent. His wife was murdered, and all he cared about was whether he could use the pool. Then he wanted to kill her little dog. The man is heartless. We should tell the police."

"Tell them what?" Jeff said. "That Kent didn't want his wife's dog? Do you think Detective Crayton would want a foo-foo dog? He'd probably send Prince to the pound, too."

"But it makes no sense. Why would Jonathon kill Tammie? He wouldn't murder her because she barged into the grooming room."

"No, he wouldn't," Jeff said. "But the police keep asking me questions about Jonathon's missing grooming shears. The ten-inch ones. The detectives were in here this morning, before the store opened. This time they wanted to know if Jonathon had reported their loss to me."

"Tammie was stabbed in the chest with grooming shears," Helen said, then quickly shut her mouth before she spilled more. What a babbling idiot I am, she thought. I'm not supposed to know that the scissors were the murder weapon—or where Tammie was stabbed. Jeff will know I saw the body.

"That's my guess, too," Jeff said.

Helen breathed a little sigh of relief. Jeff hadn't noticed her slip.

"Someone is trying to frame him," Jeff said.

"So what did you tell the police? Did Jonathon mention that he was missing his scissors?" Helen said.

"No," Jeff said. "But he was busy."

If he was busy, Helen wondered, wouldn't he need his ten-inch scissors? But that was a question she couldn't ask. She didn't want to ask it. She didn't want Jonathon to be the murderer.

"Kent stole them," she said. "He heard the whole fight. He was there. I saw him standing in the doorway. He could have slipped in and taken the scissors and none of us would have noticed him."

Jeff pulled out the pot-roast sandwich and began munching. Once again, Helen realized she'd missed lunch. Her stomach growled. Jeff didn't notice that, either.

"The police also asked me if he'd ever shown any violent behavior," Jeff said, taking a big bite. The sandwich dripped warm gravy. Helen wanted to lunge over the counter and grab it. "I think the cops may have heard the stories that he killed the man in Miami."

"Wasn't it self-defense?" Helen said. She couldn't believe the theatrical Jonathon was a killer. It wasn't his style, and Jonathon was all about style. She liked his retro disco suits and platform shoes. The world would be a dull place if all men wore Ralph Lauren and ate pot roast.

"Yeah, but a gay guy is easier to arrest and convict," Jeff said, taking another bite of the boundless sandwich. "How do you think a flamer like Jonathon would do with a jury?"

Badly, Helen thought. South Florida, for all its wild ways, could turn suddenly conservative. Get a Bible-thumping jury and he'd be convicted for his ungodly lifestyle. But she didn't say it. Jeff had enough worries.

"The police haven't arrested Jonathon," Helen said. "They're still investigating. They could be targeting the husband. The detectives have to ask Jonathon those questions. It's their job."

"But are they any good at it?" Jeff said. "Stately Palms isn't a city like Fort Lauderdale. They're not going to hire young hotshot detectives. They'll pick up a few tired old retirees from up north who don't want to work too hard."

"You don't know that," Helen said. "They might have experienced detectives who got sick of the politics in some cold city."

"Is that how Crayton struck you—a good detective? Or that other one, McGoogan, the guy who twitched the whole time?"

Jeff had a point. "Do you know anyone in Stately Palms who could give you some inside information about the investigation?" Helen said, steering the subject to a less worrisome area.

"Not a soul," Jeff said. "If it were here in Wakefield Manor, I'd know in a heartbeat. There's the cutest sergeant on the force, and he comes in here with his rottweiler, Dixie. Buys bags of organic chow. But I don't know anyone who can help us at Stately Palms."

I do, Helen thought. Phil would make some inquiries if I asked him. He has the law enforcement contacts. But he's in Washington now. And I didn't tell him about Tammie's murder when he called last night. So what do I say now? By the way, Phil, I forgot to mention it, but I found a body.

"I'm sure the police have a long list of suspects to check," Helen said. She wasn't sure at all.

"I hope so," Jeff said. "I hate to sound selfish, but I don't want to be known as the grooming shop that hired a murderer."

"Maybe it will be good for business," Helen said. "You know what they say, 'No publicity is bad publicity, as long as they spell your name right.' "

The phone rang. Jeff stashed his sandwich and took the call in the back room. He came back five minutes later, pale and shaken. "That was Willoughby's attorney. Barkley is still missing. The police talked with the husband, but he denied being in the store.

"Willoughby is going to file suit Monday. Her attorney claims his client lost a valuable dog because of our carelessness and incompetence. We're being sued for the value of the dog, plus her lost income. She wants . . ."

Jeff stopped and took a deep breath. He could hardly get the words out. "Fifty million."

"Dollars?" Helen said. What else would it be? Monopoly money?

Jeff nodded. It was all he could manage. He pulled out the monster pot-roast sandwich and held it. Maybe its warm weight was comforting.

Fifty million dollars. The sum was staggering. The suit would swallow Jeff's store and leave him with nothing, not even a bone. Helen appreciated the fact that Jeff said "our carelessness." He was generously sharing the blame, she thought. Jeff did take the call from the husband. But I gave that dog to Francis. At least I think it was Francis. Now a sweet little pup was facing possible destruction—and so was Jeff.

"We might survive a killer groomer, but we can't lose a dog," Jeff said. Helen thought there were tears in his brown eyes. "Our customers won't trust their precious babies to us again. This is like losing a child. When this story hits the news, I'm ruined."

"You mean it hasn't yet?" Helen was surprised.

"No. Willoughby has managed to hush it up so far. She told the Davis department stores that the dog has an upset stomach. It will buy her some time. She knows they'll cancel her contract at the first sign of trouble. The publicity would ruin Barkley's career. But the dog has to show up for that shoot on Monday or else. It's only a matter of time before the story breaks. Willoughby is afraid her vengeful husband might blow the whistle. When the suit is splashed all over the media on Monday, I'm dead. There's nothing I can do to stop this disaster."

"Sure there is," Helen said. "You worked all morning to rescue Prince. You can figure out some way to save yourself."

"This is different. I don't know how to fight this. It's hopeless," Jeff said. His shoulders slumped. The pot-roast sandwich sat untouched by his side.

Helen wanted to say, If you won't try to save yourself, I will. But that would sound silly. She said nothing. But she had a plan. She slipped into the back room and made a phone call.

When she came back out, Lulu was on the counter, eating the pot-roast sandwich. Jeff didn't notice.

He was staring at his boutique as if it might disappear.

CHAPTER 10

The hammering was like nails being driven into a hundred coffins. It came with the hellish shriek of electric saws. The sound never stopped. People were boarding up their windows. They hoped for salvation from the hurricane. But they didn't know if their buildings would survive. The hurricane heading for Fort Lauderdale could be the big one.

Floridians lived in a hurricane zone. They knew someday a storm could destroy their lives. But it was like the certainty of their own deaths. It would happen someday, later.

Now the inevitable was coming tomorrow. The TV weather maps showed the hurricane as a pulsing red blob bigger than the whole state. This mass of destruction was aimed at Florida's Atlantic coast.

Helen had no doubt now that a hurricane was on the way. Strangely dark clouds scudded across the sky. The air felt like warm, wet cotton pressed against her face, but there was cold under the smothering heat. She shivered. The hurricane was supposed to hit about eight o'clock tomorrow night.

That was twenty-eight hours away. Helen had work to do if she was going to save Jeff's shop—and herself. Any publicity on the dognapping would be fatal. Her ex-husband would find her for sure.

After she got off work at four p.m., Helen began phase one of her plan. She headed for Willoughby Barclay's house. She was going to throw herself on the woman's mercy. She knew it would be a stony surface.

Helen didn't tell Jeff what she was doing. She knew he wouldn't want her talking to a woman threatening a lawsuit. He'd think it was too risky. She figured they had nothing to lose.

Helen had looked up Willoughby's address in Jeff's files. The Barclay couple had moved into a new mansion shortly after their pup snagged her big contract. Willoughby told Detective Brogers that she'd kicked out her husband, but she still lived in their new home. Like most mansions, it was near a bus route. The rich needed their houses cleaned, their dogs walked, and their children watched.

Helen bought an energy bar for a late lunch and ate it while she waited for her bus. The passengers sat tense and straight-backed, clutching shopping bags crammed with water jugs, peanut butter, and bread. Hurricane food. The air was electric with their edgy energy and end-of-the-day sweat. Babies cried. Mothers snapped at their children. Men complained about their jobs and their wives. Helen was glad when the bus reached her stop.

The Island of Malta was in a cluster of man-made islands off Las Olas in downtown Lauderdale. Five years ago the islands had been lined with charming old Florida homes, sensible one-story houses with breezeways and jalousie windows.

Many were gone now, torn down for three-story stucco mansions. Squeezed into minilots, the new mansions looked like elephants herded into tiny pens.

Willoughby's mansion had a portico with gawky white columns, like a teenager who'd grown too fast. The half-circle drive was barely wide enough for a Mercedes. Helen counted at least four styles of windows on the house, from Palladian to bulging bay. It reminded Helen of her own tract mansion in St. Louis. She didn't miss it.

Helen rang the doorbell. Willoughby answered. When she saw Helen, her face turned into a primitive mask of hate. "You husband stealer. What do you want?"

Helen was stunned. She'd expected any reaction but this. "Husband stealer? What are you talking about?"

"I heard you were flirting with my husband at the shop. You let him grope you, you slut. You just want a rich man. Well, let me tell you, when I finish with him, he won't have a dime."

Helen was still trying to figure this out. Someone must have told Willoughby about Francis feeling her up, but they put a nasty spin on it. Did a customer see that humiliating scene? Did Todd or Jonathon tell Detective Brogers to save their own skin? That damned detective was capable of twisting the truth.

"Wait a minute," Helen said. "I don't know where you heard that, but it's a lie. I wasn't flirting with him. Your husband put his hand on me, and I stomped him good and hard. You must know he's handy. I guess that's one reason why you're divorcing him."

Helen didn't add that she couldn't steal what this woman didn't want—or that she wouldn't let Francis touch her if she spent six months alone in a lighthouse.

"Now can we talk about what's really important—getting your dog back?"

"You'd better be here to tell me you've found Barkley," Willoughby said. But there wasn't much threat in her words. The bounce was gone from her curls and her step. She had great dark circles under her eyes. Willoughby was worried. Helen suspected this stucco splendor would go on the sheriff's auction block if the dog wasn't found.

"I have an idea about how to get her," Helen said. "But I need to come in and talk to you."

Willoughby opened the door reluctantly. Helen slid in before the woman changed her mind. The front hall glared with mirrors and marble. Tiny spotlights set off a gold-framed painting of Willoughby signed by Rax. She looked like a young queen about to ascend her throne. Helen thought the least the couple could do was put up a portrait of Barkley. After all, the dog bought the place.

Willoughby didn't look like the confident woman in the painting. She was wearing something pale and ruffled that undoubtedly had a designer label. But in her own home, Willoughby seemed overwhelmed by her expensive outfit, as if it were wearing her.

Helen followed Willoughby into a great room with a view of the pool. She watched the wind rip pink and purple flowers off the bushes and toss them like confetti. The pool deck led to a boat dock, where a white Hatteras cruiser rocked wildly in the water.

Willoughby went to a wet bar. With silver tongs she dropped ice in a wineglass, then poured herself an Evian water and topped it with a thin lemon slice. She didn't offer Helen a drink. Helen was thirsty after her bus ride, but she said nothing. She was inside the house. That was enough.

Willoughby plopped down on a pale beige leather couch. Helen bet Barkley never got near it. Helen sat down on another slippery leather sofa section and set loose an avalanche of needlepoint pillows. She picked them off the floor, then said, "I'm very sorry about Barkley."

"You should be," Willoughby said. "You gave my dog to my husband. She's gone and you're responsible."

Helen felt her tact tearing away like the flower petals. "You should have warned us you had sole custody of your dog. You didn't tell us your husband couldn't pick up Barkley."

"I did. Besides, did I have to give you a list of all the people who couldn't pick up my dog?" Willoughby said. "I dropped it off at your store and I should have picked it up. Period. I don't have to give you any information about my private life."

"It." Barkley was an "it" to her owner. Willoughby didn't really love the perky puppy, just the money she brought in. Maybe my plan has a chance, Helen thought. She took a deep breath and started in. "Jeff will lose everything if you sue, Willoughby. His reputation, his shop. I'll lose my job." Helen didn't mention that she had much more to lose, including her freedom, if this story went public.

"And I've lost my income," Willoughby said. "I'm bankrupt if that dog isn't found. Do you know what the payments are on this house? Or the maintenance? The pool service alone costs a fortune."

Not to mention the landscaping, Helen thought, as a palm frond sailed through the air. It's already gone with the wind.

"Suing us won't help you," Helen said. "Jeff doesn't have one million dollars, much less fifty million. The only one who'll get any money is your lawyer. Please give us a chance to find Barkley. You don't want this story getting out to the media. A catfight over a dog won't help you."

I could have used a better choice of words, Helen thought.

But Willoughby was listening. She leaned forward and said, "What choice do I have? Barkley has to be on the set in Miami Monday or the department store contract is canceled."

"There's a hurricane coming," Helen said. "It's supposed to be a bad one. When it hits, electricity and phone lines will be down, bridges will be out, roads will be flooded. Barkley's shoot will be canceled. Things won't get back to normal for weeks. No one will expect you to produce Barkley during a major hurricane. The papers will have other news to print besides a lost-dog story. You have some time to save the situation. Please let us find Barkley for you."

Willoughby considered Helen's words. She could almost hear the wheels turning in the blonde's frilly brain. Finally she said, "You have one week."

Helen nearly collapsed with relief. It was the first time she'd felt at ease since Willoughby screamed at her in the store. Helen wanted to sink into the sofa's soft surface and snooze on the piles of pillows. Her plan would work if the weather cooperated. She was probably the only person in Broward County who hoped the hurricane would hit.

"Then we've got a deal," Helen said. "But you'll have to help me."

"I'm not giving you any money," Willoughby said in a hard, flat voice. Her hand shook slightly, and the ice clinked in her glass.

"I'm not asking for any," Helen said. "I need you to answer some questions. Do you think anyone besides your husband could have kidnapped your dog?"

"No," Willoughby said. "The police aren't sure he did it, but I know it was Francis. He hates me. He's never forgiven me for filing for divorce and getting temporary custody of Barkley."

Willoughby didn't mention that she'd also exiled her husband from the McMansion. Francis had lost everything—his wife, his income, and his home. Helen wondered how much rage was in that pale little nonentity with the restless hands.

"I thought Detective Brogers was going to talk to your husband."

"He did, for all the good it did. Francis claimed someone impersonated him at your store. He says he never took Barkley."

"Could the police get a search warrant for his home?"

"They didn't need one," Willoughby said. "Francis let the detective inside his condo to look for the dog. He made a big deal out of inviting him in to search. Brogers says he checked the entire place, including the closets and the storage room. There was no sign of a dog, not even any food or water bowls. But I know Francis has it. He's hidden it somewhere. Francis is too smart to keep Barkley at his condo. Oh, there's another thing. Francis has an alibi. He says he was at the mall when the dog was stolen."

"Which mall?" Helen said. Florida had more malls than mosquitoes.

"Sawgrass Mills."

"The outlet mall?" Helen said.

"The one with more than four hundred stores," Willoughby said. "It's supposed to be the biggest mall in Florida. It's two miles long. They bring shoppers in on tour buses. You can buy mall tour tickets at the big hotels."

Helen wondered if Willoughby had statistics on all the major malls. The woman was definitely a power shopper.

"I never shop there for my clothes, of course," Willoughby said. "They would be at least a year out-of-date in an outlet mall." She paused dramatically.

The awkward silence continued. Helen finally figured out that Willoughby was waiting for her to admire her outfit. "I can see your clothes are up-to-the-minute," Helen said.

Willoughby smiled and took another sip of Evian. "Francis doesn't care about fashion. He likes to roam around and look at things. He calls it people-watching." Willoughby clearly could not understand her husband's fascination with others. People were supposed to watch her.

"Francis knows that on a Saturday afternoon some fifty thousand shoppers can swarm into the Sawgrass stores. He showed Detective Brogers a dated and time-stamped receipt for a meal at the mall. He was supposedly eating a hamburger when Barkley was taken from your store. Except I don't believe it. Who keeps a receipt like that? It was for cash, too. That's how I knew it was a phony. Francis pays for everything with a credit card."

"Did you tell the police?" Helen said.

"Yes. Francis explained that, too. He said he couldn't afford to use his credit cards since I filed for divorce. I don't believe that. I think he went through the mall trash cans until he found a receipt with the right time on it. It wouldn't be difficult, not with thousands of shoppers eating there. Somebody would throw away a receipt he could use. There are more than thirty places to eat in that mall."

Helen wondered if Francis was really that crafty, or if his soon-to-be ex was so blinded by hatred that she wanted Francis to be the kidnapper.

"Where did he eat?" Helen said.

"He didn't," Willoughby said. "He lied."

Helen tried again. "At what restaurant did he claim he had the hamburger?"

"The Golden Calf."

"Do the police think your dog was kidnapped for money?" Helen asked.

"I haven't received a ransom demand. I would have been contacted by now. Who else would take it?"

"There are a lot of sick puppies out there," Helen said. Why am I dogged with animal puns? she wondered.

Willoughby was too intent on blaming her husband to notice. "Francis took that dog," she said. "He didn't kidnap it for ransom. He's doing this to spite me. He doesn't need the money. We got a nice chunk of money up front when we signed exclusively with the Davis stores. He took his share and invested it."

Willoughby blew her half on the house and the boat, while Francis saved his. The little bland man had brains.

"Francis has stashed that dog somewhere," Willoughby said. "He's going to keep Barkley until the Davis department stores contract is canceled and my dog's career is ruined. I know how Francis thinks."

"Where do you think he hid Barkley?"

"I have no idea," Willoughby said, and drained her glass. "I just know he did."

"Does he have family here in Florida?"

"No, his mother is his only relative, and she lives in Connecticut," Willoughby said. "Mrs. Barclay wouldn't steal my dog. She's a lovely woman. She's also eighty years old."

"What about his friends?"

"Francis doesn't have any," Willoughby said.

Helen could believe that. "Lovers?" she said.

Willoughby looked uneasy. "He doesn't have a girlfriend."

Ha, Helen thought. Your husband is a hound and you know it. But she'd been revolted by his touch. She suspected other women would feel the same way. Maybe he didn't have a girlfriend. Why the careful wording? Was his ass-grabbing an act? Fort Lauderdale was the gayest city this side of San Francisco.

"Boyfriends?" Helen said.

That got a reaction. "Francis is not gay!"

The lady doth protest way too much, Helen thought, but she let the subject go. "Do you have Francis's new address?"

"Why do you need it?" Willoughby sounded suspicious. Was she still afraid Helen would cross over to the enemy?

"In case I want to follow him for surveillance," Helen said.

Willoughby liked that idea. She handed over the address.

"One last thing. Do you have a photograph of Francis?"

"Why?" Willoughby said. She still didn't quite trust Helen.

"I'd like to ask around at the mall and see if anyone can identify him."

Willoughby went to a cherry-wood secretary near the window. She opened a slim drawer and took out a silver-framed photo. It had been lying facedown. Helen saw it was a wedding photo of Willoughby and Francis. Willoughby was radiant in white lace and ribbons. Francis had no more expression than the plastic groom on a wedding cake. What had the beaming bride seen in him? Was it only money? Helen studied his blank face. It was the man who'd felt her up. She'd definitely given Barkley to Francis, but Helen didn't know whether to be relieved or not.

Willoughby slid the photo from the frame, then took a shiny pair of scissors from the same drawer. They had to be at least ten inches long. She cut the groom out of the picture with one swift, sharp stroke.

"Here," she said. "Take this."

CHAPTER 11

Waiting for a hurricane was like sitting on death row, Helen decided.

She knew the lethal hour, but still hoped for a reprieve. Hurricanes were as unpredictable as governors, and subject to as many unseen pressures.

Maybe the monster storm would suddenly swing up to Palm Beach. (Dear God, please hit the rich for a change, instead of the poor mobile-home dwellers.) Maybe it would head even farther north to Orlando. (Smite Disney World, o Lord.) Or go south into the Keys. (They're used to it.) Best of all, let it blow harmlessly out to sea. Please let it hit anywhere, anyplace, but my place.

That was the prayer for the hurricane-zone dwellers, and Helen recited it when she left Willoughby's house.

Yes, she needed a hurricane to make her plan work. But now that she was getting a taste of the oncoming storm, she wasn't sure she wanted to go through with it. The wind battered the palm trees and sent trash in swirling circles. Flying particles of sand stung her eyes. Street signs flapped and hummed, ready to pull loose and fly like Frisbees.

Helen felt restless and uneasy. She did not want to go home. Phil was still in Washington, and she couldn't face her lonely apartment. It was only five o'clock. She had

Francis's picture stashed in her purse. Helen caught a bus to Sawgrass Mills Mall.

The bus ride took nearly an hour in vicious traffic. Cars scurried like scalded roaches through red lights, over yellow lines, into wrong lanes. Pickups flipped off anyone who was in their way. SUV drivers yelled into their cell phones and ran pedestrians out of the crosswalks.

Helen's bus lurched past gas stations with angry, honking lines at the pumps. At one gas station, Helen saw a burly man take a swing at a guy who blocked his access. For once she was glad to be riding the bus.

At last she reached the sprawling Sawgrass Mills Mall. The bus let her off at the Pink Flamingo entrance. Each entrance was named after a different tropical animal—Pink Flamingo, White Seahorse, Yellow Toucan. As she approached the doors, recorded reminders said, "You are entering the Pink Flamingo entrance...."

For Helen, the mall was a preview of hell, where she would forever long for what she could not have. Her shoes were resoled and her black Escada pants were shiny with age, but the mall's designer styles, even heavily discounted, were too expensive for her. She was six feet tall and couldn't wear the sensibly priced brands most women bought. They were too short for Helen's extra-long arms and legs.

A sleek designer pantsuit with a long coat caught her eye in a shop window, and she stood there, wondering if maybe she could hold up a convenience store and buy it. She was almost grateful when a short woman shoved her out of the way. Helen tore her eyes from the displays and started searching for the Golden Calf, where Francis claimed he was eating when Barkley was stolen.

The stores were as frantic as on Christmas Eve. Nothing stopped the relentless shopping, not even the threat of a category-three hurricane. People had to buy before it all blew away.

The food court smelled deliciously of fried grease. Helen realized she was hungry. Not "I'd like some dinner" hungry, but "I could eat a side of beef" ravenous.

Hurricanes did that. The energy bar she'd downed on the way to Willoughby's house was long gone. Helen stopped at a chocolate shop for a big bar of Cadbury dark chocolate, then studied the mall map for the Golden Calf.

By the time she figured out where the restaurant was, the whole Cadbury bar had disappeared. Stress, she told herself. Helen bought two more bars for hurricane supplies. Desperate times called for desperate measures. She now carried a shopping bag, which would make her less obvious to store security when she questioned people.

The hike to the Golden Calf seemed to go on for miles. She was hungry again when she finally found the restaurant. The Golden Calf served twenty-dollar slabs of prime rib in dark-paneled booths. It was nearly empty at six thirty. Helen wondered if the storm kept customers away or if the Golden Calf was headed for the last roundup. She looked at the leather-bound menu. Francis hadn't ordered a hamburger. He'd had a twelve-dollar chopped steak. She could afford a small salad and an à la cart baked potato. The rest of her assets were tied up in Cadbury's stock.

The server had an expensive black uniform, a worn face, and tired hair. Her name tag said she was Eunice. When she poured Helen a glass of water, Eunice's hands were red and calloused, with veins like tree roots. What did she do for her other job? Clean houses? Wash dishes? Work in a factory?

Helen was almost embarrassed to order, but Eunice said, "Can I bring you extra rolls and butter, no charge?"

Our kind recognize each other, Helen thought. She noticed that the Golden Calf's tables were clean and the floor was vacuumed. There were no soda-straw wrappers or receipts on the floor. Maybe Francis really had eaten there.

When the server returned with her salad and potato, Helen pulled out the picture of Francis. "Have you seen this man in here recently?"

"What did he do?" Eunice said.

"Deadbeat dad," Helen said. Well, it was true, sort of. Helen suspected that story would appeal to Eunice.

"I'd like to say I did, but he looks like a lot of guys," Eunice said.

"He would have been here this weekend," Helen said.

"I may have seen him, but I'm not sure it was this weekend," Eunice said. "We get a lot of men in here on Saturday and Sunday while their wives are shopping. He looks familiar, but he doesn't look like anyone in particular. Does that make sense?"

It made a lot of sense. Francis had the kind of face that was hard to get a fix on. There wasn't any feature to catch the eye—no big nose or blue eyes or bulldog jaw. He wasn't tall, bald, or hairy. He was average, with brown eyes, brown hair, and no scars. Life had left no marks on him, and he'd left no marks on it.

Helen remembered his one distinguishing characteristic. "He's kind of handy. He might have tried to feel you up."

"Honey, that won't help," Eunice said wearily. "I can't remember all the men who've hit on me. You'd think I was on the menu."

Helen asked at the shops and restaurants in the section and got the same story. Salesclerks told her: "I'm not sure." "It could be him." "I think I've seen him before, but I can't say it was Saturday." She didn't have the nerve to mention Francis's hobby.

By eight o'clock, Helen knew her search was hopeless. She'd walked the mall until her feet ached. She sat on a bench near the exit. She would come back after the storm. This wasn't a good time to interview people. The salesclerks seemed distracted and anxious to close early. The shoppers were clearing out, their burst of manic buying over. A man and a woman struggled with a huge box marked PORTABLE GAS GENERATOR on a dolly. It didn't seem very portable now, but that generator would be worth its weight if the storm knocked out power lines.

As the couple wrestled the unwieldy box through the door, a blast of warm wind blew leaves and plastic bags onto the mall's polished floor. A small woman with unnaturally black hair came out of the restroom with a cleaning cart. She looked at the fresh mess, shook her head, and started sweeping up the windblown trash.

Trash.

This woman would notice a man rooting through the trash. Helen dug deep in her wallet for her emergency twenty. When she had made six figures a year, twenty dollars was lunch money, "yuppie food stamps," because ATMs issued so many twenty-dollar bills.

But now, in her minimum-wage world, twenty dollars had new respect. It represented nearly half a day's pay.

Helen held out the creased and folded bill. "Excuse me, ma'am," she said. "May I ask you a question?"

"What did you lose?" the black-haired woman said. Her English was accented but clear.

"A man," Helen said. "He is causing problems for his family." The woman swept the floor with a long-handled broom nearly as tall as she was. She moved it expertly while she shook her head at the wickedness of men.

Helen gave her the photo and the twenty. The woman took both, and studied the photo as she pocketed the twenty. The light gleaming off her dead-black hair gave it a purple cast.

"Yes, I saw him," she said. "It was Saturday about five thirty. I know the time because I start work at five o'clock, so I was not so tired early in my day. He was looking for something in the trash can by the Gap store. I remember, because I don't see a white man do that very much. He was not a bum or an old man looking for aluminum cans for the recycling. He took some paper out of the trash and overturned a full coffee cup. He made a big mess and left it for me. I had to mop the floor."

She handed Helen back the photo. The cleaning woman was about thirty-five, an anonymous servant like Helen. She bet there was another reason this woman remembered Francis. "Did he make a pass at you?"

The woman's face flushed with anger and shame. "He touched my—" She couldn't continue, she was so upset. "I am a respectable married woman. I will not forget him."

A break at last. "Could I have your name?" Helen said.

The woman backed away. Her English deteriorated as her fear grew. "No, please. I no talk to you about this. Make trouble for me." She pushed her cart before her like a shield and hurried down the hall. Helen didn't follow. She had what she needed. The police could track down the woman if they had to.

Helen called Willoughby collect from a pay phone at the mall. Barkley's owner was desperate enough to take Helen's call and ecstatic when she heard the news. "I knew Francis didn't have an alibi," Willoughby said. Helen could almost see her blond curls bobbing emphatically. "I'll call that Detective Brogers. We'll have my dog back in time for the shoot."

For the first time Helen felt a surge of hope. Barkley would be found. The lawsuit would disappear and so would her troubles.

She braced herself for the walk to the bus stop. The sky was black and moonless. The night was alive with wind-borne debris. Helen's bus pulled up as she arrived, her second lucky break. All the way home she felt a surge of excitement that she tried to push away. She had to ignore the feeling. It was too soon to celebrate. That wasn't the right word to describe her situation. There was still the Tammie horror. But half her burden had been lifted. She felt lighter.

Even the perpetual pounding of hammers as she walked home from the bus stop didn't ruin her good mood. At the Coronado, the dancing palm tree was jigging in wild circles. Magically, there was no wind by the pool itself. Margery and Peggy were stretched out on adjoining chaise longues, drinking white wine and eating pretzels. Pete moved restlessly up and down the back of Peggy's chair, like a soldier on perimeter patrol.

"You look like you've got good news," Margery said. She sat up and poured Helen a big glass of wine. Helen wished she could wear purple clam diggers like Margery. On tall people like Helen, those pants looked like she couldn't find anything long enough.

"Did you find the missing dog?" Margery asked.

"I've got a lead," Helen said. "The husband was lying about his alibi. A cleaning woman saw him digging in a trash can." She told Margery and Peggy the story.

"I hope that woman's still there if the police want to question her," Margery said.

"Why wouldn't she be?" Helen said.

"Green card," Peggy said.

"Awk!" Pete said. Those were scary words in Florida.

"She might not have one," Peggy said. "Or she could have a fake card that won't stand a close look. What nationality was she?"

"I'm not sure," Helen said. "I don't think she was Hispanic. She might have been Eastern European. She was short with dead-black hair and dark eyes."

"Did you get her name?" Margery said.

Helen shook her head. She didn't get anything. She could feel her hope leaking away.

"It sounds like she was telling the truth," Margery said. "That's what you should be doing. Have you told the cops what happened at Tammie's?"

Helen looked at Peggy, who was studying the pretzel bowl as if it contained the secret to world peace.

"Don't underestimate the police, Helen," Margery said. "They're going to find out you were in Tammie's house when she was dead."

"Awk!" Pete said. Peggy's wine sloshed in her glass, but she said nothing. She'd been in places she shouldn't have been, too.

Margery continued her lecture, a professor in purple clam diggers. "Look how fast you learned Willoughby's husband was lying, and you don't even know what you're doing."

"Thanks a lot," Helen said. "I got information the police never bothered to find out."

"True. But if that cop was half-awake, he would have figured it out in five minutes. How long will it take two real homicide detectives to discover your shenanigans?"

Helen looked over at Peggy. She was feeding Pete a pretzel. Maybe his diet was discontinued for the storm.

"I wiped down everything before I left Tammie's," Helen said. "But so what if they find my fingerprints? I was in the house when I picked up the dog."

"You were there too long the second time."

"No one will know that," Helen said.

"You went through a security gate in that pimpmobile."

"Pupmobile," Helen said. "The guard was asleep."

"The security camera was wide-awake," Margery said.

"The police are too busy building a case against the star groomer, Jonathon."

"Are you sure?" Margery said. "Maybe the cops are building a case against you."

"Me?" Helen's voice came out a croak.

"Maybe they think you're an accomplice. Look at it from their viewpoint. You work with Jonathon. Tammie made a pass at you. Jeff must have seen her waving her tits at you at the store. Didn't you complain to him that she was naked?"

"Yes, but—"

"You had a grudge and you helped kill Tammie. That's how they'll see it. It's time to call in Phil, Helen. He can help you."

"I can help myself," Helen said.

"So far I haven't seen you do much but flap around in circles—kind of like that palm tree out there. That reminds me—what are you doing when this hurricane hits?"

"Hiding in my closet," Helen said. "It's got plenty of legroom."

"Come on over to my place," Margery said. "My friend Elsie is staying with me, plus everyone from the Coronado: Cal the Canadian and the women in 2C, Doris and Alice. Peggy and Pete will be there, so you can bring what's-his-name."

"Thumbs," Helen said. "I'd better keep my cat locked

in your bedroom. He might consider Pete dinner on the wing."

"Awwk," Pete said. He looked more nervous than ever.

"They'll get along fine," Margery said. "Your cat is too lazy to eat anything that doesn't come with a can opener. We'll have ourselves a real old-fashioned hurricane party. I'll make screwdrivers as long as the electricity holds out. We'll drink, eat too much, and sit out the storm."

"It's a date," Helen said. "Now I'd better head home and check on Thumbs."

The women in 2C were out on the balcony. They waved to Helen.

"Which one is which?" she asked Margery.

"That's Doris on the left, with the wineglass," Margery said. "Alice is pouring."

"And it's wine from a bottle with a real cork," Helen said.

Doris was a tanklike woman with practical gray hair. Alice was thin with a gray-black bob. They seemed to regard the approaching storm as their evening's entertainment.

What a change from the last bunch in that apartment, Helen thought.

She was almost to her door when Margery came running after her, cell phone glowing in the dark. "Phil's on the phone. He wants to talk to you." She grinned like a purple-clad Cupid.

Helen's fingers trembled when she took the phone. Margery melted into the wind-whipped shrubbery, leaving Helen alone with her lover.

"Helen," he said, his voice warm with love and worry. "I'm coming back. I'm catching the next plane down there."

Margery had told Phil she was in trouble. Her landlady couldn't resist meddling. "Why?" Helen could only manage that one word.

"Because I love you," Phil said. "Because you're mixed up in something ugly."

Margery ratted me out about Tammie's murder, Helen thought.

"Margery told me about that dognapping at your store. It's a custody battle. Divorces can get ugly, Helen."

She was giddy with relief. He didn't know. "Tell me about it," she said.

"I can save you," he said.

"I don't want to be rescued," Helen said. "I can take care of myself. Phil, please don't come to Florida. There's a hurricane coming. I'd feel better knowing you were safe."

"I'd feel better with you," he said. "What kind of life would I have without you?"

What kind of life will you have with me, when you find out how I've lied to you? Helen thought as she closed the phone.

CHAPTER 12
· ·

Helen felt like she was being walled up alive.

Two men were nailing plywood over the Pampered Pet windows. As each sheet blacked out another slab of light, the boutique grew more claustrophobic.

The store's lights were on, but they never quite reached into the room. Unsettling shadows slid around the back corners. Furtive movements flickered through the lower shelves. Helen thought they might be Lulu nosing around, but when she checked, the dog was at the other end of the store. The wind caused odd creaks and rattling thumps. Helen wondered what was working loose on the roof.

The storm was now eleven hours away. Helen couldn't see the hurricane coming in, but she could hear it. The wind had developed a horror-movie howl. A lashing rain slanted sideways across the parking lot.

Dripping customers struggled to open the shop door against the screaming wind. Jeff rushed forward to keep the door from slamming against the building. No one bought cute toys. They wanted thirty-pound sacks of pet food, emergency rations against the storm.

Everyone discussed the hurricane.

"It's supposed to hit us directly," a husky man said, as he hoisted sixty pounds of chow on his shoulders. He looked like he could stand up to any category windstorm.

"I heard the storm may miss us and go up to Palm Beach instead," a thin blond man with one earring said. "I'm evacuating to Weston, and my friends have a cat. I wanted to bring it something."

He bought the wild salmon treats and headed for his refuge on the edge of the Everglades.

Rumors flew faster than wind-scattered trash. Each customer proudly brought in a new one, like a dog dragging in a smelly piece of garbage.

This was the big storm, as big as Hurricane Andrew, with one-hundred-fifty-mile-an-hour winds. Fort Lauderdale would be flattened.

The Weather Channel said it would be downgraded to a category two and go up toward Palm Beach. Heck, hundred-mile-an-hour winds were nothing.

The Internet said it was a category three and would land at Port Saint Lucie. A hundred-thirty-mile-an-hour winds? If you didn't live in a mobile home, you were OK.

No, wait, the radio said it would hit at Melbourne and it would be—

Nobody knew anything for sure, except they were restless, fretful, and plagued with odd impulses to stock up on strawberry Pop-Tarts and peanut butter, bleach, and bottled water.

No matter how scary the storm rumors grew, people still brought in their dogs for grooming. A standing appointment with Jonathon was sacred, come wind or high water.

Jonathon groomed the dogs alone in his room, his golden mane gleaming. He looked splendid enough for a Las Vegas stage. Elvis would have envied his rhinestone-studded orange disco suit, but the king of the Lauderdale groomers lacked the last ounce of star glow. Jonathon seemed remote and worried. Helen couldn't tell if he was brooding on the impending hurricane or his possible arrest. He was trimming the ears on a fat chocolate poodle, and didn't look up when Helen entered the grooming salon. The dog was perfectly still and absolutely trusting. Helen didn't disturb him during the delicate operation.

Todd was pouting. Jeff had banished the hunky young groomer to the cage room with a new three-speed fan. The windowless room reeked of wet dog.

"Are you ready for the storm?" she asked him.

"No, and I can't get ready when people interrupt me," he snapped.

Helen put Todd's bad mood down mostly to the weather. Hers wasn't much better. She was keyed up, tired, and lethargic, all at once. The customers' dogs were shrill and yappy. Even Lulu was snappish. She tore off her daisy collar and refused to model anything else. She took an instant dislike to a large man in a very wet parrot shirt who wanted a bag of organic dog food. "Hell, I can't remember what brand she feeds that mutt," he said. "Let me call my wife."

He speed-dialed her on his cell phone and said, "Hey, you still in bed or on the can?"

Lulu nipped his pants leg.

"What's wrong with that crazy dog?" Parrot Shirt said. Lulu nimbly dodged his kick.

"I'm so sorry," Jeff said. "The storm has her upset."

Helen slipped Lulu a cheese-and-bacon treat. She would have bitten the guy, too, if she could have gotten away with it.

Jeff helped Parrot Shirt to the car with his sack of food and came back drenched. He dried his sopping hair with a dog groomer's towel, and used one of the big dog hair dryers to get the water off his clothes.

"The storm is getting worse," he said. "I think we'd better close about four p.m."

The door opened with a wind-snapping sound, and two water-soaked men entered. One was short and solid. The other shook himself like a wet dog. It was homicide detectives Crayton and McGoogan. Helen's heart sank.

"Could we talk to you a minute?" Detective Crayton asked Helen. The rain had not improved his mood.

McGoogan brushed water drops off his suit like dandruff.

She looked at Jeff, hoping he'd say that he needed her behind the register.

"I can handle this," Jeff said. "Go on back to the stockroom where you can have some privacy." And the customers won't see you, Helen thought.

The curtains to the grooming side twitched. Helen wondered if Todd or Jonathon were watching. She did not hear the roar of the dog dryer. Was someone trying to listen? Helen hoped the flirtatious Lulu would join them and distract the detectives, but she stayed with Jeff.

Detective Crayton did not sit down this time. He remained standing. His bald head barely came to Helen's nose, but the detective seemed to fill the room. "Just wanted to ask you a quick question about the second time you came to the victim's house and attempted to deliver the dog," Crayton said.

"Yes?" Here it comes, Helen thought.

"A neighbor said your store's pink Cadillac was parked in front of the victim's house for nearly twenty minutes around four o'clock that afternoon. That's a long time to knock on anyone's door. Are you sure you didn't go inside the house on that second visit?"

Detective McGoogan scratched his ear.

"Why would I do that?" Helen said.

"I don't know," Crayton said. "Maybe to kill Mrs. Grimsby."

McGoogan scraped a splash of mud off his trouser leg.

"No!" Helen said. "Never. How can you say that? The neighbor was wrong. I knocked on the door and no one answered, so I took the dog back to the store."

"We have the tape from the guard's shack," Crayton said. He leaned forward. Helen took a step back. "You came into the country club grounds at three fifty-nine p.m. and you left at four twenty-four p.m. That was a long time to knock on a door."

Detective McGoogan wound his watch.

"I got lost," Helen said. "Very twisty roads in that development."

"That so?" Detective Crayton said. He looked like a brick wall. An angry wall. "Because you had no trouble finding your way back the first time. Took you about three minutes. But that's your story, right, and you're sticking to it? Sure you don't want to change anything?"

Detective McGoogan was staring straight at her, eyes fixed on her lying face.

"I can't," Helen said. "That's what happened."

"Don't go anywhere, Miss Hawthorne. We'll be talking with you again."

They left. Helen heard the door slam in the wind. She could feel the panic clawing at her guts. She stayed in the stockroom for a moment, trying to recover. In the small windowless bathroom, she plastered on more lipstick, then wiped it off. It looked like a bloody slash in her dead-white face. Helen splashed water on her face, then took a deep breath and went into the store.

"Everything all right?" Jeff said.

"Fine," Helen said. She was glad when a little woman in a yellow rain slicker struggled against the wind to enter the shop. Helen ran to help her inside. It was Elsie, Margery's friend.

Elsie pulled off the slicker and draped it over the counter. Jeff's eyes bugged. Elsie was seventy-eight. If her heart was as young as her wardrobe, Elsie's ticker was about eighteen. She wore tight green satin low-rise pants, a yellow halter top, and turquoise high heels. Her substantial breasts hung low, which was good. They covered most of her bare middle. Helen thought the barbed-wire tattoo on her arm was probably henna. Elsie's fluffy hair was orange with green streaks. The effect was surreal but oddly appealing, like an old colorized photo.

Elsie had a sweet, dithery manner. "Helen, dear, Margery didn't tell me you were working here. I came in to pick up my Corkie. Today is her first cut. That's an important time in a doggie's life, and I didn't want to miss it."

"I'll get her," Helen said.

Corkie was a fluffy white dog with a black button nose, who'd waited patiently in her cage. She yipped ecstatically when she climbed into Elsie's arms, then licked her face, removing most of her mistress's makeup. Helen thought Corkie's instincts were good, but she was in no position to be giving fashion advice today.

In the middle of the reunion, Jonathon stalked into the boutique side like a rock star, rhinestones flashing in the fluorescent light, orange satin shining, long mane waving. As he strode by Elsie, Helen was nearly blinded by their combined colors.

Elsie didn't realize protocol required her not to speak to the star groomer. "Excuse me, young man," she said in her soft, slightly trembly voice. "Don't I know you?"

"I don't think so," Jonathon said. He looked at Elsie like she was a hair in his butter.

"I think I saw you at a pet shop in Tampa," Elsie said, stopping his sparkling progress. "You worked there about four years ago."

"I've never been to Tampa," Jonathon said. He stepped around Elsie and talked briefly to Jeff about his schedule. The next thing Helen knew, Jonathon had packed up his scissors and left.

"I don't think I am mistaken," Elsie said. "I'm very good with faces. Well, it's not important. I want a case of puppy food and some treats for Corkie. She's a teacup poodle. Very expensive, she was, but I bought a lot of love."

"She's adorable," Jeff said, and scratched the little dog's ears. Corkie wagged her tail and whimpered happily. She was still a pup, but big for a teacup poodle. Helen thought Jeff was giving Corkie a close examination. Was there something wrong with Jonathon's grooming?

Elsie packed Corkie into her carrying case and tottered out on her turquoise spikes. Helen followed with the dog food. The wind hit the women so hard, they had trouble talking. Helen made sure Elsie and her pup were safely in her red Miata. Then she stowed the dog food and treats in the backseat.

"I'm sure I've seen that young man before," Elsie said, once she was inside the car. "That groomer. What's his name?"

"Jonathon," Helen said.

"I don't think so," Elsie said. "That's not the name he used when I knew him."

CHAPTER 13

....

Helen's hair hung in wet tangles. Her soaked shirt stuck to her skin. Her shoes squished. All she did was carry Elsie's dog food to the car, and she was drenched.

"The parking lot is flooding," she told Jeff.

"The storm drains must have backed up," he said.

"I'll say. The water was up to my ankles. It will be over the curb and into the store soon."

"I'd better get some dog towels to pack around the door," Jeff said. He opened the grooming room dryer and threw Helen a warm towel.

"Ahh," she said as she dried her face. "That's heaven."

Jeff draped a second warm towel around her shivering shoulders. "How well do you know Elsie?"

"She's a friend of my landlady, Margery Flax," Helen said. "Elsie is a sweetie." Her hair was dripping on her soggy shoes.

"Maybe she's too sweet," Jeff said. "I think she was ripped off. Corkie isn't a teacup poodle. Teapot is more like it. That dog is too big to be a teacup. Adult teacups weigh between three and four pounds, and that puppy is nearly five pounds now. It's not even a full-blooded poodle. Did you see her nose? A poodle nose is pointed. Elsie's dog has a button nose, like a bichon."

"Elsie got scammed," Helen said. "It isn't the first time. She's a con artist's dream."

"She probably spent a lot of money for that cute little mutt," Jeff said. "Want some coffee?"

"Yes, I'm freezing in this air-conditioning."

Jeff poured Helen a cup. She wrapped her hands around it to warm them. "Happens all the time," Jeff said. "Naive dog lovers are willing to pay several thousand dollars for the current fashionable pedigreed pup. Instead, they get a mixed breed. They're easy to cheat when they don't know anything about dogs. I see it so often in this business. I hear so many sad stories from my customers who got clipped.

"There's a couple of local pet shops that pull these scams. They display the dogs behind glass, like works of art. They wait for suckers like Elsie, who can't tell a poodle from a Pomeranian. They'll hand her a puppy. 'Just hold it,' the pet store people say. 'Love is free.'

"Once Elsie has that lovable puppy in her hands, she's hooked. She'll pay whatever they want. The price depends on how rich Elsie looks. Since your friend has designer clothes and a new Miata, I bet she paid two or three thousand dollars for Corkie.

"The store tells Elsie she has a registered, pedigreed teacup poodle. The teacup isn't even an AKC variety. The store gave her fake papers. It's a swindle, but dog owners rarely complain. By the time they find out they've been cheated, they're in love. They wouldn't dream of returning their dog."

Helen knew they'd never pry Corkie away from Elsie.

"The crooked shops get away with their con jobs. It makes me sick. You know what really gets me?" Jeff said. "A lot of people can't afford those fake pedigreed pups. The crooked shops sell the pet on credit. The dog owner winds up paying on a high-interest loan forever."

"Poor Elsie. That sounds like something she'd do," Helen said. "She never reads the fine print in contracts."

"Are you going to tell her that Corkie isn't a teacup poodle?" Jeff said.

"Why?" Helen said. "Elsie would never return that little dog. Besides, I saw the scar on her tummy. Corkie has been spayed. She won't be bred. Telling Elsie the truth now would only upset her."

"I guess it's never good to know the truth about the one you love," Jeff said. He went back to make more coffee.

Was it? Helen wondered, as she dried her damp hair with a dog dryer. The blast of warm air felt good, but the sound nearly deafened her.

Would Phil feel that way? He was flying into a hurricane for her, if the airport was open in this weather. She longed for her lover, but she was afraid to see him. When Phil looked into her eyes, would he believe her reasons for not telling him about Tammie? Would he wonder what else she was hiding from him? Would she tell him?

After she smashed her marriage with her swinging crowbar, Helen had dated a prize collection of drunks, druggies, and deadbeats. For a while she'd had a crush on Cal, her Canadian neighbor at the Coronado. She'd loved the charming way he said "a-boot" for "about." His habit of forgetting his wallet when they went out to dinner was less charming. Helen had also dated a man who forgot he was married, and one who forgot she was single. He'd given Helen bruises when she'd talked to another man.

Helen was a loser in the dating game until she met Phil. She'd given up on the male species. Then he'd walked into her life. Actually, he'd been living next door for months on end. But she didn't see him—literally—until a few months ago. It wasn't love at first sight. Helen's first encounter with her dream lover had been an embarrassing nightmare. But then she'd saved him from drowning, and he'd saved her from getting in too deep with the law. Now, after the beating her heart took from her ex-husband, she was slowly learning to love and trust another man. When she thought about their last night together on Phil's black silk sheets, Helen felt hot, and it had nothing to do with the roaring hair dryer.

"Helen," Jeff called. "Can you take care of Mrs. Thompson?"

The store was suddenly deluged with customers. Helen didn't have time to think of Phil, Elsie's nonpoodle, or her mysterious remark about Jonathon: "That's not the name he used when I knew him."

As the weather worsened, people were frantic to buy for their pets. Helen hauled out bags of dog food and cans of cat food until her arms ached. Customers did not stop to talk anymore. They no longer speculated on the path of the storm. They wanted to run their essential errands and get home. Streets were flooding. Shops were locking their doors. Drawbridges across the Intracoastal Waterway were closing. People bought, paid, and rushed out the door. They all gave the same touching good-bye: "Be safe."

Be safe. It was what we wish most for ourselves and others, Helen thought.

Helen and Jeff worked for more than an hour before there was a break in the flood of customers. Todd came out of the grooming room looking dazed about the same time. His white T-shirt was covered with brown dog hair, and his jeans had stains Helen didn't want to examine too closely. Todd smelled like a wet dog. Only his diamond Cartier watch retained its rich glow.

"I'm starved," Todd said. "I'm going to the Briny Irish Pub for a bacon cheeseburger."

That was the bar two doors down. "Is it still open?" Helen said.

"Before a storm?" Todd said. "Are you kidding? It will be packed. People need courage to face the hurricane."

Todd was gone five minutes when Jeff said, "Have you seen Lulu?"

They searched the store for his dog, but didn't find her. Lulu's bed was empty, her toys abandoned, her food bowls untouched.

"She must have followed Todd to the Briny Irish," Jeff said. "The customers love sharing their bacon slices and seasoned fries with Lulu. My dog, the bar slut. I'd better get her. Will you mind the store for me?"

Helen sold two more bags of dog food while Jeff looked for Lulu. Jan Kurtz was the only person who didn't come in to buy food. Jan was a cool, elegant widow who lived in a high-rise on the Galt Ocean Mile with her black poodle, Snickers. Jan had a penchant for pink. She always wore pink clothes and accessories. Snickers had a pink leash, bows, and toenails.

Helen didn't recognize the Jan who stood at her counter, her hair damp and flattened, her clothes crumpled. Jan's eyes were puffy and her makeup was carelessly applied. She looked bedraggled, and it wasn't entirely due to the storm.

Jan held up a rain-spotted pink gift bag. "This is for Todd," she told Helen.

This new Jan moved constantly, like a worried hummingbird. She tapped her fingers on the counter and her heels on the floor. Her car keys jingled. Did the storm have her that rattled?

"Todd's out right now," Helen said. "He should be back in half an hour. Do you want to wait for him?"

Jan looked uneasy. "I need to get to my friend's house in Plantation before the roads flood. I've been evacuated, and the traffic is terrible. I just wanted to drop this bag off for Todd."

"I'll make sure he gets it," Helen said.

"You promise?" Jan sounded desperate.

"Absolutely," Helen said, hoping she looked trustworthy. Jan hesitated. A gust of wind rattled the plywood. She handed Helen the gift bag, then rushed out into the storm.

Todd got gifts all the time, but his ladies didn't usually act so spooked. And who would bring a gift for their boy toy during a hurricane? Helen had to peek inside that bag. I need to know, she told herself. This could be part of a murder investigation. I'm not stealing anything. The bag was handed to me. If God didn't want me to see this, She wouldn't have put it in my hands.

Helen parted the damp pink tissue paper. It hid a big

chocolate brownie with gooey icing. What was so vital
about that? There had to be something more in that
bag. It was too heavy for one brownie. Besides, nobody
carried on that way about a brownie, not even if she
made it with Alice B. Toklas's favorite recipe.

Helen lifted the brownie and found another layer of
paper. She shoved it aside and saw a roll of hundred-
dollar bills nesting inside. Helen quickly counted them.
Jan had packed two thousand dollars in cash under the
brownie. That was one sweet treat.

Helen heard the warning jangle of the boutique bell,
and shoved the brownie back on top of the money just
as Jeff entered. He was carrying a wet and sullen Lulu.
Todd trailed behind them with a foam go-box.

"Todd, Jan Kurtz left this bag for you," Helen said.

Todd yanked the bag from her hand so fast he nearly
dislocated her fingers. "Oh, she knows how I love
brownies," he said, but he didn't look inside the bag.

"It looked very rich," Helen said, and could have
kicked herself.

Todd clutched the brownie bag to his chest. He did
not stash it on the back-room shelf where the employ-
ees kept their belongings. He carried it into the cage
room with him.

By two o'clock, a deathly quiet descended on the
store. There were no more customers. Most of the major
nearby businesses, including the bank, were closed. The
drawbridges over the Intracoastal Waterway were
closed, too. Police cars with flashing lights guarded the
entrances to the beach. More patrol cars moved slowly
down the deserted streets, light bars strobing red, tires
kicking up great fishtails of water. The city had an eerie
war-zone feel.

A lashing wind beat on the boutique's boarded windows. The plywood creaked and groaned. The flooded
parking lot was almost empty. The store lights flickered
once, then twice.

"We'd better close," Jeff said. "The electricity is going
out soon. I want you all safely home. I'll balance the
cash register."

"I'll take the last grooming dog home," Todd said. "Call Mrs. Carter and tell her I'm on my way. She can't get here until four."

"Is that Brandy, the Saint Bernard?" Jeff said. "Will she fit in your car?"

"Brandy is a good dog," Todd said. "She's not a problem."

Helen wondered if Todd had kissed the Saint Bernard. You didn't trifle with the affections of a dog as big as Brandy.

Helen was sweeping the grooming room when a woman came rushing into the store. She was about fifty, with the stiffly sprayed hair that announced "standing appointment." "I need a thirty-pound sack of dog food, and then I'm going to the salon next door for an emergency manicure."

"A what?" Helen said.

"I broke three nails putting up my hurricane shutters," she said, waving her hand. "I can't stand it."

Helen thought the woman would have plenty of time to do her nails by candlelight when the storm hit.

"Can I help you with that bag?" Helen said.

"No, no, just hold the door," woman said. "I have to run to my manicure."

Helen held the door and the woman struggled into the storm. Lulu zipped out after her.

"Lulu!" Helen said. "Get back here."

But the skittish Lulu ignored her. Helen could see the dog's little bottom bobbing above the flooded sidewalk before she disappeared around the corner.

"Lulu's heading for the bar again," Jeff said, and dashed after her. He was back ten minutes later, wet and worried, curly hair plastered flat on his head. The wind was howling now, a nightmare sound.

"I can't find Lulu," Jeff said. "The bar is closed. Someone at the salon saw her running toward U.S. 1. She could get hit by a car. Drivers can't see her in this rain. What am I going to do?"

"Go after your dog," Helen said. "I'll lock up and go home."

Jeff handed Helen the spare key. "Don't stay long," he said. "This store can flood in a bad hurricane. During Andrew, the water was four feet high in here."

Then he was gone, racing out into the storm, crying, "Lulu! Lulu!"

The wind seemed to be coming from all directions now, swirling and slashing. Helen had to get out of there while she could still walk home. She piled some towels by the door to soak up the water, then did a quick walk-through check of the shop.

She was ready to lock up when she noticed a huge deposit in the Saint Bernard's cage. Damn. Todd should have cleaned that up. She'd have to pick it up or the place would smell foul, especially if the electricity went off. The unpleasant pile was way in the back of the cage.

The Saint Bernard cage was the size of a child's playpen. In fact, Jeff told her the previous owner of the grooming shop used to lock his kids in there on hectic Saturdays. Helen didn't know if he was joking or not. It had a padlock that was occasionally used for dogs good at jailbreaks.

She crawled into the cage with a roll of paper towels and a plastic bag, cussing the incontinent Saint Bernard. The lights flickered for the third time. Helen had to get out of here. If the wind got any fiercer, she wouldn't be able to walk home to the Coronado.

Something heavy hit the boarded windows. A coconut? A flowerpot? A lawn chair? Common objects turned into deadly missiles during a hurricane.

The wind was shrieking like a tortured soul. The building rocked and swayed. Each blast set loose frightening thumps and flapping bangs. Now there was a sound like ghostly footfalls. Helen shivered. She didn't like being alone in here.

Well, then, she told herself briskly, get it over with and get out. Helen crawled the length of the cage, glancing down at the newspapers lining the bottom. That was a mistake. SINGLE WOMAN MURDERED IN LAUDERDALE CONDO, screamed one headline. UTAH SERIAL KILLER BELIEVED IN SOUTH FLORIDA, said another.

Helen moved faster. She'd crawled all the way to the back of the cage when the lights went out.

"Shit!" she said, and put her hand into the warm dog pile.

"Double shit!" she said.

That's when she heard the cage door slam shut. "Hey! Who's there?" Helen said. She was too angry to be afraid.

No one answered. Above the howling, she heard a metallic snap. The cage lock. Helen saw a figure moving in the blackness toward the door. She couldn't tell if it was a man or a woman. She didn't know if it was short or tall. It was hunched over, shrouded in a rustling rain slicker.

"Help! Don't leave me in here. I'll drown," Helen said.

The only answer was the slam of a door.

CHAPTER 14

··

Helen sneezed. Her nose itched from the dog hair. She rattled the door again, but she knew it was useless. She was locked inside the dog cage, stuck in an ungainly crouch. The cage wasn't big enough for her to sit down or stand up. Wasn't that a form of torture? It certainly was for her.

The smell in the cage was atrocious. What did that damned Saint Bernard live on—beer and pickled cabbage? Helen had wiped her dirty hand on a paper towel and pushed the foul towel through the wire. She couldn't get the massive left-behind lump in the cage through the wires, so she buried it in more paper towels and stuck it in the plastic bag. The cage still stank.

Helen felt something wet on her feet. Oh, no. The Saint Bernard didn't leave a puddle, too, did she?

Helen dipped a finger and sniffed cautiously. It was water. She tasted it. It was slightly muddy, a little salty. This was bad news, far worse than any piddling Saint Bernard. The rainwater in the parking lot was over the curb and coming into the shop. The flooding had started.

What had Jeff said? During Hurricane Andrew the water in the store was four feet high. She'd drown, trapped in this cage. That was way over her head. Helen couldn't imagine a more humiliating way to die. She'd be found floating in a locked cage with the biggest pile of dog doo in Fort Lauderdale. She could hear the shocked whispers at her funeral as her friends stood over a cut-rate casket: "Poor Helen. We didn't realize she drank until it was too late."

Would it be worse if an autopsy found no evidence of alcohol? What if her friends thought Helen had died of acute stupidity? "We don't know how it happened, but she managed to lock herself in a cage, and when the water came up, well . . . Helen always was a little klutzy."

Who did this to her and why?

Helen must have discovered something that threatened someone—but what? Did Todd see her poking in his pink gift bag with the green lining? Did Jonathon hear her say something to the police? In that case, why didn't they just kill her? The person in the slippery slicker could have easily surprised her and bashed her head in. Why leave her locked in this cage, waiting for a slow death? Who hated her that much?

Helen was angry at herself and whoever snapped that lock. She was not going to die. She would find a way out, and from the sound of the storm, she'd better do it soon. The wind grew wilder, beating on the boarded-up windows. Strange missiles thudded against the plywood. The building creaked and sighed.

She rattled the cage door until her teeth vibrated, hoping to shake the lock loose.

Nothing.

She grabbed the wire door with both hands and pulled until the tendons stood out on her muscular arms, trying to yank the door off its hinges. It held. It was made to withstand two-hundred-pound dogs. The burly Saint Bernard weighed more than Helen did.

What time was it? It was absolutely dark in the boarded store. There was no light from the street, no winking security lights or glowing clocks. Helen couldn't read her watch, but she guessed it was about five o'clock. The storm was supposed to hit at eight. She wondered if the store would survive the hurricane. She wondered if she would survive.

Thwap! Something landed on the roof. Helen jumped

and the dirty water sloshed around her ankles. The plastic bag of dog doo bobbed on the water. Helen's feet and the seat of her pants were wet. She tried to sit on the roll of paper towels, but it quickly absorbed the water. The grooming room was warm and steamy, but she still shivered in the muddy water swirling in the cage.

Helen poked three fingers through the cage wire and found the padlock, rough and slightly rusty. She could feel a keyhole, a fairly large one. Now she needed something to open the padlock. She had nothing useful in her hair or on her clothes. Why didn't she wear a pin or a hair clip? Why didn't she carry a nail file or a Swiss army knife? Her shoes were slip-ons. Her watch was cheap plastic. Helen didn't even have a metal belt buckle.

Her stomach growled. She was hungry. Thirsty, too. Her mouth was dry with fear. She was in water past her ankles, but it wasn't fit to drink. Helen wanted to paw the cage like the yappy dogs in the grooming room. If she ever got out of here, she'd never ignore their unhappy howls again. She knew exactly how they felt.

She forced herself to make a slow, careful search of the cage, inch by wire inch. It was damp, blistered with rust, and frustratingly secure. Until she reached the far left corner, near the very top. A wire stuck her thumb so hard she bled. Helen was never so happy to feel pain. Yes! She'd found an inch-long length of loose wire. She began working the small piece off the cage. Her battered fingers were slippery with her own blood. She slowly lifted and twisted the wire, teasing another inch away from the cage. The rest was too tightly attached.

Helen kept prying and pulling. She was at an awkward angle. Her knees cracked and cried for mercy. Her hips and back ached. The wire slid and sliced her finger. She kept twisting. She broke a nail down to the quick. That stung, but Helen didn't care. The wire was loosening. She could feel it. One more good pull and a twist, and it would be free. Then she could start working the lock.

Slam!

The shop door banged open. Was it the wind or her attacker returning?

Heart beating, Helen jerked the wire free, then sloshed up against the back of the cage. She hid the wire in her palm. I'll ram it in his eye if he comes near me, she promised herself. I'll stick it in his neck. I'll rake his hand until he bleeds. I won't hesitate. Not after what he did to me.

Helen heard a voice. No, wait. Was that two voices? It was hard to tell with the raging wind. A flashlight beam hit her in the eye, blinding her. Helen gripped her wire, ready to spring.

Then she heard Margery's raucous voice: "What the hell are you doing in a cage?"

"Helen, are you OK?" It was Phil.

"Phil!" Helen said. "You made it to Florida. You're safe."

"Helen, what happened?" That was Jeff. She heard the rattle of her boss's key ring, and the cage door was open. Phil's strong hands pulled her free, and he wrapped his arms around her. Helen tried to stand, but her cramped knees gave out. They felt like they had been stung with a million needles. She sagged into his arms, her head cradled on Phil's shoulder.

"Good Lord," Margery said. "What is that smell?"

Helen didn't answer. She might smell bad, but Phil was deliciously spicy and lemony, with a slightly sweaty tang that made Helen see him stripped naked on her sheets.

Margery took care of that memory. "Pee-yew. I'm sorry, Jeff, but I have to light up or I'll gag," she said. "What stinks?" She set fire to a cigarette.

Helen pointed to the bobbing bag in the cage. "It's what got me locked in here in the first place," she said.

"Gee, we used to use pork rinds for bait," Margery said.

Jeff came back with a load of dog towels to wrap around Helen. The wind was tearing at the Pampered

Pet building with such ferocity, Helen's rescuers decided not to wait for her legs to start working. "Get her into my car, Phil," Margery said, "while I help Jeff check the water damage."

Phil carried Helen out to Margery's big white car like a bride on her wedding night. Helen threw her arms around his neck and buried her face against his chest. The chest was nice and hard. The shirt was soft, well-worn denim. The blue matched his eyes. It would have been romantic if Phil hadn't staggered under her weight.

"It's the water," he said gallantly, as the rain slapped him in the face. Helen appreciated the lie. Phil struggled to open the door and stretched Helen out on the car's wide backseat. He rubbed her cramped legs, trying to get the circulation back. Swarms of needles and pins traveled up and down her legs. She could not stop shivering. Phil took off his jacket and wrapped her in it. She was a soggy mass of ragged towels and damp coats.

Now that Helen was out of the store, she caught a whiff of herself. It wasn't something she would bottle. Phil didn't mention it. He was such a gentleman.

The wind rocked Margery's heavy car. A chunk of wood hit the trunk and bounced off. Helen was glad when her landlady fought her way to the car and flopped into the seat, breathless and windblown.

Margery lit another cigarette, then said, "Store's OK for now. Most of the water is on the grooming side, not in the boutique, so Jeff's stock is in good shape. I helped him stack the expensive bags of dog food up on the higher shelves and set out some sandbags by the door. If they hold, he won't have much damage."

Neither Phil nor Helen said anything about a seventy-six-year-old woman helping Jeff with the lifting. They'd seen Margery sling the heavy patio furniture around like it was made of paper when she hosed down the pool deck.

Headlights blinked at the far end of the lot. "That's Jeff's car," Margery said. "He made it. Let's go."

Helen settled against Phil in the backseat, grateful for his warmth. They drove home through a black soup on nearly deserted streets. Slamming winds sent the car sliding out of its lane, but Margery gripped the wheel and hung on, her cigarette clenched in her teeth. At a stoplight, a broken metal sign skittered through the intersection.

"I'm not waiting for the light to change," Margery said. "God knows what will be through here next." She ran the red light.

"How did you find me?" Helen asked.

"When you weren't home by five, Phil and I were worried. You'd given me Jeff's phone number. I called his cell and got him at home."

"Did he ever find Lulu?" Helen said.

"Yes. He told me he left you to lock up his store because Lulu escaped. That crazy mutt was at the Taco Bell on Federal Highway, begging in the kitchen. When I said you weren't home yet, Jeff was afraid something bad happened. Shops closing for the hurricane are easy targets for robbers. Phil and I met Jeff and then found you. Want to tell me what happened?"

By the time Helen gave her landlady and Phil the details, they were at the Coronado. Helen's legs felt warm and unpleasantly needle-y, but they were working. She could walk on her own.

"Look at that," Margery said, as she pulled into a parking spot. "Storm got my neighbor's old ficus tree." The massive ficus, the size of a garage, was lying on the lawn, its roots helplessly in the air.

The jolly little Coronado Tropic Apartments looked grim in the lashing gray rain. The Art Deco windows and sliding doors were boarded with plywood. The wind had stripped the bougainvillea of its purple blossoms and torn away tree limbs and palm fronds.

"What time is it?" Helen said.

"Six thirty," Margery said. "Why? You going somewhere?"

"The storm isn't due for another hour and a half," Helen said. "I can't imagine what it will do."

"Won't have to imagine anything," Margery said. "You're going to see the whole show."

CHAPTER 15

....

Helen ran through the stinging rain to her own apartment. She was greeted at the door by Thumbs, her six-toed cat. The big-pawed cat looked at her reproachfully with wide golden eyes. She bent down to scratch his thick gray-and-white fur. He looked like a stuffed toy, except for those monster paws.

"Sorry, boy," she said. "I left you here alone. You must be exhausted from having to do storm duty." Thumbs moved through the hot, darkened apartment with weary dignity, leading her to the kitchen. Helen opened a whole can of tuna to reward him. Thumbs ate it with smacking satisfaction.

She looked around her place as if seeing it for the first time. Helen guessed the turquoise Barcalounger, the boomerang coffee table, and the lamps shaped like nuclear reactors would fetch high prices in New York. In St. Louis she'd have called them tacky. They simply belonged here in her Florida home. She loved her small furnished apartment with the view of the Coronado gardens.

But the boarded-up windows turned Helen's airy apartment into a dank cave. After being locked in the cage, she could hardly breathe in the small closed-in rooms. She was glad she wouldn't have to stay here for the hurricane. Margery's place wouldn't be much bigger, but it would have noise and people to distract her.

Helen checked her windows and sliding doors for leaks, then took a quick hot shower and put on fresh clothes. No point in drying her hair. It would be soaked again by the time she ran across the yard to Margery's home.

She put Thumbs's food and litter box into a shopping bag, then packed bread, chocolate, pretzels, peanut butter, sliced turkey, a box of wine, and other hurricane essentials. As she locked her door, she wondered if it would be there to open in twenty-four hours.

Thumbs howled his protests as Helen carried him through the slashing rain, the bags of groceries bumping against her tortured legs. Margery's door opened before she had to knock. The other storm refugees were already there.

Margery's friend Elsie was sitting in the purple recliner with her unpoodle, Corkie. Doris and Alice, the new renters in 2C, were drinking screwdrivers on the couch. They were both in their fifties, no-nonsense women in jeans and T-shirts. Doris was built like a Humvee with short gray hair and a big bumper. Alice was the thin one with the long gray-black bob.

Helen put the struggling Thumbs on the floor.

"Here, kitty." Doris gave Thumbs a big smile and reached for the cat.

Thumbs rudely ran past her and disappeared under the couch. Helen was relieved that her cat showed no interest in Pete. The tubby parrot was sitting on Peggy's shoulder, restlessly pulling at his feathers. His exotic owner ran her fingers through her dramatic splash of red hair with the same gesture. Peggy's face was not conventionally beautiful, but that made it all the more compelling.

Helen saw why Peggy was tearing out her hair. Another Coronado resident, Cal the Canadian, had her blocked in a corner. As usual, Cal was praising his home country and cutting down the U.S.A. "Not only don't you Americans have health insurance like we

do, but now your government is going to take away
your Social Security. You know that, eh?"

Peggy gave Helen a wild-eyed look, and Helen promised herself she'd rescue her friend as soon as she could.
She worked her way to the kitchen and added her bags
to the loot on the table.

Margery was running her orange juicer. "I'm making
screwdrivers," she said over the high-pitched whine.
"Help yourself to the food and drink."

Helen suddenly remembered she was hungry and
found herself a paper plate. A cooler was packed with
iced soda, water, and wine. She helped herself to a cold
bottle of clean water.

The table was overflowing with platters and dishes.
Helen spotted a big bowl of Thai chicken salad, Peggy's
special recipe. The rest was comfort food: green beans in
mushroom soup smothered with crunchy canned onion
rings, sliced meat loaf, tuna casserole, chocolate cake,
boxes of brownies and doughnuts, trays of deviled eggs,
and thick ham sandwiches. Two bruised tomatoes sat
unsliced on a plate.

"Did Cal bring the tomatoes?" Helen said.

"Again," Margery said. "They look like the same ones
he brought to the Labor Day picnic. That's all he
brought, too, except for the beer he's drinking. Cheap-
est man on earth."

There were better men to discuss, Helen decided.
"Where's Phil?" she asked.

She felt his long arms around her and his warm
breath on her neck. He had a cold beer in one hand, and
his kiss tasted deliciously bitter. Helen forgot all about
her food.

"If you're going to do that, go into the hall back
there," Margery said. "I can't concentrate with you two
making goo-goo eyes."

They escaped gratefully into the dark hallway. Phil
put his beer bottle on the floor. He had his hands under
Helen's shirt and was working them down into her
jeans. Helen began quickly unbuttoning Phil. She gave a

soft moan and pressed her hips against him. God, he felt good.

"Are you as hot as I am?" Phil said, as he feather-kissed her neck.

"Yes," Helen said. "What is it about hurricanes?"

"The bedroom is full of sleeping bags, but maybe we can—"

"Oh, dear. Oh, my. Excuse me. I didn't mean to interrupt. I was on my way to—"

It was dear, dithery Elsie. Helen and Phil pulled apart. Helen was breathless and dizzy from Phil's kisses, and embarrassed that her bare breasts were nearly hanging out of her unbuttoned shirt. It didn't matter. So were Elsie's. The punked-out septuagenarian was wearing red toreador pants, a blue satin push-up bra, and a black lace shirt. Lumps of bare flesh popped up everywhere, like a colony of prairie dogs.

Elsie took a step forward on her red spike heels and knocked over Phil's bottle, sending cold beer across Margery's hardwood floor. Helen could almost see the sticky alcohol eating the finish.

"I need to put Corkie to bed," Elsie said, petting her fluffy white dog. "She's sleeping."

"We were about to head for bed, too," Phil said. Helen kicked him.

"Oh, not so early, I hope," Elsie said. "You'll miss all the fun. You need to join the party."

"Excuse me. Sorry, but this is the only route to the restroom," Cal said. "And I need to get my sweater out of the bedroom." He walked between them and stepped in the beer. "Did you know there's beer on the floor here?"

"I was just going to the bedroom so my little dog, Corkie, can get a nap," Elsie said. "Are you still coming, Phil?"

"Not a chance," Phil said.

Helen kicked him again. "I think you're right, Elsie," she said. "We'd better join the party."

Phil looked unhappy, but they both knew there was no privacy in Margery's crowded apartment. Staying

with each other was slow torture. It was better to separate for now. Phil rummaged in the hall closet for a
towel to mop up his beer. He held the empty bottle
strategically in front of him.

Helen went back out to the kitchen for her plate, then
wandered into the living room. Peggy and Pete were
watching the Weather Channel. It was strange to see the
storm as a pulsing red blob on the TV map, when they
could hear its lost-soul howls outside their walls.

"It appears now that the category-three hurricane
may land at either West Palm Beach or Port Saint Lucie
to the north," the announcer said.

"That's good news, isn't it?" Alice asked.

"Not if you're in Port Saint Lucie," her cleaning partner, Doris, said. Helen and Elsie sat down on the couch
to talk with the new neighbors in 2C.

"You clean houses for seniors," Elsie said. "Isn't that
lovely?" Instead of her little dog, she was holding a
screwdriver in a glass the size of a vase.

"We'd really like to clean your home," skinny Alice
said.

Burly Doris nodded enthusiastically. "We can help you."

"Thank you, dear, but Gert has been cleaning for me
for thirty years," Elsie said. "I wouldn't dream of using
anyone else. She knows all the old remedies, the ones
my mother used. Much better for the environment than
some of those products they have now. When I had my
new closet put in and the workers left plaster dust all
over my tile floors, Gert got it up in two shakes with
warm water and white vinegar."

"White vinegar?" Doris said. "That's for salads."

"It's the most useful cleaning product this side of
baking soda," Elsie insisted.

"Now it's baking soda. Are you a cleaner or a cook?"
Alice said, laughing.

Helen wondered how good they were at houseclean-
ing. Even she knew about baking soda and white vinegar. But Alice and Doris seemed to lose interest in the
subject. They drifted toward the TV to watch the
weather report.

Helen settled in for a talk with Elsie. It didn't take long to learn that she'd bought her little dog on credit, just as Jeff suspected.

"Teacup poodles are so expensive," Elsie said. "The bank wouldn't lend me the money, even though I told them it was an investment. She'll only grow more beautiful. But that nice store gave me the money. I pay them fifty dollars a month."

Helen didn't have the nerve to ask how many months Elsie would be making those payments. She concentrated on her plate of food instead.

Elsie took a healthy sip of her screwdriver. "I just love fresh orange juice," she said, and belched delicately. Helen didn't think that was from the orange juice. "I wanted to ask you about that young man who groomed Corkie. He did a very nice job. But I'm sure he worked at a store in Tampa. I know it was him, but he went by another name in those days. He didn't look so picturesque, either. His hair used to be very short, almost a military cut, when he lived in Tampa."

"Tampa?" Helen said. "Jonathon has never mentioned Tampa. What was the name of the store?"

"It's out of business," Elsie said. "It had a bad reputation. Charged high prices for its puppies, but their papers and shots turned out to be fakes. The store said they had a vet look at the animals, but they never got any treatment. So many of the little puppies and kittens died. They were supposed to be treated for their coughs, infections, and other newborn illnesses, but they weren't. The ones who survived didn't have any of the shots they were supposed to have. The pet shop gave the owners a certificate for a free visit to a veterinarian—then sent them to the same crooked vet who signed the fake papers. That's how they stayed in business as long as they did. It was a terrible story. Terrible."

"How did you know about it?" Helen said.

"My granddaughter, Allison, worked there. She quit because her conscience hurt her. She couldn't stand all those poor puppies dying."

"Did she report the store to the authorities?"

"No," Elsie said. "She couldn't, dear. She helped fill out the fake papers for the crooked vet. Then he'd sign them. The owner told her to. Allison was only seventeen. She didn't know it was wrong at first. Then she figured it out. Allison wanted to go to law school. It wouldn't have looked good on her record to be involved in a fraud. Not at all. Allison's father is an attorney, a real straight arrow. He would have had a fit. She came to me and I said it was OK to stay quiet. Allison had her future to consider. Besides, the store closed, and I don't think that vet is practicing anymore."

Elsie took a tea-party sip of her screwdriver, then a good long gulp.

"Who was the crooked vet? Was he called Kent Grimsby?" Helen said.

"Oh, dear, no," Elsie said. "Nothing like that. His first name started with an L. Lenny? Lester? No, it was like a romance novel. Lance. That was it. Very muscular he was, but not handsome at all. I wish I could remember his last name, but I'm not sure I ever heard it. My niece called him Dr. Lance. Silly name, that, don't you think? Lance was married to a very pretty girl. I think she was his assistant or accountant or something."

"Was her name Tammie?" Helen said.

"No, no, it was Wanda. A very old-fashioned name. You don't hear it much anymore. Wanda, yes. That was it."

"Do you remember anything else about her?" Helen was desperate for more information.

"Well, she was blond and had a very large chest," Elsie said. "I think they were implants. But that's not very helpful, is it? So many young women get that surgery. I'm lucky I am naturally well-endowed." She stared down toward her waist at her large bosom. "Let's see. There must be something else I can tell you about them. Wanda was very much into physical fitness."

That sounded like Tammie, too. "Is she a friend of

your niece's? Did they stay in touch after the store closed?" Helen asked.

"I'm afraid not," Elsie said. "Wanda did something rather awful, you see. She asked my little niece to be part of a threesome. Wanda had only been married a year or so, too. Can you imagine—asking an innocent seventeen-year-old? She offered her drugs, too."

"Yes," Helen said. "I mean, no." Sex and drugs were an easier way to identify Tammie and Kent than any scar or tattoo. "What happened to the couple?"

"They moved out of the area. I don't know where," Elsie said.

I do, Helen thought. They swung over to Fort Lauderdale and changed their names. But Kent Grimsby still had his same love of animals. No wonder he didn't care what happened to poor Prince. He didn't care about any animal.

"I'm glad he's not a vet anymore," Elsie said. "He shouldn't be. That shop was terrible. It had the worst groomers. One shaved off a poor dog's nipples. Shaved them right off."

Helen winced and grabbed her chest. Her plate sat untouched beside her, forgotten in the tales of cruelty and mutilation.

Elsie took another gulp of her drink. Those screwdrivers were aptly named, Helen thought. They definitely unlocked something in Elsie.

"Another groomer hurt a show dog, a lovely standard poodle," Elsie said. "It was supposed to compete in a big Tampa show. Everyone thought it would win best in show. The groomer gave the owner special drops for the dog's eyes. Supposed to brighten them, he said. The drops were special, all right. They were liquid soap. The dog's eyes watered so much it couldn't be in the show. Temporarily blinded that sweet animal. It recovered eventually. The winner was a complete surprise—a Westie. Nice dog, but no one had expected it to win. There were rumors that the groomer was paid to ruin the favorite's chances, but they were never proven."

"That's terrible," Helen said. "Who would do that to a defenseless dog?"

Elsie finished off the rest of her screwdriver. Helen waited patiently.

"Why, that young man with the long blond hair," Elsie said. "The one who calls himself Jonathon."

CHAPTER 16

At midnight, green fireworks exploded outside the window. Helen peered through a slit in the plywood and watched the gorgeous, glowing green show high on an electrical pole near the Coronado. Sparks in shades from tender lettuce to bright lime shot straight up. Then there was an eerie green glow.

Suddenly the lights went out.

"Transformer blew," Margery said.

Helen thought the destruction was beautiful. Some guilty primal part of her was thrilled to see trees crack and fall. She liked to watch gas grills fly through the air and coconuts turn into torpedoes.

But when the green explosion died, everything in and around the Coronado went black. The darkness extended into infinity. The only other light was a single candle flickering in a distant window.

That lonely sight unnerved Helen. She wasn't frightened by the fireworks or the theatrical howling of the wind, but the isolation got to her. They were alone together in this little apartment. They might as well have been adrift on the ocean. Helen couldn't even run to that single candle in the distance. She'd be cut down by flying debris.

The storm grew more violent, until the glass slats rattled in the boarded-up jalousie door. The wind snagged on a piece of aluminum and made a raucous blatting sound.

Phil slept through the hurricane, and that irritated Helen. Why couldn't he be afraid like a normal person? He slept in a peaceful curl, oblivious to the roaring storm. His blue eyes were closed. His long, dramatic white hair swept his shoulders. Normally she thought Phil looked sweet when he slept, like an innocent little boy. Tonight she wanted to slap him.

Elsie and the two cleaning women, Doris and Alice, were also out cold. But they'd chugged screwdrivers until they passed out. Now the three women snored together on the living room floor, wrapped around one another like kittens in a basket. Margery had thrown a blanket over them.

Peggy had also had a few too many. She snoozed on the couch, mouth open. Peggy was one of those rare women who actually looked attractive sleeping that way. Pete slept beside her, his head tucked under his wing.

Cal was stretched out in the purple recliner in a miasma of beer fumes, making occasional smelly eruptions.

The booze that knocked out most of the hurricane party only made Helen restless. She and her cat Thumbs paced as the storm screamed around them. The wind-blown assault on the building was constant. Frightening, unknown objects battered the plywood with pops and thuds. Helen thought it was like being stuck in an endless MRI.

Thumbs stayed at Helen's side as she stepped past the sleeping bodies. The golden-eyed cat took his patrol duties seriously, carefully placing his big paws so he didn't step on anyone or anything. His tail was curled into a question mark as he solemnly padded beside Helen.

The wind was so intense the sliding glass doors bulged in and out. The doors were boarded and Margery had covered them with slanting zigzags of tape so the glass wouldn't explode in the room. But now they moved. Helen and Thumbs stopped and stared, mesmerized by the pulsing doors. Each time, the doors' bulge was a little bigger. Helen was sure they were going to blow apart. She was right in the path of the glass shards, but she couldn't tear herself away. The doors seemed to be breathing, sucking her toward them, like the doors in that novel, *The Haunting of Hill House.*

Margery broke the spell. "Why don't you get the hell away from those doors before you get hurt?" she said. Her landlady was standing in the doorway between the living room and the kitchen, carrying a Coleman lantern. The yellow glow gave her purple cutoffs and eggplant T-shirt a burnished sheen. Her cigarette burned like a distant beacon.

"Wind getting to you?" Margery asked.

Helen nodded.

"Let's let the folks in here sleep. Come into the kitchen and talk. I have some iced drinks in the cooler or coffee in the thermos. In the morning, when Cal and Phil are awake, we can get the generator going and make more hot coffee."

Margery moved as carefully as Thumbs in her red tennis shoes. The kitchen was warm, but bearable. The Coronado's thick old walls held in the last of the cool air-conditioning. Helen decided caffeine would make her more jittery. She took a bottle of cold water and cut a big piece of chocolate cake. She remembered Phil staggering when he tried to carry her to the car, but she wasn't going to worry about her weight now. She could be blown away any minute. Besides, calories didn't stick when she was this scared. The fat would slide right off her shaking bones.

Margery and Helen talked for an hour about what happened at the Pampered Pet, who might have locked her in that cage and why.

"Maybe it has something to do with the dognapping," Helen said. "After all, I found out the husband, Francis, probably picked his alibi receipt out of the trash."

"Did you tell him about your suspicions?" Margery said.

"Uh, no," Helen said. "Of course not."

"So he read your mind, rushed over to the Pampered Pet, and locked you in a cage?"

"It sounds pretty stupid when you say it that way," Helen said. "But it all sounds stupid."

"Maybe it was Jonathon or Todd. Do you think it's connected with Tammie's murder?" Margery said.

"Todd was wrestling with a big dog in a small car," Helen said. "I don't think he'd feel like coming back to the shop to lock me in a cage."

"But he could have, couldn't he?" Margery took a generous swig from her glass. Amazingly, Helen's landlady was still pounding down screwdrivers, but she showed no sign of being drunk. The woman had the capacity of a shipload of sailors on leave.

"It's possible," Helen said. "But I don't think he did it. Todd's not serious enough. You know what I mean?"

"That boy may have more depth than you give him credit for. What about Jonathon?"

"I can't believe it's Jonathon," Helen said.

"You always were a sucker for a pretty suit," Margery said.

"It's true Jonathon's wardrobe keeps me entertained. I can't believe he did it. He's accused of stabbing Tammie." He stabbed a man in Miami, a small voice whispered. "So why didn't he stab me?" It was more an answer to her thoughts than to Margery. "Why attack me at all? What do I know?"

"Something you don't know you know," Margery said.

"You sound like a riddle," Helen snapped, then felt bad for her ill temper. "I'm sorry. I didn't mean to snap at you. Elsie thinks there's something off about Jonathon." Helen told Margery about Elsie's revelations, then said, "Do you think what she says is true?"

"Yes," Margery said. "Elsie may be a little dippy when it comes to money, but her memory is sharp. If she says she knew Jonathon under another name, then she did."

"I can't imagine Jonathon working at a bad grooming shop and hurting dogs. Elsie says he blinded a show dog. It was temporary, but it ruined the dog's chances in a big show. The Jonathon I know loves animals. I've watched him when he doesn't know I'm around. He doesn't kiss dogs like Todd, but they respect him and respond to him."

"People change," Margery said.

"For the better?" Helen said.

"Not usually," Margery said. "OK, you don't know enough yet. You have to find out more about him. Let's say for now you have some doubts about Jonathon. Do you think Todd is in the clear?"

"Not totally," Helen said. "He's getting bags of money."

"He's what?"

Suddenly the night was calm and quiet. The wind quit shrieking. The silence was overwhelming.

"That's the eye of the hurricane," Margery said. "It's over us now."

Helen started to open the kitchen door for some cool air, but Margery stopped her. "Don't!" she said. "The pressure isn't equalized. You open that door and every window in the place will crack."

Margery and Helen sat back down at the kitchen table. Helen felt like she'd been shut inside a box. She wanted to claw her way out of the boarded windows.

"Walls closing in on you?" Margery said, as she stubbed out her cigarette and lit another.

"Yeah," Helen said. "It's that cage. I hated being trapped. I can't sleep. If I close my eyes, I can feel the water slowly rising around me in the dark. I could have died, Margery."

"Talk to me," Margery said. "You'll feel better."

"I've just thought of one good thing," Helen said. "The police have plenty of suspects to work with. Maybe they won't bother me about being in Tammie's house and running off with her robe."

"Don't bet on it," Margery said.

"You've done wonders for my anxiety," Helen said.

"Sometimes you're supposed to be afraid. Like when you do something stupid during a murder investigation. It's not too late to call the cops, you know."

"Speaking of knowing," Helen said, making a clumsy attempt to change the subject, "do you think Jeff knows his star's past history? Do you think he knows his other groomer, Todd, is getting bags of money from customers?"

"Let's back up a little here," Margery said. "This is the second time you mentioned Todd and the money. It went by me last time when I got distracted. This Todd is getting bags of money?"

"Bag. A very sweet widow, Jan, dropped off two thousand dollars in a pink gift bag for Todd, right before the hurricane hit."

Margery raised an eyebrow in surprise. "She told you that?"

"Of course not," Helen said. "I peeked. She had the cash stashed under a brownie. It was a heck of a tip, even for Todd's adoring women customers. I wondered what kind of services he was rendering. But now I think he's blackmailing her. I heard him make an ugly phone call back in the stockroom. He said, 'Listen, I don't care how you get the money, but I want it.' Then he said, 'That's your problem, not mine.' "

"And he was talking to this Jan?"

"I don't know who he was talking to," Helen said. "But he certainly wasn't very polite. It could have been someone who borrowed money from him. But ever since I saw that bag, I'm wondering."

Margery puffed thoughtfully on her cigarette. "How was this Jan person when she brought in the money? Excited, happy, a little twinkle in her eye?"

"Frightened," Helen said. "Worried. She looked ready to jump out of her skin. She's usually a well-groomed woman, but she was a mess that day."

"Sounds like blackmail to me," Margery said.

"But Jan seems like such a nice woman," Helen said. "Why is Todd blackmailing her?"

"Why don't you ask her?"

"You're kidding," Helen said.

"No, if she's truly a nice woman, I'm guessing she didn't do anything too terrible," Margery said. "She might even be relieved to talk to you."

The wind had picked up again. Now it screamed and pulled at the plywood on the kitchen windows. One wooden sheet flapped loose and went whirling off into the night, leaving the window looking raw and exposed. Helen could see the dancing palm tree doing a wild jig. Another surge of wind sent water rushing in under the kitchen door.

"There are towels in the cupboard by the sink," Margery said, as they ran to clean it up. Helen's landlady stuffed towels and throw rugs at the bottom of the door. Helen crawled around the kitchen floor, wiping up the water.

As she mopped, Helen said, "So when do you think I should talk to Jan—and where?"

"At her home, when the storm is over," Margery said.

With that, the glass shattered on the exposed window and something came hurtling into the kitchen. The sound burst like a bomb. Pete woke up with a squawk. Thumbs yowled. Doris and Alice woke up and screamed in chorus.

Helen didn't think this hurricane would ever end.

CHAPTER 17

....

A single shaft of sunlight pierced the broken kitchen window and hit Helen in the eye. That solar poke in the eye woke her up. The sun was shining in a blue sky. The wind was no longer wailing. The hurricane was over.

Helen didn't know what time she'd fallen asleep last night, but she found herself sitting at the kitchen table. Apparently she'd slept on the chair with her head lying on the table. Margery must have wrapped the blanket around her.

Helen's neck felt like it had been kickboxed. Her back cracked when she sat up. Her head hurt, but that pain had a different cause: Alcohol and adrenaline don't mix.

In the dark, boarded-up recesses of Margery's apartment, the other members of the hurricane party were stretching and waking.

"Ouch, I'm too old to sleep on floors," Alice said, rubbing her back. Her cleaning partner, Doris, was examining a bruise on her bicep. "How do you think I got that last night?" she said.

Cal tried to get out of the purple recliner and nearly jackknifed it. Peggy pulled him to safety. The beer-soaked Canadian tottered around in unsteady circles, sideswiping Pete.

"Awk!" the parrot said. The hungover Alice and Doris looked like they'd had a hatchet sunk in their heads.

"No loud noises, please, birdie," Doris said, rubbing her aching head.

Elsie came out of the bedroom with her fluffy little dog, Corkie, and Doris winced again. Elsie's outfit was a lot for an alcohol-soaked brain to absorb. She was wearing green satin hot pants, a yellow bustier, and an orange bolero jacket. The hot pants and jacket were the same color as her hair. Helen thought Elsie was also wearing purple stockings, then realized those were varicose veins. Cal looked at her, groaned, and covered his eyes.

"The hurricane is over," Elsie said. "And we're all here safe and sound." She sounded disgustingly chipper.

"Where's Phil?" Helen said.

"Right here," he said.

Helen saw all the women in the room turn to him with appraising eyes, as if he were the last hunk of undeveloped real estate in Florida. Phil's hair was in a ponytail, and his shirt was open to show just the right amount of tanned chest. He looked hotter than an August afternoon. He grinned at Helen. She ran her finger along his slightly crooked nose. She preferred her men less than perfect.

Margery came out of the kitchen with a tray of orange juice and Krispy Kreme doughnuts. "The good news is the phones are working," she said. "But there's no power and we may not have any for a couple of days. That means no hot coffee and no hot showers."

"I'm just happy to be alive," Helen said.

"That will last about twenty-four hours," Margery said. "Tomorrow there will be fistfights in the stores over the last bag of ice, but right now everyone is acting like this is the prelude to heaven."

"What kind of damage did we get last night, besides the broken kitchen window?" Alice said.

"I was about to go out and see," Margery said. The denizens of her apartment followed the landlady outside, blinking and squinting at the bright sun. "Stay with me," she said. "Don't go wandering until I make sure there's no downed power lines."

A small palm was stripped clean to its gray trunk, but the others survived, even the dancing hurricane tree. A broken chair floated in the pool. The yard was full of tree limbs and debris. A two-by-four was driven into the ground by the gate, and someone's vinyl siding was lying on the flooded sidewalk. The bougainvillea and rose of Sharon had lost their blossoms.

"All your pretty flowers are gone," Alice said.

"They'll be back in a couple of weeks," Margery said. "Things grow fast down here. I don't see any downed power lines in the yard, so we can move around."

"What can we do to help?" Phil said.

Margery began issuing orders like a purple-clad general. "I need you and Helen to see if you can get out in your Jeep and go for a coffee run," she said. "Bring back some hot food if you find anyplace open. Cal, you get the gas generator started so we can have TV and air-conditioning in at least one room.

"Peggy, you can board up the broken kitchen window. I taped some plastic over it last night to keep the rain out, but I need something that will hold until the window people can come out. Then you can help pick up debris. Doris and Alice, if you don't mind cleaning on your day off, you can help me get the inside in order. Everybody ready to go to work?"

Phil slapped his backside dramatically. "Oops, I forgot my wallet," he said. "I think it's in my place."

Helen followed him to his apartment, wondering what that was all about. He locked the door behind him and practically threw Helen against the wall, he was so hungry to kiss her.

"I like to finish what I started," he said.

"Me, too," Helen said. They raced into the bedroom, ripping off their clothes on the way.

Half an hour later, Helen and Phil drove down U.S. 1 in a postcoital glow. Some side streets leading to the highway had been flooded, but the Jeep had bulled its way through. No one had any electricity on this side of town. Businesses stayed closed and boarded. The stoplights were out. Police directed traffic at the major intersections. At the smaller streets, cars cautiously crawled across the highway, dodging oncoming drivers.

The damage looked similar to the Coronado's: Trees were toppled and bushes torn up, signs broken and fences flattened. A few roofs were stripped of their shingles.

Helen switched on the radio. "The National Weather Service reports that the hurricane landed north of Fort Lauderdale in Palm Beach County," an announcer said. "Most of the major damage took place in that area. Officials estimate that—"

"Look, an open doughnut shop," Helen said.

Phil swung the Jeep into the waterlogged parking lot. They bought warm glazed doughnuts and filled four thermoses with hot coffee. Helen was tempted to dig into the doughnuts, but restrained herself.

As they drove farther south, there was electricity again. More shops were opening and more hurricane shutters were coming off. "There's a pizza place," Helen said.

Four pizzas later, they were back on the highway heading toward the Coronado when they spotted a chicken franchise.

"Let's get a roast chicken, mashed potatoes, biscuits, and gravy," Phil said, pulling into the drive-through line.

"Hurricanes make you hungry," Helen said.

"And horny," Phil said. He kissed her until the order taker shouted three times over the staticky speaker, "May I help you, sir?" Phil finally gave the woman their order.

While the Jeep idled in the line, Phil held Helen close. "Margery tells me that you found a dead woman when you went to deliver a dog," he said.

Helen tensed. Here it comes, she thought. "I did," she said cautiously.

"Did you tell the police?" Phil said. He knew she didn't. Margery had told him that, too.

"No, I got scared and ran," she said.

"Helen, the police know that people panic when they see dead bodies. But you have to tell them what you saw before they find out you were at the murder scene. Your information could be important to their investigation."

"I saw the same thing they did—a woman with a pair of scissors in her chest," Helen said. "Besides, they aren't going to find me."

"Cops aren't stupid, Helen. They will track you down. They'll be royally pissed if you don't tell them first."

They won't find me, Helen thought. I wiped off my fingerprints—and maybe the murderer's—with Tammie's robe, then dropped it in a Dumpster. I didn't tell them that, either.

"Is there anything else you're not telling me?" Phil said.

Helen felt like she was locked in that dark cage with the rising water. "Why would you say that?"

"Because you just answered my question with a question," Phil said.

The man she loved had turned into a relentless interrogator. Helen pulled away from Phil and sat up. "I can't let the police get sidetracked and have them start investigating me. And you know why—because of my ex-husband."

"The police understand abusive spouses," Phil said.

They wouldn't understand if I were the abuser, Helen thought. I took after Rob with a crowbar. Phil seemed to believe she was running from an ex-husband who'd beaten her. Helen had never corrected that impression.

"What's wrong? Is your ex-husband friends with the prosecuting attorney back in St. Louis?" Phil said. "Does he have pull with the local cops? I have contacts, Helen. I can help you. Just tell me what it is."

"It's nothing I can talk about," Helen said.

Only her sister, Kathy, knew Helen's complete story. She loved Phil, but she wasn't ready to trust him completely. She wanted to. She felt guilty that she didn't. But Helen had had such bad luck with men. What if she told Phil everything and he betrayed her, too? All it would take was one fight and one phone call, and she'd be back in front of that ugly little judge in St. Louis. She was risking everything if she told Phil what really happened, including her new life in Florida.

Besides, nothing could fix her situation. She was beyond help.

"So I'm good enough to fuck, but not good enough to talk to," Phil said. His voice was hard, and there was an angry flush on his face.

"No!" Helen said. "You don't understand."

"Here's your order, sir," the cashier said, handing him the bags of food. "Anything else you need?"

"Yes, but I can't get it here," he said, then gave her that crooked grin to soften his hard words. The cashier giggled.

As they headed home, the chicken and gravy overpowered the other tantalizing odors. But Helen had lost her appetite.

Phil and Helen arrived at the Coronado in sullen silence, but there was so much activity, no one noticed. Helen let herself into her apartment and dug her secret cell phone out of the red Samsonite suitcase. Helen had bought the phone in Kansas and sent her sister, Kathy, a thousand dollars cash to cover the bills. She usually called only once a month, but she had to let Kathy know she was OK.

Helen suspected her sister would be worried sick. As soon as Kathy answered the phone, Helen knew she'd guessed right. "Oh, thank God you're safe," Kathy said. "I've been so worried." Helen could hear the relief in her sister's voice. "Mom was over here, and kept asking why I was so jittery. She doesn't know where you live and I couldn't tell her. She'd go straight to Rob."

"It's too bad I can't trust my own mother," Helen said.

"She loves you," Kathy said. "She wants what's best for you. It's just that her idea of what's best—"

"Is the worst," Helen said. "You know I can't go back to Rob. But she can't accept that. She never will."

Helen could hear kids squabbling in the background,

and knew this conversation would have to end soon. "Kathy, please don't worry. I'm safe. I have plenty of food and water. There's no damage to my building. The electricity is off. The worst that will happen is I'll sweat a bit and lose six eggs in my fridge."

"I kept thinking of you facing the storm all by yourself," Kathy said.

"Don't worry. I wasn't alone," Helen said. "I was with Margery and my friends."

There was a piercing kid shriek and Kathy said, "Stop that! Helen, gotta go."

I was more alone in St. Louis, Helen thought, as she hung up the phone. I have such a good life down here, and I could lose it all because I was careless and a coward. Her hot, dark apartment suddenly seemed infinitely precious, far more desirable than her St. Louis mansion.

Helen packed the phone back in the suitcase and went to Margery's place. Peggy was in the yard, piling up dead branches. Cal and Phil were prying the plywood off all the windows except the broken one.

Inside, the women from apartment 2C were helping Margery clean up. Helen thought they were curiously ineffective for professional cleaners. Doris and Alice handled mops and brooms as if they were foreign objects. Even Elsie did a better job of cleaning, and she wore high heels.

Cal had the gas generator running. It was outrageously noisy, but the living room was blessedly cool. Margery had one window air conditioner running off the generator. The TV was on, except when Margery had the orange juicer going for screwdrivers, which was fairly often. The hurricane party wanted some hair of the dog.

Helen borrowed Margery's phone to call her friend Sarah, who lived on the beach in Hollywood. Sarah was fine, except for a little water on the carpet. Next Helen called her boss, Jeff.

"Lulu and I made it through the storm unharmed," Jeff said. "I'm at the store now. We have electricity. I'm going to take off the plywood and clean up the water in the grooming room. No, no, Lulu and I can handle it. Your Margery predicted it right. The water damage wasn't serious. We'll be open tomorrow, business as usual. I'll expect you here at nine o'clock."

Helen wanted to watch the news, but Margery had the TV off again while she made another batch of orange juice. She flipped the TV back on in the middle of the newscast.

The announcer looked strained from having to deliver one solemn statement after another. Helen caught the last part of his sentence. She thought he said, "Mrs. Barclay was the owner of the Davis Family Dollar department stores mascot."

"Was?" Helen said.

On the screen there was a clip of the labradoodle pup frolicking on behalf of the store, then a formal photo of Willoughby.

"That's Barkley's owner! She owns the kidnapped dog," Helen said as everyone gathered around the set. Even Margery came out of the kitchen, holding half a mangled orange.

"Mrs. Barclay was found dead in her yard by a neighbor about six this morning," the announcer said. "At first police believed that Mrs. Barclay had been killed by a falling tree branch, but now her death is being investigated as a homicide."

"Oh, Lord," Margery said.

"Very sad. She was so young," Elsie said in her fluttery voice. "And now she's dead."

Thank God, Helen thought, but she didn't blurt that out. She felt a sudden selfish surge of relief.

"There won't be any lawsuit," Helen said. "My troubles are over."

"Wrong," Margery said. "Your troubles have just begun. You're now the chief suspect."

CHAPTER 18

······································

Lulu wore a gold Lurex turtleneck and gold nail polish.

"Now that the hurricane is over, you're putting on the dog, Miss Lulu," Helen said.

The low-slung hound strutted around the store as if she were at a cocktail party, greeting her guests. The customers did everything but worship Lulu. They definitely bowed down to her.

"What a sweet doggie-woggie," a twenty-something brunette said. She had a jaunty ponytail and a white halter that said, TROUBLE. Helen thought Lulu should add that item to her wardrobe.

Ms. Trouble got down on her knees to scratch Lulu. "You are the cootest doggie," she said.

She sounded like she was possessed by the ghost of Elmer Fudd. Why did people talk to dogs that way? Helen stayed on the other side of the room, restocking the shelves. Baby talk made her fwow up. Helen wouldn't admit it, but she felt sad and sour after her fight with Phil. It didn't help that she knew she was wrong.

The boutique bell rang and a man with florid white hair and a forceful gut entered the shop. "Hew-wo, widdle doggie," he said.

Helen froze. She recognized that voice. She peered

out from behind a stack of dog-food sacks. Ted Brogers, pet detective, was cooing to Lulu. "Aren't you a booful li'l girl?"

Lulu lapped it up. She pranced for the red-faced detective, showing off her gold manicure. Helen decided to slip into the stockroom. Suddenly the golden girl turned and planted herself in front of Helen, blocking her escape. Lulu's gold clothes and nail polish glittered and winked at her.

You gave me up, you gold-plated bitch, Helen thought.

Lulu wagged her treacherous tail.

Where the heck was Jeff? Helen needed him here. Jonathon and Todd were busy grooming dogs. They couldn't hear anything over the screaming hair dryers.

Helen put on an uneasy smile for Detective Brogers and tried for chitchat. "I see you survived the hurricane," she said.

"I did," he said. "But someone else didn't. Another dog lover."

"Willoughby Barclay is dead," Helen said, then added quickly, "I saw it on TV."

"She isn't dead," Brogers said. "She was murdered. It was brutal. Mrs. Barclay was a nice woman. She didn't deserve to die that way."

"It's very sad," Helen said. "But I didn't realize you did homicides. I thought you handled lost-dog cases." The words seemed to run out of her mouth, the way roaches scurried out of a kitchen when you flipped on the light. Nice move, Helen told herself. Always insult a cop.

Detective Brogers puffed out his chest with self-importance. "I investigate major crimes. Barkley is a valuable dog. Now her owner is a homicide victim. It's still the same case."

Helen could see Ms. Trouble, the ponytailed brunette, sidle in closer to listen. She was one aisle away, pretending to study the needlepoint beagle pillows.

"The victim had words with you shortly before her murder," Brogers said. "Mrs. Barclay accused you of giving her dog to her estranged husband. She was going to sue you sideways unless you found that dog by the end of this week."

"She was going to sue the store," Helen said.

"Oh, no," Brogers said. "She was suing the store, but she told me she was also suing you personally. You handed that dog to her husband. You were flirting with him. Trying to catch yourself a rich husband? I heard about your behavior in the store."

"You heard wrong," Helen said coldly. "That man is a creepy little bottom-feeler." Where the heck was Jeff? Helen wondered. Why didn't Brogers ask to talk to him?

"That's your story now, but I know for a fact Mrs. Barclay was furious with you. She could have ruined you."

"No! You don't understand," Helen said. "The last time I talked with Willoughby, she was happy with me. I discovered her husband dug his alibi out of the trash. A cleaning woman at the mall saw Francis Barclay rooting through a trash can at Sawgrass Mills Mall. That's where he got the receipt for the Golden Calf. I called Willoughby and told her. It was a big break in the case. She was going to call you. Didn't she?"

"No," Brogers said. "I don't know anything about this. Did this so-called witness actually see Mr. Barclay with a receipt from that restaurant?"

"No, but—"

"Do you have the witness's address and phone number?"

"No, but—"

"Do you even know her name?"

"No, but—"

"Do you know where you were between four and six the night of the hurricane?"

Helen stopped, startled. Detective Brogers was asking for her alibi. "Yes," she said. "I was here at the store. Locked in a cage." Helen told him the story. It sounded stupid, even to her. Ms. Trouble leaned in so hard to listen, she nearly snagged her ponytail on a shelf.

"Can you prove you were at the store during that time?" Brogers asked.

"Three people drove over here to rescue me when I didn't come home," Helen said. "The owner, Jeff Barker, showed up with my landlady, Margery Flax, and my boyfriend, Phil. They got here about six fifteen. They saw me trapped in that cage. It was padlocked."

"All that proves is that you were in a cage when they arrived," the detective said. "You had time to murder the victim, run back to the store, and lock yourself in for an alibi."

"That's crazy," Helen said.

"Is it?" said the detective. "Why would anyone bother locking you in a cage? That's even crazier."

"It wasn't crazy at all. The prowler"—Helen thought of the figure in the rustling rain slicker as a man, even though it could have been a woman—"could have killed me, but he didn't. He wanted me locked up, alive and alone."

"You're the person who benefited most from the victim's death," Detective Brogers said.

Jeff benefited more than I did, Helen wanted to say. He has money and a business. It took all her strength not to shout that at Brogers, but she wouldn't sell out her boss. Jeff had been good to her. But where was he? She needed him. He'd know what to say. Soothing words were his specialty.

"What about her husband, Francis?" Helen's voice was shrill. Ms. Trouble jumped back, alarmed by Helen's raised voice.

"He was fighting the issue in court. He didn't have to kill his wife. He was using lawyers for his weapons," Brogers said. "Mr. Barclay had a good chance of winning, too, according to his attorneys. All he had to do was sit tight and he'd get the dog back—or half of it—and Barkley makes enough money for two."

"But he stole that dog," Helen said.

"You'd better watch what you say. I personally searched Mr. Barclay's condo and never saw any sign of a dog. But I did see Mrs. Barclay blaming you for giving her dog to a kidnapper. She was going to sue you for carelessness. She said so right in this store."

"She didn't mean it!" Helen said.

"She sounded serious to me," Brogers said. "You don't look like the sort of person who can afford lawyers, Miss Hawthorne. But you don't have to worry about that now, do you? With Mrs. Barclay dead, the lawsuit went away. Very convenient."

"You think I killed Willoughby? That's nuts," Helen said.

"Is it? Like I said, it doesn't sound as crazy as your cage story. I'll be back, Miss Hawthorne. You can count on it."

Ms. Trouble backed up, then leaped over Lulu in her dash for the door. Her ponytail bobbed like a racehorse's tail. Ms. Trouble was running from Helen, the hurricane killer. Lulu followed Detective Brogers to the door, her tail wagging.

Helen couldn't move. Now she knew who was in that rustling rain slicker—Willoughby's killer. He'd locked Helen in that cage for a reason. He wanted her to take the blame.

It worked. Helen had no alibi for the crucial time of Willoughby's murder. She was sure the cop didn't believe her story about the cage. She hardly believed it herself.

But who killed Willoughby? Was it her husband, Francis, or someone else? Margery was right: Willoughby's death made everything twice as bad. This wasn't about a missing dog anymore. She was in the middle of another murder. Her only break was that Tammie's murder had been pushed out of the news by the hurricane. So far, the detectives in the two separate investigations hadn't made the connection that the two rich dead women had been customers at this store. Worse, both had had screaming battles here before they were killed. And Helen was involved.

But so was Jonathon. Helen remembered what Elsie had told her at the hurricane party. Maybe she could find some tactful way to ask him. "Hey, Jonathon, that woman you're accused of killing—did you know her back in Tampa when she was Wanda and you were someone else? And by the way, did you blind a show dog?"

Jeff came through the front door, smiling. His teeth were white as sugar cubes. His thick dark hair hung down over one eye, giving him a sultry look. Had Jeff been flirting with someone in the parking lot?

"Hi," he said. "Anything happen while I was gone?"

"Nothing much," Helen said. "A cop accused me of murdering Willoughby, but that's all."

"Is that a joke?" Jeff asked.

Helen told him the whole story. Jeff rubbed his head and groaned. "And Brogers was harassing you in front of our customers?"

"Oh, yeah," Helen said. "He all but accused me of murder. The good news is there was only one person in the store: a brunette about twenty-five with a ponytail and a halter top that said, 'Trouble.' "

Jeff groaned louder. "That isn't good at all," he said. "That's Genevra, the biggest gossip in Lauderdale. The whole town will know by tonight. We're going to have the TV cameras here yet. I'll be ruined. Can this day get any worse?"

It could, and it did.

Half an hour later, two men in suits entered the shop. One was short and stocky. The other was tall and lean with a face like raw hamburger. Lulu pattered up to them. The all-too-solid homicide detective Crayton bent down to scratch Lulu's ears. The gangly man beside him scratched his own ears. That would be Detective Mc-Googan. The Stately Palms detectives waited a minute. Then four uniformed police officers, three men and a woman, came through the boutique door.

The color drained from Jeff's face. "Is there something I can help you with?" he asked. Helen noticed he couldn't quite keep his voice steady.

"You have a groomer here by the name of Jonathon?" Detective Crayton said.

"Yes, he's working in the back," Jeff said. "I'll tell him you're here."

The detectives and four officers marched toward the grooming room. "Wait!" Jeff said. "You can't disturb him. Please. I'll—"

The police brushed past Jeff as if he weren't there. He followed them into the grooming room, wringing his hands.

Jonathon was clipping a collie with a thick, handsome coat. Jonathon's own coat was equally stunning. His avocado disco suit with the plunging neckline was made of some shiny material that changed to gold. The effect was dazzling with his hair.

The collie stood absolutely still while Jonathon expertly snipped around its back legs. Dog and groomer looked up when the police crowded into the room.

"Are you Jonathon, also known as Bertram Reginald Falkner?" Detective Crayton asked.

"I am," Jonathon said. He was holding his ten-inch grooming scissors. They seemed menacing.

"You're under arrest for the murder of Tamara Grimsby. You have the right to remain silent—"

Crayton recited law enforcement's familiar chant while the uniformed police officers took the scissors from Jonathon, patted him down, and cuffed him. The collie whimpered. So did Jeff.

"You're going after Jonathon because he's gay," Jeff said. "Jonathon! Don't worry. I'll call my lawyer right away."

"Save your money," Detective Crayton said. "Unless you like men who kill women."

Helen was stunned. She should have expected this, but seeing Jonathon in handcuffs was frightening. A weird, silly thought bubbled up in her brain: The silver handcuffs didn't go with the gold in his disco suit, but she caught herself before she blurted it out. The exotic Jonathon looked smaller now, sad and shaken. The cops were wrong. They had to be.

"Jonathon didn't kill anyone," Helen said. "He—" She felt the two remaining police officers on either side of her. They seemed too close, even in this small room. Suddenly they both clamped down on her arms.

"Helen Hawthorne," Detective Crayton said, "I'm taking you downtown for questioning in the murder of Tamara Grimsby. You have the right to remain silent—"

The roaring in Helen's ears blocked out the rest of the recitation of her Miranda rights. This couldn't be happening. Helen didn't stay silent at all. "Jeff," she said. "Call my landlady, Margery Flax."

The female officer started patting her down. The male yanked Helen's arms backward and snapped handcuffs on her wrists. That *snap!* sound was worse than the cage door closing on her in the dark.

Helen fought back her panic. She had to get in touch with Margery. She had to let her know what had happened.

Jeff stood there, paralyzed. Helen wasn't sure if he'd heard her or not. "My landlady, Margery Flax," she repeated. She was shouting now. "You have her number."

Jeff looked at her blankly, too dazed to react.

The last thing Helen saw, as she stumbled out the door, was Todd. He was smiling slyly.

CHAPTER 19

Helen had never been handcuffed before—not even when she went after her ex-husband with a crowbar. With her hands locked behind her, Helen felt helpless, trapped, and ashamed. She hadn't done anything wrong, except maybe lie to the police. OK, she'd wiped off her fingerprints and possibly destroyed some evidence. But she didn't kill anyone.

Now she felt overwhelmed with guilt.

Helen kept her head down on the endless walk to the police car. Her face was hot with embarrassment. She prayed that no one coming out of the Briny Irish Pub or the hair salon saw her handcuffed between two police officers. The perp walk—wasn't that what this hangdog procession was called? She'd always thought those people looked guilty, with their heads down and their hands cuffed. Now she was one.

It wasn't any better inside the patrol car. All the way to the Stately Palms police headquarters, Helen wondered if the cops had discovered her real name and learned what happened in St. Louis. She hoped that Jeff had called Margery. She wished she'd followed her landlady's advice, and Phil's, too. Just yesterday her lover had warned her that the police would be furious if they found out Helen had lied.

Now she was dumped in the backseat of a police car behind a security screen.

"Excuse me, Officers," Helen said. "Do you know how long I'll be detained?"

No answer. The two uniformed officers were silent as crash-test dummies.

Eventually Helen found out exactly how long she'd have to wait: four hours and eleven minutes. Every minute was agonizing.

The uniformed officers took Helen to a box of a room. It had a table bolted to the floor, a two-way mirror, and a couple of chairs. They uncuffed her hands from behind her back, then cuffed her right hand to a chair. It felt good to get one hand free and the other in front of her.

Stately Palms was a new community, and so was its police headquarters. Was the dark gray color on the walls and floor specially chosen by a decorator to induce fear and remorse? Helen was definitely sorry.

Her neck prickled. She thought someone was watching her through the mirror.

After the second hour, the air-conditioning went off. Helen suspected that was deliberate. The single handcuff chafed her wrist. It also hurt her conscience. Why should a metal bracelet make her feel so guilty?

By the third hour she was tormented by visions of her mother and the nuns from school, all weeping with shame. She could see Dolores standing in front of her. Her mother was thin and sad, wearing a luxuriant brown wig meant for a much younger woman. Dolores kept wringing her hands and asking where she had gone wrong: Didn't she make sure Helen had a good Catholic education? Next to her mother was Sister Mary Margaret, Helen's algebra teacher. She asked how an honor student had come to this.

Helen didn't know. She had to go to the bathroom really bad. Her stomach growled. She'd confess to killing Nicole Simpson for a cup of coffee and a sandwich.

By the fourth hour she was squirming in her seat. Sweat ran down her neck and soaked her shirt. She was tormented by questions she couldn't answer: What did the detectives know about her? What did they want? What were they going to do? Did they connect the murders of Tammie and Willoughby to the shop—and to her?

At six o'clock the door opened, and homicide detectives Crayton and McGoogan entered. They looked exhausted. Helen wondered if they'd been interrogating Jonathon for four straight hours. If the cops were exhausted, what did Jonathon look like? The air-conditioning came back on with a cooling burst.

The short, solid Detective Crayton sat across from Helen. He didn't seem like a Russian doll anymore. He looked like a KGB torturer. The lanky McGoogan sat next to him and picked lint off his suit jacket.

Detective Crayton radiated anger: in his face, his hunched shoulders, and his clenched hands. "You've got one chance, and one chance only, to get this right," he said. "Do you know anything about a white terry robe left in a Dumpster in a shopping center on Federal Highway?"

They know, Helen thought. Someone saw me. She decided to tell the truth. It was her only way out. The silence stretched on while Helen found the courage to say four words: "I put it there."

McGoogan pulled at the knot on his tie.

Once she admitted that, the rest seemed easy. The words came flooding out. "I found Tammie's body. I panicked and ran. I wiped down the front door with the robe. After I drove off, I realized I still had it in the car, so I threw it away behind a little strip shopping center."

They made her repeat her story again and again. While she told this part, Detective McGoogan didn't twitch, itch, or move. He stared straight at Helen with hard cop's eyes. She felt like a germ under a microscope, but she kept talking. She hoped the truth would set her free.

"Why did you have the victim's robe in the first place?" Detective Crayton asked.

"Because I didn't want to see Tammie naked again,"

Helen said. "The live Tammie, I mean. Or the dead one, for that matter. Except I didn't know she was dead when I went back to her house."

Helen was so tangled in her sentences, she backed up and started again. "The first time I visited her house, Tammie wasn't wearing any clothes. I don't like looking at naked women. If she pulled that stunt again when I came back with her dog, I was going to hand her the robe and tell her to cover up."

"So you were angry at her," Detective Crayton said.

"Not angry. Disgusted. Just because I'm a servant doesn't mean I have to put up with that."

"Did Tammie make advances toward you?" Crayton said. "Is that why you killed her?"

"I didn't kill her," Helen said. "I don't know why the woman was naked. It may have been a power play. I didn't like it and I didn't want to see her without her clothes. So I took her robe out of the master bath."

"What was your relationship with the deceased?"

"I didn't have any," Helen said. "I saw her for the first time that day."

"Were you ever in her house?"

"Just when I picked up her dog, Prince, and then when I tried to return him."

"Why did you run when you found the victim's body? Were you afraid for your own safety?"

"I panicked," Helen said. "I guess I was afraid. I was certainly afraid to be with a dead body."

"You used the victim's robe to wipe down the front door?" Detective Crayton said. McGoogan gnawed on his pen tip like a puppy.

"Yes," Helen said.

"Did you realize that you knowingly destroyed evidence? Do you understand that's a crime?"

"I'm sorry," Helen said. "I didn't mean to. I freaked. I saw Tammie with these scissors sticking out of her chest. It was horrible. I ran, and that was wrong. But I did call 911 to let the police know she was dead."

Detective Crayton hit the tabletop with his thick, meaty hand. Helen jumped. "You didn't tell the police what really happened. You delayed our investigation because of your lies."

"I'm sorry," Helen said. How many times did they want her to apologize?

"Do you know or suspect anyone who might have wanted to kill the victim?"

Just Tammie's husband, Kent, Helen thought. But if I say I think he's the killer because he wanted to put her dog to sleep, I'll sound even more unstable. Oh, and by the way, a little old lady with orange hair and turquoise toreador pants says he used to be a crooked vet named Lance.

"No, sir," Helen said. "I don't know anyone."

"Have you ever been arrested?" the detective said.

"Me?" Helen squeaked like a mouse. "No." That was technically true.

"Are you hiding anything else?"

"No," Helen said. That was a lie.

"Write down your statement, sign it, and get out of here," Crayton said. "This afternoon was just a taste of the future. If I catch you in another lie, I'll lock you up and throw away the key."

Half an hour later Helen stumbled into the lobby, feeling like she'd crawled out of a car wreck. She looked like it, too. Her hair was limp and greasy. Her shirt was wrinkled and torn on one shoulder. She was angry at herself, but she had tear tracks on her cheeks. That made her madder.

Phil was waiting for her on a hard plastic bench. In the dark lobby his hair shone like a beacon. Helen ran into his arms and he held her, crooning to her and smoothing her hair. He smelled of coffee and something citrusy.

"It's all right, babe. It's going to be all right," he said. "Let's get out of here and get you some food."

"I can't go to a restaurant looking like this," Helen said.

"We'll go to your place. The electricity is back on. I'll scramble you some eggs while you shower and change."

Helen felt better after she was clean and sitting in

front of a steaming plate of eggs and slightly burned buttered toast. Phil treated her with tenderness, but the tension between them wasn't completely gone. Helen could feel it like a small stone in her shoe.

Phil even fed Thumbs. The big-pawed cat jumped in his lap for a long scratch while Helen wolfed down her food.

"I talked with the two homicide detectives while you wrote out your statement," Phil said. "They were more interested in pumping me about you than telling me anything."

Helen put down her fork, instantly wary. "What did you tell them?"

"That you were a complete ditz," Phil said. "I said I wasn't surprised that you ran away when you found the dead woman."

"Thanks a lot," Helen said.

"They believed me," Phil said. "I was trying to get you off the hook."

Maybe he was, but Helen still thought it was an angry thing to say. The cops weren't the only ones who were furious at her.

"They did tell me a few things," Phil said. He was scratching Thumbs's ears. The cat rolled over on his back and presented his belly. "As I suspected, they brought you in because they were mad." Phil didn't say, "I told you so." He didn't have to. "They wanted to scare the shit out of you."

"They succeeded," Helen said.

"You did the right thing, telling them the truth." Helen heard the unspoken "this time."

"The police have you on tape tossing that robe into the Dumpster," Phil said. "You picked a Dumpster by a doctor's building with security cameras. The docs have had a lot of drug break-ins.

"A security guard noticed you dumping the robe. He picked it out. It had a woman's name embroidered on it. When he saw the news later that night, and realized that was the name of the murder victim, he called the Stately

Palms police. If you'd lied about the robe, the cops would have arrested you for sure."

"They've already arrested our star groomer, Jonathon, for Tammie's murder," Helen said. "If they have a suspect, why are they asking me all these questions?"

"Because they think you might have helped him. Jonathon denies it. He also denies that he killed the woman."

"I don't think he did," Helen said. "I think her husband, Kent the ogre, did it. He was at the shop that day, Phil. He could have stolen Jonathon's shears and killed his wife. Listen, I know you have some law enforcement contacts, but why were the police telling you this?"

"Because they wanted me to deliver a message," Phil said.

"What am I going to do?" Helen said.

"You're going to let me help you," Phil said. "Maybe we can give them some leads on the real killer. I know you think it's Kent, but could anyone else have killed Tammie?"

"The police are convinced it's Jonathon. I'm not, but I admit Jonathon looks like a good candidate. He had a fight with her the day of the murder, then disappeared for part of the afternoon. I don't know if his fingerprints are on the murder weapon. But he may have killed someone years ago in self-defense."

"Did he shoot them?"

"No, he used grooming scissors."

Phil whistled. "That's not good."

"It gets worse. He may have an ugly past, Phil. Margery's friend Elsie says he used to work for a crooked vet in Tampa, and he took a bribe and ruined a show dog's chances. She claims Jonathon changed his name and his look when he moved here. The crooked vet and his bosomy assistant sound a lot like Tammie and Kent."

"What does Kent do for a living now?" Phil said.

"Nothing," Helen said. "But he has a lot of money."

"Do you think Kent conspired with Jonathon to kill his wife?"

"No. I'm not convinced Elsie's story is true."

"You don't like to hear bad things about Jonathon, do you?" Phil said.

"I like him, but I can't tell you why, except he doesn't talk baby talk to the dogs. That's some basis for a friendship."

"Anyone else?" Phil said.

"There's something odd about Todd, too. I don't think he's a killer, but he may be blackmailing a customer. He's jealous of Jonathon. Jonathon was in a snit when Todd worked in his room, and he held a pair of scissors to Todd's throat."

"Jonathon again. Are you sure he's a good guy?" Phil said. "He sounds violent."

"He's a prima donna," Helen said. "He wouldn't actually hurt anyone."

"Except the man he killed."

"He tried to kill Jonathon first," Helen said. "Anyway, Jonathon didn't hurt Todd. I swear Todd cut his own throat to make the fight with Jonathon look worse."

"I can't think of any other candidates. There may be other people who wanted to kill Tammie, but I don't know her well enough to say who they are."

"What about Jeff?" Phil said.

"Jeff!" Helen said. "He wouldn't hurt a soul. Besides, he was running around like crazy at the store the afternoon of her murder."

"Did you see him at the store all afternoon?"

"I think so. I was pretty busy," Helen said.

But now she wondered. Jeff had slipped out this morning, and she didn't realize it until he came whistling through the front door. Could he have disappeared for half an hour the day of Tammie's murder?

"Maybe Jeff needs checking out," Phil said. "I'll see what I can find out about Jonathon, Todd, Kent, and Jeff. Can you get the gossip on Tammie? Any way that you can talk to someone in her crowd?"

"I can try," Helen said. "I can work on the Todd angle,

too. It's possible he's blackmailing Jan Kurtz, one of our customers. Margery thought I should talk with Jan and see if I can find out why."

"Good idea," Phil said. "Jan is more likely to confide in a sympathetic woman."

There was a knock on her door. Helen heard a smoky voice demanding, "Are you two decent? It's Margery."

"Of course we are," Helen said.

Margery handed Helen a glowing cell phone and stepped inside Helen's home. "It's your boss, Jeff. He wants to know how you are. So do I."

"I'm fine, Jeff," Helen said into the phone. "No, no. It was nothing serious. The detectives asked me some questions and let me go. I don't know why they came on so heavy with the handcuffs. Once I got to the police station, it was no big deal. I'm sorry I didn't call you sooner. I'll be in tomorrow. There's nothing to worry about."

Helen snapped the phone shut and handed it back to her landlady. Margery's face was purple with anger. "When are you going to quit lying?" she said. "Aren't you in enough trouble?"

CHAPTER 20

The high-rises on Galt Ocean Mile blocked everyone else's view of the ocean, like bullies taking over a bar.

The massive buildings made Helen feel insignificant. She should have been gliding up the curving drive to Jan Kurtz's condominium in a Mercedes or a Jaguar. Instead she got off a bus. Helen was out of breath by the time she climbed up the long driveway and grand staircase. She was also wet. When the wind shifted, the fountain had sprayed her like a stray dog.

The magnificent doorman eyed the dripping Helen as if she were a burglar. Helen was nearly blinded by the light from the chandeliers bouncing off the mirrors and the marble floors. The young man at the front desk gave her a superior stare.

"Helen Hawthorne to see Mrs. Kurtz."

The superior young man made a call, put the phone on hold, and said, "Mrs. Kurtz is at home, but she's not expecting anyone."

"Tell her I want to talk to her about her gift bag."

The young man spoke into the phone again, then said, "You may go upstairs. Seven-seventeen."

The elevator was paneled in dark wood. On three sides it had long brass rods like coffin handles. It traveled faster than Helen's bus.

Jan opened her condo door cautiously, blocking it with her small, trim body. Her pink Capri pants and fitted top had been stylish three years ago. Her makeup and blond hair were flawless, but Jan's smile looked like it might slip off her face. Her hands trembled slightly, and she clung to the door frame to steady them. Jan was a frightened woman. Helen hated to make her feel worse, but she needed some answers, and the only way she would get them was by asking Jan questions that would hurt her.

"I know about you and Todd," Helen said, deliberately talking a little too loud.

Jan swiftly beckoned Helen inside. Condos had notoriously sharp-eared neighbors. Helen stepped in and stopped, stunned by the view of the blue-green sea stretching into infinity. A little black poodle came running up, danced around Jan, then barked protectively. Jan scooped up the dog and put her hand over its muzzle.

"Shush," she said, hugging the dog. "You know we can't make noise."

Jan turned to Helen. There was fear in her eyes and a desperate courage. "I don't have any more money," she said defiantly. "I told Todd that. He said this would be the last payment, and now you're here. I swear I'll go to the police this time. I have nothing to lose. I'm broke."

Helen looked past the splendid view and saw the slightly lighter rectangles on the green wallpaper where paintings must have hung. A long, lighted display cabinet for smaller artworks was dark and empty. The carpet was worn and the curtains were sun-faded.

Helen had guessed right: Todd was bleeding this woman. "Sit down, Jan, and talk to me," she said. "I don't want your money. I think I can help you."

Even though she was in her own home, Jan took a seat in a mint-green wing chair, as Helen directed. Helen sank into the couch. The pillows shifted, and she saw they hid a stain on one cushion.

"I don't think you can help me," Jan said. Tears streaked her perfect makeup. "I'm trapped. Todd's tried this 'last payment' routine before. I gave him all the money I had, but he'll be back for more in a few months and I'll have to sell my condo."

"How long has this been going on?" Helen said.

"Three years."

"Tell me why he's doing this to you," Helen said. "I'll understand."

"It's Snickers," Jan said, and hugged her dog tighter to her chest. Helen looked at the small curly-coated poodle with the long pink tongue. Maybe she couldn't understand after all.

"Snickers is illegal," Jan said. "I live in a condo that doesn't allow pets."

"That's all?" Helen said.

"All? It's everything. The condo association can take my Snickers away from me. Ever since Todd discovered I lived in a no-pets building, he's been blackmailing me. I couldn't bear to live without my little doggie. With my husband dead, I have no one else."

Snickers jumped out of Jan's lap, then returned with a slobbery squeaky toy, as if the rubber duck would cheer her up. Jan took it and scratched the dog's ears. "See?" she said. "See how sweet he is? He gave Mommy a present."

"How did Todd learn your secret?" Helen said.

"At your store. I bought a special bag to hide Snickers in when I carried him into the building. It looked like a designer purse, except it had mesh on the sides, so Snickers could breathe. Todd sold it to me."

Todd had preyed on a customer. Jeff would be furious and mortified.

Jan kept her head down and her voice so low Helen had trouble hearing her. "I . . . I made friends with Todd. You know, good friends. I know it was a mistake, but I'm only forty-five. I'm still an attractive woman, and I'd dated such awful men. One got drunk and made a scene in a restaurant when I refused to go home with him. I was so embarrassed, I never went to the restaurant again."

Helen had made a few mistakes herself. She hoped she looked sympathetic.

"After that episode, I didn't date," Jan said. "Then I met Todd. He seemed so nice. He was a little young, but that didn't matter to me. We had fun together. We went shopping. I could never get a man to go shopping with me before. My late husband, Thomas, hated stores. They bored him.

"I enjoyed buying Todd presents. I gave him platinum cuff links, a gold key ring, and a silver ID bracelet. I felt so sophisticated. I liked shopping for nice clothes for Todd. I helped him with his rent sometimes, but I'd do that for any friend in trouble. Todd made me laugh. For the first time since Thomas's death, I felt young.

"Then Mrs. Morris—she's another widow, an older woman who lives in the penthouse—said, 'So you've taken up with the neighborhood gigolo.' Suddenly I saw what I was: a foolish middle-aged woman with a much younger man."

That interfering old busybody, Helen thought. Jan wasn't hurting anyone. Why couldn't that woman have left her alone?

"I was so ashamed," Jan said. "I was the laughing-stock of the building. I couldn't go out with Todd again. Thanks to Mrs. Morris, I realized Todd wasn't my friend. He was my boy toy. I gave Todd a nice present and said I didn't want to see him anymore.

"That's when he turned nasty and threatening. He started blackmailing me. He said if I didn't pay him, he would tell the condo association about Snickers. They took away Mrs. Chaney's peke and nearly broke her heart. So I paid him. But Todd wanted more and more. I tried to give him what he wanted, but then the stock market crashed, and suddenly my investments weren't doing so well."

"That's a terrible story," Helen said. "But I have to ask, couldn't you move to a building that allowed pets?"

"I wish I could. But I can't afford to anymore. After I lost so much money in the market, this building started undergoing a massive renovation. The salt air destroys these condos. We need a new roof, new elevators, and new balconies. The air-conditioning system has to be replaced. There are huge assessments against each condo—seventy thousand dollars for this unit. I had to take out a home equity loan to pay it. If I tried to sell now, I'd take a big loss. Nobody wants to move into a building when there's construction going on. It's noisy and inconvenient, so the prices go down. It will take at least two years before all the work is done. I can hardly afford to stay here, but I can't afford to leave."

The bare room said Jan was telling the truth.

"I am so sorry," Helen said. "Our store owner will be horrified that this happened. When I tell Jeff—"

"You can't! Please. Jeff would fire Todd, and Todd would smear my name all over the neighborhood. I have to live here."

"But—"

"No!" Jan was shaking with fear. "I've thought about going to Jeff a hundred times, but I know what would happen. I couldn't stand it. I faced down the gossip about Todd once. I lived through the giggles and smirks on the elevator, the little remarks in the lobby. It's over now, but I couldn't take it again. Promise me you won't tell Jeff."

"I promise," Helen said. "But I also promise that you'll never make another payment to Todd. Don't you worry, Mrs. Kurtz—"

"Please call me Jan." For the first time, she managed a tentative smile.

"Don't worry, Jan. If Todd threatens you again, call me at the store and I'll take care of him."

"What are you going to do? How will you make him stop?"

"I'm going to blackmail him," Helen said.

As Helen walked to the bus stop, she saw the Galt Ocean Mile in a new light. Now it seemed bold, rich, and optimistic. That's what she was. Well, two out of three, anyway.

Helen felt so energized, she started the second phase of her investigation. She needed some accurate information about Lauderdale society. Margery could help with that.

When Helen got back to the Coronado, she saw a tall ladder leaning against the old white building. At the top of the ladder was a tanned and shapely pair of legs in purple kitten-heeled sandals.

"Margery!" Helen said. "What are you doing on the roof?"

"Checking for storm damage," Margery said.

"Get down here," Helen said. "You'll fall and kill yourself."

"Quit fussing at me like I'm an old lady." Margery leaned over at an angle that made Helen dizzy, and glared down at her.

Helen was not going to remind her landlady that she was seventy-six. "Those shoes worry me. They're not safe."

"Of course they are," Margery said. "I can hook them on the ladder rungs for traction. I can't find a decent roofer to go up and check for me after the storm. They're all busy doing hurricane repairs. So I did it myself. The roof is fine. Hold the ladder if you're worried about me. I'm coming down. Why aren't you at work?"

"I don't go in until noon," Helen said.

"Where's Phil?"

"He's digging up information for me. I need some from you, too."

Ten minutes later Helen sat in Margery's kitchen drinking coffee and running a list of names by her landlady. Margery didn't know the dead Tammie or Willoughby or the blackmailed Jan Kurtz. "I don't run with the Galt Ocean Mile crowd. Too rich for my blood."

Helen was afraid she'd strike out completely, until she mentioned Betty Reichs-Martin. Margery gave her a wide smile. "Oh, yeah. Betty's a good old girl. Very down-to-earth, despite her money. You know she actually goes to the shelter and shovels sh—"

"Yes," Helen interrupted. "She's generous with her time and money."

"She also picks up the donations for the animal shelter charity auction," Margery said. "She hounds—no pun intended—all her friends into giving something for those stray dogs. Betty's not afraid to take some risks."

"What do you mean?" Helen said.

"She's been arrested once or twice for animal-rights issues. She beat up a neighbor who was abusing his dog. Punched out a guy twice her size when he left his dog outside with no water on a blistering summer day. Betty can't stand to see animals suffer. She'd do anything for them."

Even kill for them? Helen wondered.

"Betty should be able to tell you something about the people you're interested in," Margery said. "She's been in most of the houses on the moneyed side of Lauderdale, collecting for her animals."

"How long has Betty lived in Lauderdale?"

"You'd think forever, but she's only been here a couple of years. Used to live on the other side."

That's how the east coast Floridians referred to the west coast of Florida, as though they'd stepped through the looking glass. Maybe they had. The state's east coast was stranger, darker, more dangerous than "the other side." Some people feared the east for that reason. Helen liked it. She'd lived on the safe side too long.

"I've talked with Betty at the store," Helen said, "but I don't know her well enough to call her, and I don't want Jeff involved."

"Let me make a phone call," Margery said. "What time do you go in tomorrow? I'll try to set something up with Betty for you."

Half an hour later Helen was walking to work, cheerfully singing out of tune. Margery had gotten her an appointment with Betty tomorrow. Her meeting with Jan Kurtz went well. Now there was only Todd to deal with, and that sleazy little gigolo was no match for her.

When Helen got into work, Lulu greeted her at the door in a black dress, but there was no sign of Jeff. Todd was working in the stockroom, stacking cases of dog food. His sullen, slightly sweaty good looks might set some female hearts thumping, but Helen thought there was an ugly weakness in his pretty pink mouth. When he saw Helen, he started for the door with a case on his shoulder. Helen blocked his way.

"I know what you did to that woman," she said.

Todd dropped the case, and cans of organic dog food rolled everywhere. He turned whiter than his T-shirt and backed away from Helen.

"You're blackmailing Jan Kurtz," Helen said. "I know it. I can prove it. If you ever talk to her again, I'll tell Jeff. He'll fire your ass and blacklist you with every grooming shop in Lauderdale."

Todd simply nodded, but he seemed relieved. His color was coming back. "I promise I'll never do it again," he said. "I don't know what got into me." He hung his head and looked fetchingly contrite.

Todd was guilty, all right, Helen decided. But he wasn't a hardened criminal. Look how quickly he promised to reform. Todd was young and pretty and he found rich, older women easy to manipulate. All their attention went to his handsome head. Look at him now, on his knees, scrambling to pick up the dog-food cans. Confession was obviously good for Todd's soul.

Helen decided that since she had him where she wanted him, Todd should tell her more.

"The day of Tammie's murder, was Jeff at the store all afternoon?" she said.

"No," Todd said. "He slips out a couple of afternoons a week and meets a man. He leaves Lulu at the store and everyone thinks he's still around somewhere."

"Do you think he's cheating on his interior decorator? They seem so happy together."

"I don't know," Todd said. "But I've seen him with a man about five years older, a good-looking guy, drives a black van. Sometimes they sit in the van with the windows up and the air conditioner running. Sometimes they disappear together. I've seen him take big, thick envelopes with him, but I don't know what's in them."

"Is he meeting with his silent partner, Ray Barker?"

"No, Ray lives in New York most of the year," Todd

said. "They talk by phone several times a week. Ray has gray hair. Doesn't look like the man in the black van at all. I don't know who this person is. Jeff has only started seeing him in the last four or five weeks."

Helen went home that evening, satisfied with her day's work. She'd solved a mystery, stopped a black-mailer, and helped a woman in trouble.

Too bad none of it helped her.

CHAPTER 21

Helen heard Phil unlocking his front door about eight thirty that night. He seemed to be fumbling with the key. Hmm. Had he been drinking? Was he hurt? What did he have to do to get her information?

Helen came flying out her door. She hardly recognized Phil. He was scruffy and unshaven, his shining white hair in dirty gray tangles. Phil wore a stained Sturgis T-shirt and a rebel-flag tattoo. His wallet had a long, thick chain, and his scuffed boots looked like they were made for stomping faces. His greasy jeans showed his butt crack.

Yuck. If Phil was undercover, he was a little too authentic. Her dream lover had turned into her nightmare man.

"Phil?" Helen said. "Is that you?"

"I'm a little unsteady, babe," he said. "I've had to drink beer in redneck bars up near Okeechobee."

"Poor you," Helen said, with a touch of sarcasm. "I bet they pried your mouth open and made you drink that disgusting beer."

"I had to drink it or the customers wouldn't talk to me," Phil said. "Cheap beer gives me a headache. Before that, I had to drink puckery lemonade with a sweet old lady, and that was almost as bad."

"An old woman let you in her kitchen looking like that?"

"She kept me on her front porch," Phil said. "In full view of the neighbors. Miss Bonnie didn't live to be eighty-seven by taking risks. But I wasn't dressed like this. She was my first stop of the day. She saw me in my respectable investigator's suit. Somehow she got it into her head that I was with the police."

"I wonder where she got that idea," Helen said.

"Can't imagine," Phil said, and hiccupped.

"Come in for coffee and a sandwich and we can talk," Helen said.

Phil followed Helen into her kitchen. Thumbs came out to greet his pal. He sniffed Phil thoroughly, then walked away, tail in the air.

"Thumbs doesn't like your brand of beer," Helen said.

"Ungrateful beast," Phil said. "After all the scratches I've given him."

While Helen fixed Phil a turkey sandwich on rye and a mug of black coffee, he told her about his adventures in Okeechobee. She poured herself a cup, set the coffeepot on the back burner, and joined him at her kitchen table.

"I had to get some information on Todd," Phil said. "I started with the high school, looking at the yearbooks. I figured he was somewhere between twenty-one and thirty. He's twenty-six. First thing I learned was that Todd wasn't his real name. He was called Jarrod back then. He was in the freshman and sophomore classes, but Todd never graduated. I found Miss Bonnie, his freshman English teacher. She was retired, and willing to talk to me if there was a chance of saving the young man. She believes there is good in him."

"He seems willing to reform," Helen said, "if you put the fear of the Lord in him like I did."

"Miss Bonnie felt sorry for Todd and gave him special tutoring. She also says a great wrong was done to him as a boy. I got some of his story from Miss Bonnie, and the raunchier bits in a run-down bar near the Dixie Highway. Turns out the old-timers knew Todd and his family. They told me his mother was a prostitute, but she gave it away about as often as she got paid. His father was a burglar who surprised a woman in her home and beat her to death. After that Todd—or Jarrod—was in several foster homes, and didn't do well in any of them. Miss Bonnie says he was small for his age, shy and sensitive, and had trouble getting along with bigger, tougher boys."

"If Todd is pretty at twenty-six," Helen said, "he must have looked really girlish as a kid."

"That was Todd's problem. Kids can be mean, and school bullies picked on him. He was poor, effeminate-looking, and he wore castoffs. Miss Bonnie said he had a crush on a pretty cheerleader. Followed her like a puppy. She was a coldhearted little number.

"The cheerleader's name was Mindy, and she dated the captain of the football team. When Todd was fifteen, Mindy invited Todd to a party at her house. Miss Bonnie still remembers the way his face glowed. She said, 'He looked like Saint Peter had invited him into heaven.' Todd thought he was finally going to be accepted by the high school in-crowd. He told Miss Bonnie about it. She gave Todd some money to buy himself a new shirt. She saw him walking to the party, his hair slicked down with water. His new shirt still had the package creases in it.

"Mindy got Todd drunk at the party, and he passed out. He woke up the next morning in front of the school. He was naked, and his manhood—that's what Miss Bonnie called it—was tied up with pink ribbons."

"That's awful," Helen said.

"The whole school knew about it," Phil said. "They taunted him. Called him 'Pinkie.' It was like part of Todd died. He lost all interest in school."

"I can't imagine what that would do to a fifteen-year-old boy," Helen said. The story made her sick. She still didn't like Todd, but at least she understood why he made his living off women.

"Miss Bonnie blamed Mindy and her bully-boy

friends, but the incident took place off school grounds and there was nothing she could do about it. She did tell me that Mindy married a shoe salesman who knocked her up and then left her for another woman. Mindy now works at Wal-Mart. Miss Bonnie thought it served her right.

"Todd drifted around school like a ghost for the rest of the year, trying to make himself invisible. He got a summer job working in the fields, and the hard work filled him out and toughened him up some. At sixteen everything changed, including his name and address. Todd met a rich, older Palm Beach woman. By then, the skinny little boy was a handsome young man. Todd left school, left the area, and moved in with this rich woman."

"Didn't the authorities go looking for him?" Helen said.

"Not really. Even Miss Bonnie thought Todd was better off gone, even if he was 'living in sin,' as she said. His rich lady friend taught him how to dress, how to talk, how to walk, how to eat in the best restaurants. She sent him to a good dentist to straighten his teeth. She bought him a Cartier diamond watch."

"He still wears it," Helen said.

"When Todd turned twenty, the woman tired of him. She'd found a younger, prettier boy. She bought Todd a condo at Sailboat House in Fort Lauderdale."

"I've heard of that. It's fairly expensive. His lady friend was smart enough to send him to another city," Helen said.

"Yep. She also sent him to dog-grooming school."

"Sort of like those Victorian dandies who set up their castoff mistresses with a hat shop when they tired of them," Helen said.

"Exactly," Phil said. "Dog grooming was the perfect trade for Todd. He loved animals, plus he'd always have a steady supply of older women to buy him presents and pay his condo fees. I can't find out much else about him. Todd has no arrest record and no history of violence. He lives beyond his means sometimes, but when he needs money he goes to the pawnshops with cuff links, rings, watches, and cigarette cases from places like Tiffany's. I talked with a couple of pawnshops."

"Let me guess," Helen said. "Somehow they got the impression you were a cop."

Phil shrugged and grinned modestly.

"Sounds like Todd is exactly what we expected," Helen said. "A young man who makes his money off wealthy older women. At least I understand why he seems so heartless."

"There's only one oddity," Phil said. "Recently he began buying expensive women's jewelry at the pawnshops. He purchased a tennis bracelet, a diamond pendant, and yellow diamond earrings."

"Think he fell in love with someone?" Helen said.

"A gigolo like Todd? I doubt it. More likely he has a rich woman on the string," Phil said. "An heiress likes a man to buy her expensive presents. Then she can kid herself that he's not after her money. Once he has the heiress hooked, she buys the presents for him."

"So the pawnshop gifts would be an investment," Helen said.

"That's how I see it. Appreciate the sandwich and coffee," Phil said, taking his empty plate to the sink. "Did I get you good information?"

"You did indeed," Helen said, and threw her arms around him. He smelled slightly beery. His beard was nicely scratchy. She gave him a long, lingering kiss. "Hmmm. I think I could learn to like lowlifes."

"Wait a minute," he said. "I've worked all day for you, lady. I want my pay."

"Wanna take it out in trade?" Helen said, and kissed him again.

Phil unbuttoned her blouse. "I think we could work out an easy payment plan," he said, as he freed her breasts from their tight bra.

Helen was surprised her slightly wobbly kitchen table could hold their weight. She didn't notice that the coffee turned to sludge on the back burner. They both ignored the problem that had them fighting so bitterly just days ago.

Betty really did shovel out dirty cages at the animal shelter. Today Helen was right beside her, both of them dressed in cutoffs and baggy T-shirts. Betty's fat old bichon, Barney, waddled behind her, snuffling and sniffing, picking up the scent of other not-so-lucky dogs.

The things I do for information, Helen thought, as she grabbed piles of soiled newspapers with her gloved hands. Betty scrubbed the cage bottoms and sides with brisk, efficient movements.

Helen was grateful for the hard work. It kept her mind off the heartbreaking shelter scene. All those beautiful animals, unloved and abandoned. Some tried so hard to make new people take them home. They put on desperate little shows, begging, wagging, dancing. Others slumped despondently in their cages.

Betty knew all the animals' stories. "See that gorgeous little Maltese?" she said, pointing to a small white dog pawing at her cage bars. "Her owner abandoned her because she didn't match the new couch."

"The dog as an accessory," Helen said. "How cruel."

"You won't believe what people do. That big gray Persian cat? He was dumped off because the new boyfriend didn't like him. His person had that cat ten years, but she abandoned him for a man she knew one week. People who do that should be shot. How can they hurt helpless animals?"

"The same way they hurt helpless children," Helen said.

"I could go on all day about the animals here," Betty said. "But Margery says you need help. I know everybody worth knowing in Lauderdale—that means everyone with an open wallet. Ask away, and I'll try to answer your questions."

"Did you know Tammie Grimsby?"

"The woman who got murdered? Sure did. I'm not surprised she came to a bad end. She was headed for trouble, one way or another. She and Kent had too much money and not enough sense. Some people take scuba lessons or join a book club. They did coke and threesomes. Did you know Tammie once asked me to join them?"

Helen sucked in her breath, and not because she had a smelly load of newspapers.

"Don't look so surprised. I clean up pretty good."

Helen looked at Betty's thin, weathered face with the high cheekbones and elegant nose. When her hair wasn't scraped back, she'd be a good-looking woman.

"I'm surprised she didn't come on to you," Betty said.

"I think she did," Helen said. "I pretended not to notice."

Betty crawled into a cage on the bottom row. Helen had a brief attack of the fantods looking at that small space.

"Here." Betty handed Helen more smelly paper. Helen smiled. She couldn't brood around Betty. That woman was too brisk and practical to indulge her fantasies. Helen went back to cleaning cages.

"Tammie did the hunting for her husband, Kent," Betty said, giving Helen some useful dirt. "That's not a good sign. Kent was bored with his wife. He'd probably find a replacement soon—maybe one of the women Tammie brought home. I suspect that's why she went after older broads like me. Thought we'd be flattered, and we'd also be no competition for her. Tammie was no spring chicken. Did you ever talk to her?"

"Yep. Tammie was dumber than a box of rocks," Helen said.

"But sexy," Betty said.

Helen remembered the disturbing feelings the naked Tammie had stirred in her, and said nothing.

"Still, that wears off after a while," Betty said. "Especially if you had to listen to Tammie. I think Kent wanted rid of her. But he couldn't afford to divorce her. I heard he had no prenup."

"He must have been really in love to marry her without legal protection," Helen said.

"The only one Kent ever loved was himself. I figure

she had something on him," Betty said. "I had a pretty good idea what it was, too. Kent used to go by another name."

"Lance," Helen said.

"That's it. Then you know Kent used to be a vet, but he doesn't practice anymore. He told me he was retired. But I got a detective on it. I have the money to satisfy my curiosity. He'd made millions in the business and left under a cloud. Tammie helped him in some way, as his accountant or office assistant."

"Kent made millions as a veterinarian? Is that possible?" Helen said.

"If you're dishonest enough," Betty said. "Most vets I know are kinder than the average people doctor and treat their patients better. But there's a market for vets without consciences."

"Was he involved with a crooked pet store?" Helen said.

"So you do know the stories. Kent—or Lance, as he was then—was in cahoots with a pet store that sold puppy-mill dogs. Customers paid for shots and treatments that never happened. Doc Kent would sign the papers stating that he'd given the pups and kittens their shots, or treated them for health problems, when all he'd done was autograph a big blank block of paper.

"When the little animals died, well, that happens, doesn't it? The owner would get another puppy, and if it was a hardy soul, it would survive. Maybe Doc Kent told himself he was improving the gene pool. I don't know how people like that think. I do know the good people of Tampa were catching on to the pet-shop scam. Doc Kent changed his name, packed up his money and his wife, and moved to this side. He never mentions how he used to make a living. He can't. The animal lovers would lynch him. We tolerate a lot of things in Lauderdale, but not that."

"Why do you?" Helen said.

"Oh, I hurt him—right in the wallet. I hit those two up for donations for the shelter. We're talking staggering amounts. All I have to do is mention the word 'Tampa' and they write me big, fat checks. If that's blackmail, well, I do it for a good cause. But if you know about it, their secret must be out."

Helen shrugged. She didn't want to reveal that Elsie was her source. "What happened to the crooked pet shop?" she said.

"It's closed and the owner took off. There's no proof and no witnesses."

Except for Elsie's granddaughter with the guilty conscience, Helen thought. That young woman couldn't complain to the authorities. She was part of the scam. She wanted to be a lawyer, and puppy abuse wouldn't look good on her résumé. She'd never turn in Doc Kent.

"That's good information about Tammie," Helen said. Betty had confirmed everything she'd learned from Elsie. Well, almost everything.

"I deal in grade-A gossip," Betty said, sweeping up a large pile of dog doo. Barney was curled up in the corner, sound asleep. "Who else can I help you with?"

"What do you know about Willoughby and Francis Barclay?" Helen said.

"Not much. I tried to get their dog, Barkley, as the featured guest for a shelter event, but the Barclays wanted to charge us an arm and a leg. Refused to waive the dog's personal appearance fee, even to help other animals. They're a greedy couple."

"Not anymore," Helen said. "She's dead."

"Well, I'll be." Betty looked at the long row of clean cages. "We're done. Good job. I owe you a drink. Did you bring extra clothes, like I told you?"

"Sure did," Helen said.

"Wash up and change in the restroom. I'll take you out for a beer and a Greek salad. I hope you have an appetite after mucking out those cages."

Helen was surprised to find she did. The sun was shining when they left the shelter, and it was a pleasant day. They drove in Betty's lumbering SUV to the Sea Ranch Diner near a little beach community called Lauderdale by the Sea.

The Sea Ranch was in a beige shopping center with a Spanish-tile roof. It had one remarkable feature: The center was topped by a vast, improbable half of a concrete dome. It looked like someone had dropped the Hollywood Bowl on the shopping center and painted it bright blue with fat white clouds.

"I love it," Helen said.

"We all do. Makes no architectural sense whatsoever," Betty said.

They took a table outside under the preposterous dome. Barney followed them as fast as his short legs would carry him.

"He wants his usual," Betty said.

"Barney! How's my boy?" the waitress said, as she set down a bowl of ice water for the dog.

"I'll have my usual, too," Betty said. "And she wants the same."

"You serve dogs?" Helen said, when the waitress brought them salads mounded with snowdrifts of feta cheese.

"Dogs, cats, birds, we serve them all," the thin blonde said. "People, too."

"Fort Lauderdale isn't exactly Paris, but it has a lot of restaurants where you can take your dog," Betty said. "OK, who else do you want to pump me about?"

"What do you know about Jonathon, the star groomer?" Helen asked.

"Nothing, except he's the hottest groomer in town. Does wonders with little dogs. Everyone wants a Jonathon cut."

"Know anything about his love life?" Helen asked.

"I suspect he's gay," Betty said, "but I've never seen him with anyone, male or female."

"Margery's friend Elsie says she recognized Jonathon. He used to work at a pet shop in Tampa," Helen said. "She says Jonathon temporarily blinded a show dog. Sound familiar?"

"No," Betty said. But she wouldn't look at Helen. Instead, she made a big deal of bending down to scratch Barney, which kept her face hidden.

She's lying, Helen thought.

"Think it's the same crooked shop that Kent was connected with?" Helen said.

"Don't know," Betty said. She lavished more attention on the sleeping Barney. Another lie, Helen decided.

"So you don't know if Jonathon was in cahoots with Kent in Tampa."

"I doubt it, but I don't know," Betty said.

Odd. She could tell Helen everything about the other people connected with that crooked pet shop.

"Didn't you used to live in Tampa?" Helen asked.

"It's a big place," Betty said. She still wouldn't look at Helen. "I can't know everything."

But Helen knew that Betty loved animals. Jonathon had abused a dog once upon a time. And now he was arrested for Tammie's murder.

She also knew Tammie had propositioned Betty. Betty claimed to be flattered. But Helen didn't find Tammie's attention flattering. Tammie lived off the money of an animal abuser—and maybe helped him.

Betty said people who hurt helpless animals should be shot. Should they also be stabbed? How much did Betty love animals? What exactly would she do for them? Would she frame one animal abuser for the murder of another? That would be a neat bit of justice.

Maybe the murder was much simpler. Maybe Tammie refused to shell out any more money, and mocked Betty and her love of animals. Would Betty strike back in anger? One swift stab with the shears would be easy for a woman who played golf and did weekly bouts of manual labor.

Helen asked one last question. She figured she had nothing to lose. "Was that your car I saw leaving the country club when I was delivering Tammie's Yorkie?"

"You mean the day Tammie was killed? Are you asking if I was leaving the scene of the crime?"

"Yes," Helen said. There was a long silence, broken only by Barney's snores. He was sleeping with his head resting on his water dish.

Betty put three tens on the table and picked up her fat little dog.

"I won't dignify that with an answer," she said. "You can find your own way home. A long walk might clear your head."

CHAPTER 22

"**B**etty is a killer? My friend Betty? What have you been snorting?"

Margery's laughter was loud, but there was nothing merry about it. She was purple with fury. Even the dark veins on the backs of her clenched hands were throbbing with rage.

Helen was afraid Margery would rip the wineglass from her hand and smash it on the Coronado's pool deck.

Margery marched back and forth on the concrete, as if the only way she could control her wrath was to keep moving. It boiled and bubbled inside her, a red-hot geyser ready to explode. Anger aged her. Margery looked gnarled and witchy.

At first Helen was stunned by Margery's violent reaction. On second thought, it made sense. Margery was loyal to her friends, and that included Betty. She would protect them all. Margery had given Helen a friend's name, and now Helen had made an ugly accusation against her. Under other circumstances she would have admired Margery's passionate defense of her friend. But it was scary facing her landlady.

Peggy, sitting in the chaise longue, seemed paralyzed. Pete didn't say a word. He huddled in the curve of Peggy's neck, as if seeking shelter from the storm of Margery's rage.

So much for a quiet sunset by the pool, Helen thought. They were supposed to be having a posthurricane celebration in the wind-stripped garden. The night was balmy. The remaining palm leaves rustled invitingly. Everything said to relax. Except Margery, who crackled with electric irascibility.

How was Helen going to defuse this? She felt like she should be in a bomb cage, wearing a padded suit. She took a deep breath and said, "Margery, it's just a theory. I'm sorry it made you mad. But since you know Betty better than I do, I'd appreciate it if you'd tell me what's wrong with it."

"What's wrong? Everything!" Margery said. "Betty might shoot you, but she'd never make up some twisted plot. She's not devious. She never lies."

Yes, she does, Helen thought. She lied to me today—twice. I'd bet a week's pay she was not telling me the truth about Tampa. But you're in no mood to hear that, so I'll keep my mouth shut.

Helen was familiar with those so-called hearty honest types from her time in the corporate world. She knew that backslapping men and "straight-talking" women could be as devious as anyone. More so, because Helen didn't expect them to lie to her. But they did just the same.

"Why would she commit murder?" Margery shouted. Pete scooted in closer to Peggy for protection. "Betty has no reason to kill Tammie."

"Betty loves animals," Helen said. "Tammie helped that goon she married when he was the vet for that crooked pet shop in Tampa. They killed kittens and puppies. Jonathon worked there, too, and blinded a show dog."

"You can't prove any of that," Margery said. "You're guessing. So let me give you a fact. Here's one: I know for a fact that Betty would haul off and slug Kent if she caught him abusing animals. She did it before, and she was arrested for it. But she would not murder Kent's wife and then frame Jonathon for it. That's the stupidest thing I've ever heard.

"Besides, Kent didn't care about Tammie. He was

bored with her, and a divorce would be expensive. Tammie's death was convenient. Why would Betty help him by killing his wife? I swear, Helen Hawthorne, ever since you got locked in that cage, your head hasn't been screwed on straight."

Well, that last sentence was true enough, Helen thought.

Margery was still raging. "If Betty wanted revenge on Kent, she'd go after him. What reason does she have for killing Tammie?"

That was the problem: Helen didn't know the reason. But that didn't mean there wasn't one. Betty's conversation had been full of strange hints and detours.

Betty had said that Kent and Tammie were into threesomes, and she'd turned them down. But what if she didn't? What if she said yes and Tammie had humiliated her? Betty had been oddly, touchingly proud of her looks. "Don't look so surprised," she'd told Helen. "I clean up pretty good." Had Tammie made a bitter enemy during a wild night at her home in Fort Lauderdale? Or had Betty known the couple in Tampa—in the biblical sense?

"Well?" Margery said.

"How did you meet Betty?" Helen asked.

"She rented a furnished apartment here for two months while her house was being built."

"Did she live in 2C?" Helen said. That would be proof, at least in Helen's mind, that something was off about Betty.

"No, she lived in your place." Margery's smile was triumphant, but not very nice.

"Why was Betty speeding out of the Stately Palms Country Club moments after Tammie's death?" Helen said. "She was there when Tammie died."

"Did you ask her?" Margery said.

"Yes, she refused to answer," Helen said.

"Exactly what an innocent person would do," Margery said.

Or a guilty one, Helen thought.

Margery had quit pacing. She settled onto a chaise and lit a cigarette with slightly trembling fingers. The smoke seemed to calm her.

"What do you know about Betty?" Helen said. "She's not from here, is she?"

"No," Margery said. "At least, I don't think so. I know she lived on the other side for a while."

"Tampa?" Helen said.

"Someplace like that." Margery waved her hand vaguely toward the west. Either that, or she was swatting a mosquito. "She had a mansion in some gated community. Betty claimed it was too white-bread on the west coast and moved over here. It's obvious Betty has had money all her life. She said once that she went to private schools. That's all I know about her. Betty's not one to brag."

Was Betty naturally modest, or deliberately hiding her past? Helen kept that question to herself, too. She felt oddly disoriented. She'd thought she could talk to Margery about anything, but she'd bungled this badly. Now Margery felt betrayed, and so did Helen.

Peggy kept a tactful silence in the chaise longue, sipping wine and waiting for the two women to work it out.

Helen wasn't good at confronting problems. She'd run from her husband, she'd run from the court, and now she ran from this. Instead of telling Margery her doubts about Betty, Helen changed the subject.

"Maybe you can help me with something else," Helen said. "I'm looking for someone who would talk to me about the threesomes at Tammie's house."

Besides Betty the good old girl.

"Excuse me. You're asking me?" Margery said. "I already gave you the name of one friend and you decided she was a killer. I'm not helping you this time. I don't know anything."

"Yes, you do," Helen said. "I bet you know someone who could tell me about society's risque side." She tried a lopsided grin. Peggy and Pete stayed motionless on the chaise longue, as if under a spell.

"And after you talk to that person, what would you do? Turn her over to the vice cops?" Margery said. "No, thanks. Get Phil to help you."

"I'd rather not have him investigating that side of Lauderdale," Helen said.

"I don't blame you," Margery said. "If he were mine, I'd put him on a short leash. Helen, I'm seventy-six years old. For most of my friends sex is a distant memory. You're on your own." But this time Margery managed a smile. She blew out a big puff of white smoke, as if her anger had burned away.

Peggy finally spoke. "If you need information, maybe you should talk to Tammie's grieving husband."

"Kent?" Helen said. "You want me to talk to that scuzzball?"

"He likes attractive women," Peggy said. "He might invite you to one of his parties. Then you'd get an inside look at what goes on there."

"Awwk!" Pete said.

"I don't think so. Anyway, I'm not his type," Helen said.

"Yes, you are. I bet he made some sleazy comment about your figure when you were at his house."

Helen looked surprised. "How did you know?"

"Horndogs like Kent always do," Peggy said, and shrugged.

"He'd love to chat you up." Margery gave an evil smile. "Show you around. Get to know you better."

"Ewww." Helen shuddered at the thought of the overmuscled Kent hitting on her.

"All kidding aside, Peggy's got a good idea," Margery said. "Kent wouldn't talk to Phil. He's not going to tell a man anything, especially a younger, handsomer man. You have the perfect excuse to see him. You can offer your condolences."

"I don't want to be alone in that big house with Kent," Helen said. "What if he killed his wife?"

"I thought you said my friend Betty was the killer." Margery would not let it go.

"If Kent turned on me, I could scream for hours and no one would hear me," Helen said.

"Make sure you're not alone," Peggy said. "Doesn't he have a housekeeper? Call first. If she's there, she'll answer the phone. Don't go to the house unless she's at home. And tell Margery when you leave. If you're not back by a certain time, she can call the cops."

"Hell, I'll even drive you over there," Margery said. It was a peace offering.

"Thanks, Margery," Helen said. "But there's no place for you to park. You'd have to go sit in the country-club lot, more than a mile away."

"So I'll drive around the grounds for half an hour. Security isn't going to bother a batty old lady in a big white car. The way that guard sleeps, he won't even notice I'm there. Anyway, do you have a better plan?"

"No," Helen said. "I haven't found Tammie's killer. I haven't found Willoughby's killer. I haven't even found her dog."

"You're not supposed to do that," Margery said. "Those are jobs for the police."

"What are they doing?" Helen asked. "Nothing. I know who murdered both those women—their worthless husbands. I don't understand why the police don't believe those men are guilty."

"Maybe they do," Margery said.

"Not in Tammie's case," Helen said. "They've already arrested Jonathon. And I know he didn't kill her."

"Why? Because you like him?"

"Well, yes," Helen said.

"Some reason," Margery said. It was the same reason why Margery wouldn't hear a word against Betty. But Helen didn't mention that, either.

"You're damn lucky the hurricane pushed Tammie's murder off the front page," Margery said. "Right now there are too many other stories for the media to cover. Nobody's made the connection between Jonathon, Tammie, and Willoughby."

"Oh, come on," Helen said. "You're really trying to nail Jonathon."

"And you're going out of your way to ignore the obvious," Margery said. "He had the fight with Tammie. He disappeared for hours, and it was his grooming shears sticking out of her chest. The police were right to arrest him for her murder."

"They haven't arrested anyone for Willoughby's murder," Peggy said. Her voice was so quiet, they had to lean in to hear her.

"That's because they think I killed her," Helen said. "I'll never be able to convince Detective Brogers to look at her husband, Francis. Brogers couldn't find lint on a dark suit. How am I going to find the real killer? I can't do that. I don't have the resources."

"You're really thinking positive tonight," Margery said.

"If you can't find Willoughby's killer, find her dog," Peggy said. "She was killed for that animal. Once you have the dog, you'll have the murderer."

That made more sense than anything else they'd said tonight.

"It sounds a lot safer than talking to Kent Grimsby," Helen said.

She was wrong about that, too.

CHAPTER 23

....

Eight thirty a.m.

Even coffee didn't help Helen this morning. She felt tired and dragged out after the scene with Margery last night. They were friends again by the end of the evening, but Helen was discouraged. She wasn't getting anywhere. She wasn't doing anything to clear her name. The cops could come for her any moment, the way they'd come after Jonathon, and then where would she be?

Back in St. Louis, facing a judge who looked like E.T. with a hangover.

Helen rummaged in her closet for a pair of pants with no holes and a blouse with all the buttons. That was the best she could do.

She was combing her hair when she heard the screech of tires and brakes in the parking lot, then the slamming of doors. It sounded like four or five cars. Who would be coming to the Coronado at this hour? And why so many cars?

The police!

Helen grabbed her purse, slipped out her sliding doors, and tiptoed to the end of the walkway. Four police cars blocked the Coronado parking lot. Helen sprinted across the grass. She started to knock on Margery's door when her landlady opened it and yanked her inside.

"It's the cops," Margery whispered.

"They're coming to arrest me," Helen said.

"That's what I figured," Margery said. She dragged Helen into the laundry room, past a chugging washer and a warm, humming dryer. She pushed Helen out a side door she'd never noticed before.

Helen found herself standing by a throbbing window air-conditioning unit, next to a pile of abandoned pool furniture and a rusted-out water heater that should have been hauled away years ago. Spiderwebs were strung everywhere. The walkway was so narrow Helen would have to slide out sideways.

Margery picked a wide-brimmed straw hat off a hook by the door and plopped it on Helen's head. "This will hide your face. Go to the end of the gangway, turn right, and you'll come out behind the Dumpsters next door."

Margery handed Helen a reeking bag of trash. "Here, take this," she said. "Drop it in old lady Murphy's Dumpster like you live there. Then pretend you're going for a morning walk. Don't forget to act curious about all the cops. That's the natural way to behave. You got some money?"

"Twenty dollars." Helen held up her purse.

Margery pushed a wad of bills into her hands. "This will get you through today. You may need more. You can pay me back later. Call me in an hour. I'll tell you if the coast is clear. Don't say your name when you call. If I tell you I don't want anything, call me back in another hour. Keep calling till you get the all-clear."

They heard pounding on Margery's front door.

"Take care of Thumbs," Helen said. "Tell Phil I love him."

"The cops are here. You'd better get going," Margery said, and pushed Helen forward.

Helen scooted down the gangway between the buildings, feeling oddly disoriented. She'd never spent much time on this side of the Coronado. She'd never seen this strange little passage between the two buildings. Helen had to pick her way carefully. The walkway was cracked and overgrown with weeds. Hairy spiders crawled along the walls. Cobwebs brushed her hair, and something slithered over her foot. Helen hoped it was a lizard. The gangway was only about thirty feet long, but it seemed endless. She came out by a short fat palm tree and an overflowing blue Dumpster.

Helen threw the bag of trash in and hoped the crabby woman next door didn't come out and yell at her. She had a clear view of the Coronado. She saw the police cars and more uniformed officers than she could count.

"Come on, move on, there's nothing to see," a tough male voice said.

Helen jumped.

A uniformed officer was directing traffic on the street in front of the Coronado, making the gawkers move along. Helen decided she'd shown enough interest. Hanging around any longer wasn't a good idea. Margery's hat hid her hair and part of her face, but Helen couldn't do anything about her height. Any smart cop would spot her.

Helen made her way to the sidewalk. She kept expecting a cop to yell, "You, there, stop!" She tried to stroll, but it was hard to look casual when her heart was hammering hard enough to knock her flat.

Helen made it down the street and turned toward Las Olas and the safety of the tourist crowds. Once out of sight of the Coronado, she burst into a frantic run that she told herself was a power walk. She didn't stop until she came to an outdoor café. Then she sat in an empty chair and collapsed. Her rapidly beating heart made her dizzy. Her hand hurt, and she realized she was clutching Margery's roll of bills so tightly she had nail marks in her palm.

Helen counted the money. Margery had handed her two hundred dollars in tens and twenties.

"May I help you?" the waitress said.

Helen jumped, then tried to pull herself together. "Coffee," she said. "And . . . and a bagel with cream cheese."

That sounded normal, didn't it? She was a tourist on a fine day, having a cup of coffee. Except she was supposed to be at work. What time was it? She checked her watch. Nine o'clock.

Helen found a pay phone and called Jeff. "I may be a little late," she said. "About an hour."

If I'm lucky. Otherwise, I'll be gone twenty to life, she thought.

"It's OK," Jeff said. "It's a slow morning. Lulu and I can handle it."

"How is Jonathon? Can I visit him in jail?"

"He's holding up as well as can be expected. He says no visitors. He doesn't want anyone to see him. He's trying to raise the money to make bail. He wouldn't let me help with that, either."

Helen pulled a free newspaper from a stand and held it in front of her face. Between the paper and the big straw hat, her face was well hidden. The waitress returned carrying Helen's steaming coffee. It smelled sharp and strong, but her stomach rebelled when she tried to sip it. Helen felt jittery. Food. That would calm her. She slathered her bagel with cream cheese, then stared at it. She couldn't take a bite.

Helen was sick with fear, worry, and loss. Even if she escaped the police, her life was over. She'd have to flee Fort Lauderdale, like she had St. Louis, except this time she wouldn't be so lucky.

The Coronado had become her second home, and she loved this life better than the one she'd left behind. Now she was going to lose everything—again. She'd been happy at the Coronado. Her new life wouldn't be so easy to give up. Margery and Peggy had become her family. Margery had protected Helen better than her own mother.

Helen liked her offbeat apartment and her big-pawed cat. She loved Phil. Would she ever see her lover again? He couldn't have an affair with a fugitive. She'd have to leave behind the man she loved.

Helen wept silent tears. She cried for this new life in Florida, which gave her so much, and her old life, which gave so little. That was what she'd finally realized about St. Louis—how easy it was to leave it. Her sister, Kathy, was the only person she missed. Helen thought she'd had friends in St. Louis, but now she knew they were only acquaintances. None of them would do what Margery did this morning—give her money and help her escape the police.

But then, Helen never needed to escape the cops in St. Louis, not until she shot off her mouth in court. Helen had been ultrarespectable, with a closet full of designer suits, a Dunhill briefcase, and the sore neck and aching back that went with a demanding corporate career.

She'd made a hundred thousand a year in those days. Most of it went for things she didn't want: a house and a car to impress people she didn't like, and gifts for an unfaithful husband who stayed successfully unemployed.

She didn't know Rob was unfaithful. Or rather, she didn't want to know. She kept her eyes firmly closed until that afternoon when she'd come home from work early and found Rob on the back deck with their next-door neighbor, Sandy. Helen couldn't close her eyes then, no matter how hard she tried. Her husband was screwing another woman on Helen's teak chaise longue.

Something had burst inside Helen. She could feel it rip loose and explode. She picked up a crowbar and started swinging. Rob and Sandy started running. They looked like skinny hairless animals, loping naked across her deck. Rob abandoned Sandy and ran for the protection of the Land Cruiser that Helen had bought him.

He scrambled inside and locked the doors. Helen demolished the SUV with the crowbar. She never laid a finger on Rob, but destroying his SUV probably hurt him more. Meanwhile, Sandy called the cops on her cell phone. Sandy and Rob didn't press charges for attempted assault. Sandy was afraid her husband would find out how she spent her afternoons. She'd told him she was a charity volunteer. Helen thought that described most of Rob's girlfriends.

Helen filed for divorce. She expected to lose the house, or half of it, even though she'd paid for the whole thing. She'd prepared herself for that. It was the price of Rob removal. But she didn't count on the rest. Rob got a smart lawyer and she got a dumb judge. The lawyer painted Rob as a supportive househusband who kept his unstable wife on a career track by sacrificing his own livelihood. Helen's high-priced lawyer sat there like a department-store dummy. He refused to fight for her.

The judge awarded Rob half of Helen's future income. That was when quiet Helen crossed the line the second time and never came back. She stood up in court and swore that Rob would never see another penny of her money.

"You're in contempt of court," the judge had told her.

"Yes, I am," Helen had said.

She went home, packed her suitcases, dropped her wedding ring in the Mississippi River, and took off, driving in wild zigzags around the country until her car broke down in Fort Lauderdale.

Helen took a series of low-paying, cash-under-the-table jobs. She refused to have a credit card, bank account, or phone. She had to keep her name out of the computers. She knew the money-hungry Rob would track her down and take half of even her minimum-wage income. South Florida and her dead-end jobs were her refuge. Now that part of her life was over.

Helen looked down at her plate. The bagel was torn to pieces, and her coffee was cold. It was nine thirty. Time to call Margery. She wondered where she would wind up living next: Idaho? South Dakota? She couldn't take the cold winters. Maybe she'd take a bus to Arizona or New Mexico.

She took a deep breath and dialed. This must be what it felt like to call a doctor for your cancer test results, she thought.

Margery picked up the phone on the first ring.

"It's me," Helen said, her voice cracking with fear.

"You're safe," Margery said.

Safe? The words didn't register at first. Then they finally sank in. "The police didn't come for me? Who did they arrest?"

"The women in 2C, Doris and Alice."

"I can't believe it," Helen said. "You rented to crooks again?"

"You were right," Margery said. "They weren't housecleaners. Those two had a scam going. Preyed on the elderly."

"But they looked so nice," Helen said. "I thought you checked them out. Didn't you call some foundation?"

"It was an accomplice in New Jersey," Margery said. "She got a cut for posing as the foundation director and giving them references. They were clever, I'll give them that. One of them—Alice, I think the cops told me—would sit in the kitchen and try to sign up a senior citizen for their phony cleaning service. It wasn't free, either, like they told me. They charged prices so high, any sane person would naturally refuse. But Alice wouldn't tell the old people the price until last.

"While she sat there explaining all the services they offered, Doris went through the house giving it an 'evaluation.' Actually, she was helping herself to jewelry, checks, knickknacks, and anything else she could shove into her mop bucket and purse. She took little items, all easy to hide."

"And people let her do that? Just wander through their houses?"

"Only the trusting ones. Or the poor souls who were slightly addled. You saw those two women. They looked like the salt of the earth."

Helen remembered how hard they'd worked to interest Elsie. "Thank goodness Elsie was loyal to her housecleaner," Helen said. "She would have been a prime target."

"Those two crooks knew exactly what to take," Margery said. "Sometimes the victim didn't miss the items for days or even weeks. They were cleaners, all right. They cleaned those old people out."

"That's really dirty," Helen said.

CHAPTER 24

....

Helen had escaped again.

She'd had two warnings. First there was her handcuffed ride to the police station. Then the cops raided the Coronado. They'd hauled away Alice and Doris. Next time they would come for her.

She had to do something. The police had stopped investigating Tammie's murder. They'd pegged Jonathon as the killer, and they'd caught Helen in an embarrassing lie. They could still come after her as an accomplice.

The Willoughby situation was even more desperate. She expected Ted Brogers, pet detective, on her door step any day, arresting her for Willoughby's death.

Even if the cops left her alone, the publicity would ruin her. What if they forced her to testify about finding Tammie's body? She could see the video of her throwing the robe in the Dumpster on the evening news. Her ex, Rob, would track her down for sure.

Phil had promised to check out more names for her, but Helen had work of her own to do. This was her problem, and she wanted to solve it herself.

She was at the Pampered Pet by ten o'clock, anxious to talk to Jeff, but the store was overwhelmed with a burst of business. She'd barely said hello before a young woman with a Westie asked for a case of organic dog food. GRAMMY'S POT PIE, the dog-food label said.

CHICKEN, RED-JACKET NEW POTATOES, CARROTS, SNOW PEAS, RED APPLES.

Helen wondered what her own dinner would look like on a can: SINGLE WOMAN'S SPECIAL: WATER-PACKED TUNA, STALE WHEAT BREAD, OLD TOMATO, LOW-FAT MAYO. Maybe she should pick up a can of dog food for dinner.

She hauled the case out to the Westie owner's MINI Cooper. When Helen came back into the store, she heard Jeff on the phone. "You need the parts shaved. Yes, ma'am. Bring her by and we'll fix her. Fortunately, we have Jonathon to help you."

He hung up the phone.

"We do?" Helen said. "Jonathon is back?"

"In all his glory. He's working on a sheltie right now. He made bail yesterday. I really need him. That poor woman has a white dog and she shouldn't. She can't keep it clean. Now we'll have to shave that pretty white hair. People want these long-haired fluff muffins when they should have a short-haired dog like Lulu. It's like wearing white pants. Some people have the knack. Others don't."

Jeff was wearing white pants and he didn't have a speck of dirt on them, despite a morning when dogs had piddled all over the store. It's a gift, Helen decided. Her own jeans smelled a bit funky. She must have knelt in something.

Even Lulu looked better than Helen. Today the glamour hound was modeling a black Lurex turtleneck sweater that Helen would have worn on a date with Phil. Lulu's nails were painted black and gold, and her strawberry-blond hair was freshly washed.

Upstaged by a dog, Helen thought, as Lulu strutted around the store. Helen couldn't afford Lulu's pampering—not when she made six-seventy an hour.

Jeff was back on the phone again, and this time something was very wrong. "I'm sorry you feel that way, Mrs. Curtis," he said. "Are you sure you want to do this?"

He was white-faced when he hung up the phone. "Another cancellation. She heard about Willoughby's dog.

She doesn't trust us to care for her baby. I knew this would happen."

"Was Barclay's dognapping on the news?" Helen said.

"Not yet. So far it's just word of mouth. But that can kill me. There's the phone again."

He picked it up as if it were a loaded gun and put it to his ear. "You know, if you cancel a standing Jonathon appointment," he said, "I may not be able to get you another one if you change your mind. Yes, yes, I understand. Your baby's safety comes first."

The salon doorbell rang, and Helen was rushing to find dog collars, dog beds, and biscuits. In between she'd see Jeff on the phone. Sometimes he accepted the cancellation stoically. Sometimes he'd resort to pleading. Neither one worked. She counted at least four cancellations in the appointment book.

It was eleven thirty when the crush of customers cleared out and the phone calls died down. Helen cornered Jeff in the stockroom. "If we're going to clear Jonathon's name, I need someone who can tell me about Tammie's sex parties," she said.

"Don't look at me," Jeff said. "I spend my evenings with Bill." That was his interior decorator.

"I don't know anything, either," Helen said. "I'm with Phil."

"Some swinging singles we are," Jeff said. "In the sex capital of South Florida, we go straight home to our honeys." He looked at Helen. "Well, some go straighter than others."

"Neither one of us knows anything about the wild side," Helen said.

"How did we get so boring?" Jeff asked.

Helen didn't think her nights with Phil were dull. "Somebody has to know something," she said. "Too many people come into this store."

There was a thoughtful silence as Jeff and Helen wandered through the shop, running lists of customer names through their heads in the search for a decent— or indecent—source. Helen studied the shelves and displays, thinking of who bought dog clothes, jewelry, and treats, picturing one customer after another, dismissing them all as too respectable. She conjured up a parade of women as sweetly innocent as their small dogs.

After a storewide circuit, Jeff and Helen ended up at the same place: the rack of spiked and studded dog collars.

"Lucinda the dog-collar lady," they said together.

"How do we get her back in the store?" Jeff said. "She shows up when she feels like it. She could come in tomorrow or next month."

"That would be too late to help Jonathon," Helen said. "What about telling her there's a sale?"

"We never have sales," Jeff said. "Our customers think those are down-market. I know! I'll tell her I have new stock in from New York. I just got in those great winter coats for dogs, the fur-lined toy boxes, and the fainting couches—"

"What's a fainting couch?" Helen interrupted.

Jeff pulled a miniature pink velvet Victorian chaise out of a box. It was exactly the right size for a small dog.

"These are new. They'll bring Lucinda in, probably with another boyfriend."

Jeff made the call while Helen paced impatiently. "Lucinda said she's tied up right now," he reported.

"Probably to a bedpost," Helen said.

"She says she'll be in later this afternoon."

"When do you think Lucinda will show?" Helen asked.

"Who knows?" Jeff said. "Could be three or four o'clock. Could be tomorrow or the next day. Time doesn't mean much for Lucinda. I've planted the idea in her foggy little brain, so she'll show up sooner rather than later."

"Could it be right now?" Helen said hopefully.

"No. It's only noon. Way too early for the likes of Lucinda. Party animals rarely get going before two or three o'clock."

Helen faced another frustrating wait, another day of going nowhere. "Why don't you lend me the Pupmobile? I'll collect Prince's grooming fee from the new widower, Kent."

"It's nice of you to try, but I don't think you'll get any money out of him," Jeff said.

"What can we lose?" Helen said. "If I'm not back by two o'clock, promise me you'll call the cops. That guy is weird."

"Are you sure you want to go?" Jeff said. "I don't need the grooming fee that badly."

"Definitely," Helen said. "Let me call first and make sure he's home."

A young woman with a heavy Hispanic accent answered the phone.

"Hello," Helen said. "I have a delivery from the Pampered Pet for Mr. Kent Grimsby. I'll be bringing it over in thirty minutes."

"*Sí*, yes," said the housekeeper. "We are here."

Margery had offered to drive Helen to the Grimsby home, but she was afraid her outspoken landlady might attract the wrong kind of attention. Helen was glad she'd made that decision when she got to the guard's kiosk at the Stately Palms Country Club.

Security was much tighter since Tammie's murder. The dozing oldster was gone, replaced by an alert, muscular woman who looked like she might be ex-military. She studied Helen's fake driver's license until sweat ran down Helen's forehead, then called the Grimsby home to make sure they were expecting someone from the Pampered Pet. She and Margery would have had a hard time bluffing their way past this woman.

Helen parked the pink Pupmobile in front of the outsize Grimsby home. Both seemed outrageously exaggerated, but their styles clashed. This time the door was opened by an attractive young housekeeper. Her uniform was embroidered with the name Lourdes. Small and voluptuous, Lourdes had an engaging giggle.

"I'm Helen." She stuck out her hand. Lourdes seemed surprised, but shook it tentatively and smiled. "I didn't meet you on my other visits," Helen said. "Are you new?"

"No. I work two years here." Lourdes held up two fingers and smiled again.

Helen wondered where the housekeeper had been the day Tammie died. Maybe Kent gave her the afternoon off so he could kill his wife. Helen couldn't ask that question. Instead she dug into her purse and pulled out a twenty.

"Lourdes, before you get Mr. Kent, could I ask you a question?"

"I don't know," Lourdes said. Her eyes were riveted on the twenty. "This is a very good job. I could lose it talking about Mr. Kent."

Helen pulled out another twenty. "I won't ask anything about Mr. Kent," she said.

Lourdes stared at the forty dollars as if willing it to fly into her hands. "But Mr. Kent and the police both said I should not talk about Mrs. Tammie."

Helen pulled out a ten. Fifty dollars, one quarter of Margery's emergency wad. It was nearly a day's pay for Helen. It was all the money she could afford to give Lourdes. It meant she'd be living on spaghetti and scrambled eggs for a month to pay Margery back. Helen was going for broke—literally.

"I just want to know if anyone visited Mrs. Tammie the afternoon she died," Helen said.

Lourdes grabbed the money and started talking. "I run the errands," she said. "I go to the grocery store. I go to the dry cleaner. I do not know. I only saw one person that day."

She looked hopefully at Helen. Helen started to take back one of the twenties, but Lourdes talked faster and hung on to the cash. "It was the dog lady, Betty. I see her come here before. She tried to get Mrs. Tammie to give money to the shelter for the lost dogs again."

"And did she?"

"Mrs. Tammie laughed at her. She said, 'I gave you enough last time, Betty. You still feeling guilty about living off those blind rabbits?'

"Miss Betty, she got angry then. She said, 'You have lots to feel guilty about yourself.'

" 'No, I don't,' Mrs. Tammie said. 'That was survival of the fittest. The strongest survived. The rest didn't deserve to live.' I thought Miss Betty was going to hit her."

"Did she?" Helen asked.

"I don't know. The phone rang and I had to answer it, and then I had to leave. I no come back that day. I spend the night with my family in Hialeah. That's all I know. Mr. Kent is home. I find him for you."

Lourdes ran off, as if worried Helen might change her mind about the fifty dollars. Helen thought she had a bargain. Her trip was already worth it. As she waited in the foyer, she noticed that Tammie's grand portrait was gone, replaced by gold-framed mirrors. There must have been two dozen. Some were no bigger than a compact. Others were the size of a hubcap. On one of the smaller ones Helen saw scratches and traces of a fine whitish powder. The rumors were true: Kent did serve coke at his parties.

The master of the house came into the foyer wearing a black Speedo. The man must be in deep mourning, Helen thought. She tried to stare at his forehead so she wouldn't see that rubbery wobble when he walked toward her. Kent's body was slick with suntan oil. He had a black silk robe over one arm. She was grateful when he pulled it on.

"I've spent enough time out by the pool," he said. "I'll look like a freaking lobster if I'm not careful. Let's go into my TV room."

The TV room was a windowless cave with black walls, a black leather couch, and a silver-framed plasma television. "Can't watch TV with that damn Florida sun," he said. "You get a glare on everything. I insisted that fruit decorator of Tammie's do one useful thing. I had him design me a room where I could watch decent TV."

Kent switched on the television with the biggest, blackest remote Helen had ever seen. He stared at a horse race.

"I'm so sorry about Tammie," she said.

"Yeah," he said. "It was too bad." His eyes were glued on the set.

"When is the funeral?"

"There isn't one. I had her cremated and dropped her off the Seventeenth Street Causeway."

Helen was too shocked to say anything. Kent kept talking. "Funerals are so damn depressing. That's not how I wanted to remember Tammie. She always liked the view from the causeway, so I figured she'd want to go over the rail there. I kept it simple."

He still didn't look at Helen. "That big gray there is gonna win," he said, pointing to the horse with his remote.

"It must have been a terrible shock when you found your wife here at the house," Helen said.

"Oh, man. I came home and there were cops all over. I thought it was a bust. Turns out she was dead on the patio. Ruined a dynamite day. I'd spent the whole afternoon test-driving a new Porsche. Good thing, huh? Otherwise I could have been dead, too."

"It must have been very hard for you," Helen said.

"I had the cops crawling up my ass until they caught that killer fruit. I couldn't take a dump without them watching me."

The big gray horse crossed the finish line, winning by a nose. "See?" he said. "What did I tell you?"

The television was still blaring, but now Kent turned to face Helen. His legs were spread and his robe fell open, showing his hairy chest and bobbing Speedo.

Oh, Lord, Helen thought.

"You look like a broad-minded lady," he said. "I'm giving a little party for some special friends next Saturday. Do a little coke, have a little fun. Wanna come, if you know what I mean?"

"Not particularly," Helen said. "But I know a big spender like you won't have a little coke. You'll have more snow than Alaska in January. If you don't want the cops busting you big-time, why don't you pay the grooming and pickup fees for that sweet little Yorkie you gave away? I think a donation to the shelter would be a good idea, too. Make it in your wife's name. It will be a nice memorial."

"What?" Kent said. "You're shitting me. You wouldn't."

"Try me," Helen said. "I saw the telltale signs all over while I waited for you. A good cop could bust you in a heartbeat."

Kent looked wildly around the room, but didn't see the razor-blade-scratched and coke-dusted mirrors.

"Don't bother trying to find them. It doesn't matter if your housekeeper tries to clean up after I leave. There's so much white stuff in this place, the cops should go through here with a snowplow. One more thing, sport. Close your robe. I've seen enough of you."

The new widower huffed and snarled, but he wrote two checks.

Helen took them both and left.

CHAPTER 25

....

"Hello, beautiful. Don't you look good today?"

Helen turned around with a smile on her face. A tall, dark, handsome man was at her feet. Too bad he was petting Lulu.

"You are such a beautiful girl," he said.

Lulu kissed him.

That dog, Helen thought. Always that dog. Lulu flirts with every man in the store, and they all love her.

Lulu has a bigger wardrobe than I do. This week alone, Lulu had swanked around in a new fake-fur coat, a pink sweatshirt, a yellow sundress, a blue chiffon evening dress, and a sparkly turtleneck.

Lulu has more jewelry than I do. Her pearls are real.

Lulu doesn't have a weight problem. She eats all day and never gains a pound. In the last two hours, she's snarfed down cheese-and-bacon treats and turkey jerky, then run off to the bar for cheeseburgers and seasoned fries. That was another thing. Lulu never paid for a meal. Everyone at the Briny Irish Pub gave her treats.

I'm no match for a strawberry blonde with a big nose and bowlegs, Helen thought. But I might be smarter. Might.

Helen had enjoyed her triumph with Kent today. But now it was three o'clock and there was no sign of Lucinda. She didn't think the aging sex queen would be in this afternoon. Helen was half-crazed by the pointless waiting. She could hear poor Jeff on the phone saying, "But you've had a standing appointment with us for five years, Mrs. Richards. That's why I put you on Jonathon's preferred-customer list. If you cancel, I can't promise . . ."

Time was ticking away. She had to do something. She couldn't look for Willoughby's dog while she waited on customers at the shop.

But there was one part of Tammie's murder she could investigate. The police thought Jonathon was the killer. Once they arrested him, their investigation of other suspects stopped. Helen did not think Jonathon was guilty, but she had major questions about him, and she wanted them answered. Once he was cleared in her mind, she could concentrate on the others.

By three thirty she came up with a plan. Two phone calls, and she had it mostly in place. Now she needed some information from Jeff to complete it. When the customer rush died down, Helen dragged Jeff into the back room, where they couldn't be overheard by the two dog groomers.

"I've got some questions about Jonathon," she said.

"You and everybody else," Jeff said.

"The afternoon that Tammie was killed—where did he go?" Helen asked.

"He won't say."

"What's his real name? The police called him Bertram Reginald Falkner. Is that really who he is?"

"I have no idea," Jeff said. "I've always called him Jonathon."

"That's how you make out your checks to him?"

"Yes. 'Jonathon, Inc.' It's not unusual for an artist to go by one name."

"Where does Jonathon live?" Helen asked.

"Nobody knows," Jeff said. "Jonathon is secretive. People have tried to follow him, but he always loses them. He's on the lookout for a tail. His real home is a closely guarded secret."

"Why?" Helen said.

Jeff shrugged. "Jonathon is a mystery. Some say he lives in a penthouse with a very old man who pays for everything. Some say he lives on a boat with a very young boy. Boaters say they've seen him sailing naked near Bimini with a crew of Chippendales. That blond hair of his is distinctive."

"What do you think?" Helen said.

"I don't know," Jeff said. "But I do know whatever the reason, he doesn't want to be found. Jonathon sometimes stays at a gay guesthouse in Lauderdale, but it's not his real home."

"What if I found his house?" Helen said.

"Why would you want to do that?" Jeff said.

"Because I think it might help solve Tammie's murder. At the very least, it could answer the question about where he was when she was killed."

"Then do it," Jeff said. "This is a nightmare. I've had two more cancellations since this morning. Word about Willoughby's dog is getting out. When the customers do come into the shop, they see the police asking questions about Jonathon. It's bad for business. Besides, I'd love to know."

"Can I borrow the Pupmobile?" Helen said.

"You're going to tail him in that?" Jeff said. "It's bright pink. He'll spot it a mile away."

"That's the idea," Helen said. "I'm the decoy. I'll have two other people on him. He won't escape us with a three-car tail. But I may have to leave early today, when he goes home."

"Go for it," Jeff said.

Helen called Margery. "We're on," she said. "Jonathon's last grooming appointment is over at four thirty. Have Peggy wait outside the store for me."

"We're all set," Margery said. She sounded like she was enjoying this. "Phil's black Jeep will be in the alley behind the store. My big white car will be on U.S. 1. We have the two most anonymous vehicles in Lauderdale. They're perfect for tailing. We've all got cell phones, so we can keep in touch."

Helen avoided Jonathon for the rest of the afternoon.

Jonathon had an almost magical ability to communicate with animals. She was not sure how good he was at reading people, but she was afraid he might sense her plans for betrayal. She was relieved when Jonathon packed up his scissors at four thirty-five and left. He headed for the parking lot, long hair blowing in the breeze. His fuchsia disco suit shimmered in the sun. The rhinestones on his platforms sparkled. For all his glitter, Jonathon drove a car so anonymous, Helen couldn't figure out what make it was. She wasn't even sure if it was forest green or black. The small, dark vehicle seemed to melt into the traffic.

Jeff was right: Tailing Jonathon was going to be tough.

Jonathon pulled out in the traffic on U.S. 1 going north. Peggy jumped into the Pupmobile with Helen. The slender redhead looked oddly naked without Pete on her shoulder. Peggy settled into the front passenger seat and took out her cell phone. She speed-dialed Margery first, then Phil, each time with the same message: "Subject heading north on U.S. 1."

"He's going toward Palm Beach," Helen said. "That would support the rich-old-man theory."

"He's not there yet," Peggy said. "There's a lot of water in between. He could still live with his boy on the boat."

The three cars followed Jonathon through the dense rush-hour traffic, keeping in touch by cell phone. Jonathon took them up into Palm Beach County and the car snarls of downtown Palm Beach.

"He's trying to lose me in the traffic," Helen said.

Jonathon's car looped through one-way streets and cut through parking lots. Helen idled in construction traffic until the Pupmobile's heat gauge went dangerously red.

"That boy's done this before," Peggy said. "He's good."

Jonathon drove in circles and figure eights. He'd cross U.S. 1, then zip back along the ocean to A1A and finally turn around and roar over the railroad tracks to the Dixie Highway.

"He must have spotted Helen," Peggy reported to her cell-phone companions. "He's trying to shake her. There's no sign he's noticed either of you."

"Tell Helen to stay on his tail," Phil instructed. "We want to rattle him."

"Wait! Jonathon is making a left against the traffic. He's heading south again," Helen said.

The little car beetled through the charging cars and went back down U.S. 1. Helen followed, bulling her way into the oncoming traffic with a chorus of shrieking brakes and honking horns. Irate drivers saluted her with single digits.

Peggy gripped the armrest. "Jeez, Helen, I had no idea you drove like this," she said. "No wonder you take the bus."

"It's the first time I could goose this baby," Helen said. "Normally I have to drive like a little old lady."

"Please do," Peggy said. "I'd like to be one when I grow up."

But Helen was hot on the trail of the elusive dark car as it dodged in and out of traffic and ran yellow lights, trying every trick to elude the pink Pupmobile. Peggy did not complain again. She was too busy relaying their position to Margery and Phil.

As they reached Lauderdale, Jonathon made an abrupt swing toward the beach on a yellow light. Helen followed, though the light had turned red. More horns blared. Jonathon's car sped up as it came to a draw-bridge over the Intracoastal Waterway. The bridge's alarm bells were ringing. The yellow warning lights were on and the red-striped gates were dropping. The draw-bridge was going up for a sailboat.

The little dark car slipped under the red-striped gate. Helen hit the gas and the Pupmobile followed, its long, square body swiveling on the rough metal bridge surface. The descending gate nearly clipped the taillights. The heavy car landed on the other side with a *whump!*

"What the hell were you doing?" Peggy said. She was white as milk.

"That was fun," Helen said. "There's real power in this old Caddy. Were you really scared?"

Peggy's cell phone rang before she could answer, and Helen heard an outraged squawk. "Right, Margery," Peggy said. "I'm still alive, no thanks to Helen. She thinks this is a movie and she's a stunt driver. OK. Got it. We'll drop back out of sight so you two can tail him. Jonathon is now heading south along the beach on A1A, but he has his turn signal on. I think he's going back up to U.S. 1 again."

Peggy hung up the phone. "We've got our orders," she said. "We're supposed to stay at least four blocks behind him, out of sight."

They drove past an endless parade of strip malls. Peggy's phone rang again a few blocks later. "Jonathon's turning off U.S. 1 at State Road 84. Wait! Now he's going into Lester's Diner."

"Hope he goes inside," Peggy said. "I could use some coffee to steady my nerves."

"You can go in," Helen said. "But Jonathon knows me. I'll have to stay crouched on the floor the whole time."

"Good," Peggy said. "That's where I've been for most of this trip."

They passed a string of lumberyards and boat businesses before the phone rang once more. Peggy reported, "Phil says don't go into the diner lot. Jonathon met a woman there. He's getting into her blue minivan. Now the two of them are back on State Road 84."

"This is getting interesting," Helen said. "Why the change of cars and the woman driver?"

"I hope we'll find out soon," Peggy said. "At least they don't suspect anything. They're driving at a nice slow pace."

The three cars trailed the minivan into Davie, driving past an unlovely vista of check-cashing stores, pawnshops, and tire stores.

"What's Jonathon doing in Davie?" Helen said. "It's not the hippest place in Broward County."

"Don't they beat up people who look like Jonathon in Davie?"

"And act like him," Helen said.

Peggy's phone rang again. She listened, then snapped it shut. "Your mystery man gets more mysterious. The minivan pulled into a subdivision. Phil says it's up here on the right. If we turn at the first light, we'll see it. The van is in the driveway of a ranch house. Phil says to park around the corner where Jonathon can't see us. Then we can walk past the house like we're two suburban ladies going for a stroll."

It was the sort of neighborhood where women went for strolls on nice evenings, dads walked the dogs, and kids played basketball in the driveways. Helen and Peggy walked past neat lawns and well-tended gardens.

"This is weirdly normal," Helen said. "I can't imagine what Jonathon is doing here."

"There's the minivan," Peggy said. "I see Phil's Jeep in the driveway of the for-sale house next door. Margery must be around the corner."

Helen didn't answer. She stopped on the street and stared at the tableau before her. She was looking at a pale green ranch house with a freshly mowed lawn and beds of bright flowers. Kids' bikes were piled on the porch.

A broad-shouldered man got out of the van. He was about six feet tall with a muscular build and short brown hair. He was wearing jeans and a blue T-shirt and carrying a gym bag. A chunky blonde got out of the driver's side. The man kissed her on the forehead. Helen was close enough to see his cleft chin, chiseled Roman nose, and tiny feet, now in ordinary Nikes.

"It's Jonathon," Helen whispered.

"That can't be him," Peggy said. "He was in disco drag."

Two little blond girls came tumbling out of the house yelling, "Daddy!" They ran up and hugged Jonathon. A golden retriever raced out with them, barking happily and running in circles. A sullen teenage boy in black sulked on the front porch. Jonathon picked up both girls and put them on his shoulders. He ruffled the boy's hair.

"Ohmigod," Helen said. "Jonathon is straight."

"Worse," Peggy said. "He's a family man with three kids. And he lives in Davie."

"If word of his lifestyle got out among his fashionable clientele, he'd be ruined," Helen said.

Helen and Peggy kept walking down the street, then doubled back. Helen waited until the family was settled in the house. "Go sit with Phil," she said. "I'm going in."

Helen rang the doorbell. The teenage boy answered.

"Hi, can I see your father?" Helen gave her best grown-up smile.

"Dad, it's for you!" the kid bellowed, leaving the front door wide open. Helen peeked into Jonathon's living room. She saw a plaid sofa, wall-to-wall carpet, and two blue-velvet recliners. The surly teenager took one, flopped down, and stared glassy-eyed at a video game.

Jonathon walked into the living room with a big smile on his face—until he saw Helen.

"You!" he said.

"Me," Helen said. She jerked her head at the boy. "We need to talk. I think it's a nice night for a walk."

"Let me tell my wife," he said. "She's fixing dinner."

As they walked down the suburban street, Helen looked for any trace of Jonathon the flamboyant dog-grooming genius. All she saw was an ordinary man with a wife and three kids.

"So now you know," he said.

"That's some secret," Helen said. "Let me guess. The long hair is a wig. Where do you get the disco suits?"

"My wife makes them. Brenda's really good at sewing. I get most of the shoes at Goodwill."

"Is this where you were the afternoon of the murder?"

"Yes," Jonathon said. "Tammie had me so upset, I had to go see Brenda and the kids. The girls and I are building a dollhouse together."

"Why didn't you tell the police that?" Helen said.

Jonathon hung his head and spoke so softly she could hardly hear him. "I didn't want to drag my family into a murder case. I tried to be Jonathon instead of me. By the time I got around to telling the police who I was and where I'd been, they didn't believe me. They said I was lying. This has been a disaster. We may lose the house if I go to trial. Bail and the legal fees have already eaten up most of our savings."

"Why do you try so hard to hide your life?" Helen said. "Most people would envy what you have."

"Maybe. But when I look like a mechanic and live in Davie, I have no artistic authority. You won't tell anyone at the shop, will you? I have three children to support."

Helen didn't answer. Instead, she said, "Do the children know about your arrest?"

"Not so far. They didn't recognize me in the photo on television. I don't dress like that around them. And my real name, the one I use here, isn't Jonathon. I stayed at a guesthouse to keep the cops away from my family. The staff was very kind. Some reporters are still following me, so I only come home a couple nights a week. The kids think I'm traveling for business. But I don't know how much longer I can go on like this. If the real killer isn't found soon, it will destroy my family."

"If I'm going to keep quiet, you have to answer some questions."

"I'll answer on the condition that you tell no one my secret, not even Jeff," Jonathon said.

"I promise," Helen said. "But I want an honest answer. Did you kill a man in Miami?"

"No, I started that rumor myself," Jonathon said. "It added to the mystique and kept me from having to defend myself from the kind of people who like to beat up gay men."

"Did you really blind a show dog in Tampa?"

Jonathon stopped and looked at her. "Yes," he said. "I was stupid and the shop was crooked. I did give the shampoo to the show dog's owner, but I thought it was special eyedrops. I'd never hurt any animal on purpose. You know I respect animals. The shop owner gave me those drops. He told me to give them to the dog's owner as a gift. I'm sure he took money to ruin the dog's chances for that show. He used me. The dog recovered his sight, but I quit as soon as I found out, and moved here. I invented the Jonathon persona as a disguise. No one from Tampa would recognize me in a disco suit with long hair. But my new look and personality changed everything. People took me seriously. Now I was an artist. They started bringing me their models and show dogs. I groomed a poodle who won best in show in Palm Beach, and my reputation was made. My old life and my old mistakes were gone."

"Who do you think is the killer?" Helen asked.

"If I knew that, I'd tell the police," he said. "I want to know even more than you do. I'll lose everything."

By the time they got back to Jonathon's house, Helen could smell dinner. Jonathon breathed in deeply. "Beef stew with carrots and little onions," he said. "My favorite."

Helen let him go home to his family. She met Margery, Peggy, and Phil around the corner.

"Don't that beat all," Margery said when she heard the story.

"I have to take the Pupmobile back to work," Helen said.

"I'll ride with Margery," Peggy said, a little too quickly.

"I'll follow Helen," Phil said, "and give her a ride home from the dog store."

Helen drove the Pupmobile at a stately pace back to the store, mulling over what she'd seen. She thought Jonathon's story had the ring of truth. He'd created the whole hysterical artist persona for his business. It worked until Tammie was found dead and his splendid creation turned on him.

Then she remembered what Tammie had said in the grooming room when she barged in on Jonathon: "I know what he is, just like I know what you are."

Did Tammie know that Jonathon was a family man? If she lived in Tampa, did she know Jonathon before he adopted his artistic persona? How far would a man go to protect his family? Helen felt the sliding horror of despair again. She'd gone around in circles. She hadn't eliminated anyone. Maybe the police were right after all and Jonathon was the killer. All the evidence pointed to him.

She would keep her promise. Until she knew more, it served her purpose to keep quiet about Jonathon.

Jeff was waiting for her when she got to the Pampered Pet.

"Well?" he said.

"I found him," Helen said. "Jonathon is living with the most incredible ménage. It includes a boy, a dog, and a woman."

"No!"

"Yes," Helen said.

"What does the place look like?" Jeff said.

"Like nothing you've ever seen," Helen said truthfully. "When I walked into the living room, I saw this young man stretched out in this blue-velvet chair that opened up—"

"I'm not sure I want to hear this," Jeff said, looking deliciously shocked.

"You're probably right," Helen said.

CHAPTER 26

"I gave you enough last time, Betty. You still feeling guilty about living off those blind rabbits?"

Tammie had taunted Betty the animal lover with those words, at least according to her housekeeper, Lourdes. Living off blind rabbits? What did that mean? What had Betty done?

Helen could not imagine. But she had to find out. She certainly wasn't going to ask Margery.

She spent her lunch hour at the library, looking up information on Betty Reichs-Martin. The computer had nearly a hundred newspaper and magazine stories on the woman. Some were one-paragraph mentions. Others were long features. Almost all were about her work for animal charities.

Photos showed her cleaning cages at the shelter and hauling auction donations. Her good works were chronicled in endless detail. Helen saw nothing to explain that odd remark about living off blind rabbits. The more Helen read the stories detailing Betty's virtues, the more she'd wondered if Lourdes had heard wrong. The housekeeper's English was a little shaky.

Helen went to the information desk for one more try. A librarian was there, a slender brown-haired woman in a long blue dress. "I'm looking for information on a Lauderdale woman, a socialite and charity volunteer named

Betty Reichs-Martin. I've gone through the stories in the computer, but I'm wondering if you might have more, maybe something older?"

"Let me check if there's a paper file," the librarian said.

She came back a few minutes later and handed Helen a big envelope filled with brittle, yellowing newspaper clippings. Helen sorted through them by date. The newest was dated 1980. The oldest article went back to 1962. It was from the *New York Times*. At first Helen thought the oldest article had been dropped in the wrong envelope. The headline said, HEIRESS ELIZABETH BUCHER TO DEBUT.

But Helen looked again. It was an impossibly young Betty, her hair demurely done in a Grace Kelly twist. She was wearing a creamy full-skirted strapless formal and twelve-button kid gloves.

"Elizabeth Bucher, heiress to the Melody Magic Makeup fortune, will make her bow to society Saturday," the article began.

Melody Magic. Blind bunnies.

Helen, and every other woman who ever wielded a mascara wand, knew about the Melody Magic scandal. The makeup company made headlines two decades ago for its gratuitous use of rabbits to test its mascara and eyeliner.

The pictures in the exposé had been pitiful. A reporter with a hidden camera had crept into the company's testing lab and taken photos of rabbits who were blinded or suffering from running sores. The family was branded the "Bunny-butchering Buchers."

Helen got back on the computer and read about the scandal. The stories went on for months. But here was something interesting. A small story from the business page said that Betty had sold her shares in the company. Helen checked the date. Betty's timing was incredibly lucky: She'd sold out a month before the scandal broke. After the exposé, Melody's makeup stock had plummeted, and with it the family fortune. The reaction was so severe that the company had closed its animal lab and promised to switch to cruelty-free testing. It took Melody years to recover from that public-relations disaster. Betty was lucky in another way. She wasn't called Elizabeth Bucher by then. She was Betty Reichs-Martin. And she was living in Florida, not New York. No one would connect her with the Bunny-butchering Bucher family.

How could anyone hurt helpless animals? Betty had asked Helen. But she knew the answer. For money. Lots of money.

No wonder Betty had devoted her life to helping animals. All her money came from animal cruelty. Helen wondered if that was why a woman as rich as Betty worked knee-deep in those filthy cages. Was that her way of atoning for the maimed rabbits? That gorgeous white debut dress had been bought with bunny blood, and Betty lived off it still.

If Melody Magic was the source of her riches, it was a well-kept secret. There wasn't a whisper about it in Lauderdale. Margery was a good gossip, but she'd never heard a word. Jeff traveled in the animal-charity circles, but he didn't know either.

Was Tammie getting tired of Betty's shakedowns for the shelter? Betty had bragged to Helen about hitting up Tammie for major donations by mentioning Tampa. But Betty had her own secret, and Tammie knew it. Helen had no idea when or how she found out. The real question was: Did Tammie threaten to mention those blind bunnies—and had Betty stopped her?

Give me a reason why Betty would kill Tammie, Margery had demanded. Helen held it in her hand.

She made copies of the articles, then returned them to the librarian. It was almost time to go back to the Pampered Pet.

The afternoon was so weird, Helen wondered if there was a full moon. First there was the young woman with the white Maltese. She wanted her dog dyed pink, to match the pink extensions in her hair.

Then there were two identical toy poodles. Clarice

always had pink ribbons and nails. Her sister, Sharise, had green ribbons and nails. Todd brought the fluffy dogs out for the owner, a small bird-boned brunette. The dogs were wiggling and wagging with delight.

"Oh, my God," the woman said. Ugly creases marred her face-lift. "You mixed them up."

"What?" Todd said.

"Sharise. You have her in pink. She always wears green. You know she doesn't look good in pink," the woman screamed. "Change them now. Sharise is always green. Clarice is always pink. I can't go out with my dogs looking like that."

The two dogs yelped and whimpered as Todd took them back to switch their ribbons and redo their nails.

"How can she tell the difference? They look alike to me," Helen said.

Jeff shrugged.

Next, poor Lulu was pressed in to model for a miniature dachshund that stayed at home.

"My dog is about Lulu's size," the blond owner said.

Lulu stood patiently on the counter while the woman tried on collar after collar. Red leather, silver, black, gold, and pink stripes—they were all rejected. The final indignity was when the woman put a cowboy hat on Lulu, then stepped back and said, "I don't know if it will work. Your dog's nose is longer."

Helen actually felt sorry for her rival.

After that, a man named Rick came in with his Boston terrier. The man wore black. His head was shaved and he had a silver earring. Alice, the Boston terrier, had a smart red leash.

"Alice needs a coat for New York," Rick said.

Jeff showed him a plaid Burberry. "This is a very classic look," he said.

Rick said, "Alice is a girl. I want her in a girly outfit."

Helen stared at Rick. This man had to live with stereotyping all his life, and now he was doing the same thing to his dog.

Jeff brought out a pink coat covered with rosebuds.

Helen thought it looked silly on a Boston terrier. The dog's head drooped. Alice seemed to agree.

"Sweet," Rick said.

But he made poor Alice try on red, blue, and beige coats before he settled on a black one.

Helen liked it better than the pink, but she didn't think it looked very girly. Rick seemed to read her thoughts.

"What can I say? She's a New York dog," he said. "New Yorkers wear black."

Helen was not surprised when Lucinda the dog-collar woman came in at two thirty. She seemed to belong to the day. Lucinda's eyes were pinpoints. She was high on something, and had the T-shirt to prove it. GOT BLOW? it said.

Lucinda's low-rise designer jeans almost didn't rise to the occasion. They were trimmed with pink daisies. Her pink high heels were either really cheap or really expensive—maybe both.

"Where's your friend?" Jeff said.

"I left him at home," Lucinda said. "He gets worried when he's left behind. It's good for him. Men should be tortured, don't you think?"

"Frankly, no," Jeff said, and smiled.

"Well, I do. After all, that's what they did to us women for, like, centuries. It's time we got ours."

Lucinda was in a mood to shock. Jeff and Helen let themselves look more outraged than they actually were, hoping it would encourage her.

"Is Toddie here today?" she said. Her eyes drifted toward the grooming room, but Helen couldn't tell if Lucinda was really looking for Todd or having trouble focusing.

"He'll be back in tomorrow," Jeff said. "He's taking the rest of the day off."

"I bet he's working harder than he works here." Lucinda smiled slyly. "Toddie is such a gigolo. Not that I'm criticizing. That boy makes a lot of lonely women happy."

"Was he ever one of your boys?" Jeff said.

"No, I like them fresher. Toddie's been around a little too much. A boy can pick up some nasty bugs that way." She stared off into space.

"Lucinda?" Helen said, bringing her back.

"Where was I? Oh, yes. Todd can get it up with women over fifty. In fact, he seems to prefer the old ones, if they have money, of course. Lately he'd taken up with Tammie."

"Is she fifty? The papers said she was forty-five," Helen said.

"No. She was a well-preserved fifty-one. Pickled in alcohol. I couldn't figure out what Todd saw in her. Tammie didn't have any money of her own, and she didn't give gifts. People gave her things. Toddie should have known better. She was going to be very poor, very soon. Her husband was in the market for someone new."

"Like you?" Jeff said.

"Oh, no," Lucinda said airily. "Kent's way too old for me. Anyway, I'm not the marrying kind. But his parties could be fun on the right night. That little Hispanic housekeeper is hotter than a jalapeño pepper. You pay her enough and she'll do absolutely anything."

I did pretty well for fifty bucks, Helen thought.

Jeff didn't have to fake shock anymore. Whatever Lucinda was on took away the last of her inhibitions, and she didn't have that many to begin with.

"But the best things in life are free, like they say. I met the most surprising people at Tammie and Kent's."

"Who?" Helen said. She made it sound like a challenge. They'd managed to steer Lucinda to the right subject without much effort.

"Like Willoughby and Francis Barclay, owners of the yuppie puppy."

"They were into threesomes?" Helen said. Now she was surprised. And shocked.

"Oh, yes. Willoughby loved them. The husband, I'm not so sure about. It was his idea in the beginning. He brought wifey to the first party. But when she really got into it, Francis didn't like that. He wanted to be in control. I think he only came back to watch her—and not for fun, if you know what I mean. He didn't want his wife running off with someone else. I tried to get them to bring the dog, but they wouldn't."

Jeff's eyebrows went straight up and stayed there.

"But Tammie's last party wasn't fun. I was bored doing the same old people. I only showed up for the blow, and it had been stepped on so many times it didn't have any kick. Francis moped around while Willoughby partied. He drank too much. He talked and talked to that little housekeeper, but they didn't do anything. Mostly Francis sat there like a lump. About midnight he wanted to leave, but Willoughby didn't. They had a big fight, and he finally stormed off alone. Willoughby stayed behind."

Lucinda was picking at the GOT BLOW? T-shirt. Jeff and Helen waited patiently until she started talking again.

"They were all fighting that night, Tammie and Kent, too. Kent dragged her into the marble master bath and they had a screaming session. I heard something glass hit the wall and break. The marble walls and floors distorted the voices and made them echo, so I wasn't sure who was talking, but it was clear they were both angry. I heard someone yell, 'Get rid of her, or you're dead.' "

"Was Kent giving an ultimatum to his wife?" Helen asked.

"Maybe. But then, she could have been giving one to him. You can't tell who's doing what at Tammie and Kent's." Lucinda smiled and ran her tongue around her lips.

"So then what happened?" Helen said.

Lucinda yawned and stared at nothing.

"Lucinda?" Helen said.

"Oh. Yeah. I left with my boy and found a new one and we had our own party. Kent and Tammie didn't know how to have a good time, but I do. It's so important to be seen with great-looking guys. Says a lot about you, don't you think?"

"Absolutely," Helen and Jeff agreed.

"Have you been to any parties there since?" Helen asked.

"No," Lucinda said, and sighed. "Death is such a turnoff."

"It's no fun at all," Helen said.

CHAPTER 27

"Lucinda is from another planet," Jeff said.

"The Creature from Planet Sex," Helen said.

Jeff laughed, then fiddled with price tags and folded stock that didn't need it. He's embarrassed by that silly woman, Helen thought. And so am I.

But I wanted to know. And what did I learn?

Helen wasn't sure. The dead Tammie was everywhere, no matter who she'd talked to. She'd found out about Tammie and Betty from Lourdes, the housekeeper. Now Lucinda added other angles—or triangles: Tammie and Todd. Francis and Tammie. Francis and Lourdes. Tammie and Kent, threatening bloody murder.

Who was the woman the couple had argued about? Was she the reason that Kent killed Tammie? Why did the touchy-feely Francis spend so much time talking to Lourdes? Was he looking for a shoulder to cry on? Was Lourdes looking for a rich American husband? Why did Willoughby want to stay at Tammie and Kent's party? Why did Francis want to go home?

Tammie, Tammie, Tammie, everywhere she turned. Sharp-tongued Tammie picked fights, insulted people, ruthlessly shopped for sex partners. She gave everyone a reason to kill her.

Helen felt like she was following the dead woman in

the dark. She was stumbling around, raising more questions and finding no answers.

"Were we the only ones in Lauderdale who weren't invited to a Tammie and Kent threesome?" Jeff said.

"Kent invited me," Helen said. "It's just you."

"Kent is a pig," Jeff said. "Can you imagine throwing a sex-and-drug party right after your wife is killed?"

"How about throwing your dead wife's ashes off a bridge without a memorial service? He dumped Tammie like a full ashtray," Helen said. "Kent told me funerals were depressing. I'll tell you what's depressing—partying in the house where his wife died. I bet he does it on the chaise longue where she was rammed with those scissors."

Jeff winced.

"Kent killed her," Helen said. "I know he did. Only a murderer would be cold enough to treat her that way."

"What about Francis? Still think he killed his wife?" Jeff said.

"Definitely. Here's how I see it. Francis stole the dog. Willoughby confronted him. Francis lost his temper and killed her. Look at his behavior at the party: Francis fought with Willoughby, then left without her. I bet that's when she filed for the divorce. The timing is right."

"Yeah, but your source is Lucinda, and how good is that?" Jeff said. "Did you see her eyes? She was drugged to the gills. What do you think she was on?"

"Her shirt said it all," Helen said.

"Do you think Lucinda wanted Francis to bring the dog to those parties—or was she trying to shock us?" Jeff said.

"Either way, she succeeded," Helen said.

"I can't believe it. That innocent little puppy."

Helen felt as if she'd been hit with a jolt of electricity. "The dog!" she said. "That's it."

"What's it?" Jeff said. He looked like a puzzled pup himself.

"Lucinda said the housekeeper would do anything for money. She's right. For fifty bucks I bribed Lourdes to talk about Tammie, even though she had strict instructions to keep quiet.

"The housekeeper wasn't home when Tammie was murdered, but she told me where she was. Lourdes said she got a phone call and had to leave. That call was from Francis. Lourdes took Barkley."

"She stole the dog?" Jeff said. Now he seemed really confused.

"No, the husband, Francis, took the dog from our store. But the police didn't find Barkley at Francis's home. He'd stashed Barkley somewhere else. He gave her to Lourdes. That's why Francis spent a long time talking to the housekeeper. He was making a deal with her. The housekeeper is hiding the dog for money. I bet she has Barkley at her house in Hialeah. It's perfect. Nobody in Francis's world would go into a Hispanic community unless they were taking their maid home."

Jeff didn't look convinced. "How are you going to find out?"

"I'm going to watch the housekeeper and see where she goes. If you'll let me, of course. I'll have to leave early again."

"Are you kidding?" Jeff said. "The cancellations are killing my business. I expect the Barkley kidnapping story to hit the news any hour now. Take the rest of the afternoon off. Take the rest of the week off. If you find Barkley, it will clear my store's name."

It will help me, too, Helen thought.

The boutique door opened and a perky blonde in her early twenties came in. She weighed maybe ninety pounds, counting the ten pounds of pink ruffles. At her side was a black mastiff big enough to saddle and ride. The dark monster was tame as a kitten, unless some man tried to get near his mistress. Helen bet this dog was the terror of UPS deliverymen and mail carriers.

The Rapunzel syndrome, Helen called it. Instead of climbing a thorny tower to claim this beauty, her prince would have to get past her monster dog.

Someday, someone will do a study about small

women and big dogs. Little women came into the shop with horse-sized mastiffs, Great Danes, shelter mutts, or exotic breeds from England and France.

The little blonde stepped up to the counter and said in a breathy voice, "Is Jeff here? I want to ask him about special food for Milton. He's got some kind of skin rash."

Milton wagged his three-foot-long tail and cleared two shelves.

"I'll get him right away," Helen said. Milton could accidentally demolish the store in five minutes.

Jeff wasn't in the stockroom. She knocked on the bathroom door, but it was empty. She checked the grooming room and circled the front of the store, in case he was on the floor, stocking the lower shelves. She saw Lulu vamping in her latest outfit, but no sign of Jeff.

Helen looked out the shop window. A black van was parked at the edge of the lot. Was this the van Todd talked about? As she watched, Jeff got out of the passenger side, looked around, then jogged back behind the building. Helen grabbed a pen off the counter and wrote the van's license plate number on her wrist. She heard the shop's back door open.

"Jeff," she said, "I've been looking for you."

"You didn't look hard enough. I've been right here, Helen." He looked her straight in the eye. "What do you need?"

The blonde stepped up to the counter, patted Milton's neck, and said, "I wanted to ask you about Milton's diet."

Helen didn't hear the rest of their conversation. Jeff had lied right to her face. Helen was so angry she stayed on the other side of the store, slapping cans of dog food on the shelves with furious thuds. Jeff didn't notice. He worked up front, schmoozing with the customers and answering the phone. Talking to people seemed to energize him.

"Are you still seeing that big dark-haired guy?" he asked Milton's owner.

"Which one?" the little blonde said.

Helen slipped into the back room to call Phil. She

sighed with relief when he answered on the second ring. "Want to help me do surveillance on the housekeeper?" she said. "I think Lourdes has the dog."

Phil listened carefully, then said, "I like your theory. The more I think about it, the more it seems possible. Most housekeepers seem to leave work between four and six at the latest. I'll pick you up at three. If we miss Lourdes today, we can leave a little earlier tomorrow."

Helen had barely hung up the phone when it rang again. She heard Jeff pick it up, and scurried out to finish restocking the shelves.

Ten minutes later Jeff said, "Helen, can you come back here a moment?" His voice sounded flat and angry. What was that about? Had she done something wrong?

Jeff was standing stiffly at the stockroom table, surrounded by boxes of doggie chews. He reminded Helen of her grade-school principal, Sister Mary Monica.

"I've talked with the Stately Palms homicide detective, Helen," he said. "Why didn't you tell me you found Tammie's body when you tried to return Prince?" He even sounded like Sister Monica now. His voice was stern, but disappointed.

"I . . ." Helen realized she had no good reason. "I'm sorry, Jeff. I got scared and ran. It was stupid and the cops caught me."

"You've jeopardized my store's reputation," Jeff said. "You used my delivery vehicle to commit a crime. Everyone knows the Pupmobile. The neighbors saw it there. How could you do this to me? I can understand your panicking and running from the police, but I thought I was the kind of employer you could come to when you were in trouble."

"You are, Jeff. I am sorry."

"You know what the worst part is? You lied to me," he said.

Yes, she thought. But you lied to me. So we're even.

"I'm sorry, Jeff," she repeated.

There was nothing more to say. She expected Jeff to fire her. Instead he turned away and began unpacking boxes. Helen finished stocking the shelves. Jeff's silence followed her like an accusation.

When Phil showed up in his black Jeep forty minutes later, Helen ran to it, grateful to be out of there. Phil pulled her into the Jeep and gave her a deep kiss.

"You're so tense," he said, rubbing her neck and shoulders. "What's the matter?"

"Bad scene with Jeff." She told him what happened. "Here's what I don't understand: Why would the detective call Jeff and tell him that now?"

"He wants to turn up the heat on you," Phil said.

"It worked," Helen said. "Jeff is angry at me and I don't know how to fix it."

They were at the entrance to the Stately Palms Country Club. The same semimilitary guard was there, looking alert and official. Phil showed her some identification with gold seals all over it. The guard did everything but salute.

"You certainly impressed her," Helen said.

Phil shrugged. "That's me," he said. "Impressive." He gave that lopsided grin that made Helen wish they were parking someplace far more secluded. Phil stopped at the entrance to the tennis courts. They could watch the cars coming out of the Grimsby driveway, but not attract the attention of the neighbors.

The street was quiet. An air-conditioning repairman left, a plumber arrived, a carpenter drove away in a white truck, but no one came or went at the Grimsby home.

"I checked the records, but I didn't find anything for Jonathon under any of his names," Phil said. "No arrests, no convictions, nothing about him even being questioned for a homicide. I think he was telling you the truth. He never killed anyone, in self-defense or otherwise."

"Good," Helen said. "At least my instincts are right about someone."

"I did some checking on a Helen Hawthorne, too," Phil said. "You don't exist. No bank account, no phone, no driver's license."

Fear gripped Helen. She'd been afraid this was coming. The only thing she could do was fight back. "How dare you investigate me," she said.

Phil brushed aside her anger and looked straight at her with hurt blue eyes. "Who are you, Helen?" he said. "What did you do? Why won't you tell me? Don't you love me?"

She could have taken anger. She would have fended it off with the shield of her own rage. But Phil was hurt, and that she couldn't stand.

"I told you," she said. "My ex-husband—"

"It's more than that," Phil said.

They both saw the battered brown car chugging toward them. It was small, square, and dented. The windows were down, and Helen could hear a Spanish-speaking announcer on the radio.

"It's Lourdes," she said.

Phil waited until there were at least two cars between them, then fell in behind Lourdes's car. Tailing her was easy. The housekeeper drove slowly and carefully. She stopped at all the lights and never made risky dashes across intersections. It took nearly forty-five minutes to get to Hialeah. They drove in silence. Helen told herself they didn't talk because they were concentrating on following Lourdes's car.

The brown car turned left at a school surrounded by a chain-link fence, then into a street with cinder-block houses painted sun-faded Caribbean colors: turquoise, yellow, and pink. Lourdes parked in front of a turquoise house with a banana tree. The house had a chain-link-fenced yard filled with children. Dark-haired boys and girls were romping with a dark curly-haired dog.

It was Barkley, the yuppie puppy. Helen had never seen her so animated, not even in her commercials. She leaped and barked with sheer joy, while the kids shouted and laughed and threw a tennis ball. Barkley would fetch it and bring it back to the tallest boy. Two girls would hug her, and the game would start over.

"That's Barkley," Helen said. "I almost hate to call the police. She seems so happy."

"And Jeff seems so unhappy," Phil said.

"You're right. If Barkley isn't found, it could ruin his shop."

It could ruin me, too, she thought, but she didn't say it. Phil would only ask more awkward questions.

"This will be my peace offering to Jeff," she said. "He may forgive me when I tell him we found Barkley."

But she took one last lingering look at the little dog leaping and rolling in the yard with the children. She was going to stop their fun. Barkley would probably go back to the cold and calculating Francis.

But if I don't get the police off my back, I'll be returned to cold and lonely St. Louis. Better you than me, poor puppy, Helen thought. They drove to a pay phone near a bodega, and Helen made an anonymous call to the police.

CHAPTER 28

The turquoise house was bathed in flickering bloody light from the police cars. Neighbors gathered in tense knots on the sidewalk. Two men gave Helen and Phil dark looks, and pointed to the Jeep.

"Let's go," Phil said. "We don't belong here."

They drove off to the sound of children crying. Helen felt like something that slithered. "What will happen to Lourdes?" she asked as they crawled through the traffic.

"Lourdes is a survivor," Phil said. "She'll claim she found the dog wandering in her neighborhood, and took care of it. I doubt if the police will make the connection between Lourdes and Francis. Willoughby's husband isn't going to tell them how he met her. Francis will pretend he's happy to have his dog back. Lourdes will keep her mouth shut. She's smart."

"How do you know?" Helen said.

"Look what she did with the money Francis gave her."

"What do you mean?" Helen said. "She didn't do anything."

"Exactly," Phil said. "The police will notice nothing suspicious. She didn't quit her job or buy a new car or a designer wardrobe. She drives a junker and wears her housekeeper's uniform. She'll be fine."

Helen still felt guilty. She kept seeing that little curly-haired pup frolicking with the children. Helen had sacrificed Barkley's good life to save her own.

Barkley is a dog, Helen told herself. She'll be returned to her rightful owner.

She's going back to the man who murdered her mistress, said a small voice. She'll pine away, living with someone who doesn't care about her.

Helen sighed and looked down at her traitorous fingers. They'd held the phone, punched in the numbers, and ratted out the pup. She saw the license-plate number she'd scribbled on her wrist earlier that day. The ink was smeared, but she could still read it.

"Ohmigod!" she said.

Phil slammed on the brakes. "What's wrong?" he said. "Are you OK?"

"I'm fine," Helen said sheepishly. "Sorry, I didn't mean to alarm you. I saw this license-plate number on my wrist and remembered I didn't tell you what else happened today. Jeff disappeared again, and I went looking for him. He was in the van with that man, like Todd said. I wrote down the license number. Jeff looked me right in the eye and denied he'd left the store."

"He's probably cheating on his boyfriend," Phil said. "I bet Jeff is sneaking off for a quickie."

"No, it's something else," Helen said. "Jeff doesn't have an alibi for the time Tammie died. He could have slipped out and stabbed her."

"But why would he?" Phil said.

"I don't know yet," Helen said. "But I didn't know there was a connection between Betty and Tammie until I found it. Jeff is up to something."

"And you want me to check out the license plate and find out who he's meeting?" Phil said.

"Please," Helen said.

"It's easy enough," Phil said. "I have some contacts."

They were back at the Coronado. A soft mist dimmed the harsh white light of the tropical moon. The palm trees shivered and sighed. It was a night made for secrets. Helen knew she could make her lover understand why she had to keep her secrets, if she could sit down and talk to him.

They walked together on the old worn sidewalk to his apartment, their footsteps echoing in the dark silence. But when they got to Phil's place, he did not invite her inside. "Good night, Helen." Phil kissed her chastely on the cheek and shut the door.

Helen stood alone in front of his home, hating herself and hating her silence. She wished she had the courage to break it, but she knew she never would.

"You found Barkley? Helen, I could kiss you. You've saved my store."

Jeff was jubilant, his anger at her forgotten. His brown eyes sparkled with relief. He danced around the shop in the hot morning sun. He hugged Helen. Then he gave Lulu a treat and draped a glamorous red feather boa around her neck.

"We're saved, Lulu!" he said. "And Helen did it." Lulu strutted alongside him, showing off the newest addition to her wardrobe.

"We're not quite out of the woods. There's still Jonathon," Helen reminded him.

"Killing a customer is not as bad as losing a dog," Jeff said.

"Since when?" Helen said.

"I was joking," Jeff said, but his smile bared too many teeth. He'd meant it. "I've told you before, these dogs are children. I can survive anything except losing one. You've found Willoughby's baby. You know, we've been darn lucky. Barkley's kidnapping never made the news. All is well."

Except for Willoughby, Helen wanted to say, but she swallowed those bitter words. "I have to ask you a big favor, Jeff."

"Honey, you can have whatever your little heart desires," Jeff said.

"I need you to get Lucinda the sex queen back to the store," Helen said. "I have to ask her another question."

"Is this for your investigation?" Jeff said. There was

no sign of a smirk. Helen's detecting abilities were treated with new respect.

"Yes," Helen said.

"I can't say no, not after what you've done. I'll even make the ultimate sacrifice and give her something free. Lucinda bought one of those red velvet fainting couches for her poodle when she was in last time. I'll offer her a velvet pillow for her new couch. I'll wait till noon. That's the earliest I can call someone like Lucinda."

The word "free" worked the same magic for the rich as it did for the poor. It lured Lucinda into the store by two o'clock, the crack of dawn for her. She yawned and stretched and thrust out her implants. The bright sunlight showed the cracks around her lips and the indelible lines the long, lurid nights had stamped around her eyes.

Lucinda's tiny tight T-shirt hugged her top. She had the body of a twenty-five-year-old, and she was hanging onto it. Lucinda was wrapped around another young man.

There was nothing shy about this guy. He had a pale, foxy face and a steel earplug the size of a spool of thread. This boy liked pain. He probably had a whole wardrobe of spiked collars and whips.

"You've got a pillow for me, Jeffie?" Lucinda said in a wheedling baby voice that made Helen grit her teeth.

"A selection, my dear," Jeff said. "Pink, red, or purple?"

"Can I have them all?"

"Don't be greedy," Jeff said.

Lucinda's pout made her look like a corrupt child. The young man whispered something in her ear and she laughed.

"I'll take the pink one," Lucinda said. "It matches my— Stop that, you bad boy. Put your hand back where it belongs."

Jeff held up the red pillow. "You can have this one, too, if you'll help Helen."

"Help her how?" Lucinda said, suddenly suspicious.

"Just answer a few questions about Tammie's parties," he said.

"Are they anything delicate young ears should hear?" she asked coyly. She licked her pink lips.

Jeff rubbed his ears and said, "I think they can take it."

Lucinda giggled. She was eager to impress her young man with her sophistication.

Helen thought that was her cue. "Thanks," she said, stepping up to the counter. "I had a question about Willoughby and you're the only one who can answer it."

"The police never bothered talking to me. At least you recognize that I know something. You may ask me," Lucinda said. She sounded like a queen granting a favor to a peasant.

"Did Willoughby like to party with anyone in particular at Tammie and Kent's?" Helen said. "Was she attracted to one person?"

"Of course, silly," Lucinda said. "She was hot for Tammie."

"Tammie was bi?" Helen said. Again, she remembered the uneasy feeling she had around Prince's naked owner.

"Tammie was hot, period. I even tried her myself, and I don't go for chicks. Gay, straight, bi didn't apply to Tammie. She's more like omni . . . omver . . . oooh . . ." Her pink, puffy lips had trouble spitting out the word.

"Omnivorous?" Helen said.

"Right. Tammie wanted everyone."

Interesting word, "omnivorous," Helen thought. There's a hint of prey about it. Had Tammie preyed on Francis's naive wife? Did Willoughby start having sex with Tammie to get even with her husband, and then it turned into something serious?

"Is that why Willoughby and Francis fought?" Helen said.

"He wanted Willoughby to come home with him," Lucinda said. "I told you that. Weren't you listening? Willoughby wanted to stay with Tammie."

"You didn't mention Tammie last time we talked," Helen said. "You just said that Willoughby wanted to stay at the party."

"Oh. Well. I was pretty stressed last time. I took something to relax," Lucinda said, waving her pink-tipped hands.

Helen remembered the pinpoint pupils. "But now I have a good tension reliever." She bit the young man on his unplugged ear.

He didn't flinch.

Jeff watched the couple grope each other as they walked across the parking lot. "I wonder what will happen to my two innocent pillows," he said.

"You sacrificed them to a good cause," Helen said.

"Did you learn anything useful?" Jeff said.

"Definitely. I think Francis murdered his wife," she said. "Willoughby wouldn't come home with him. She wanted to stay with Tammie. It was bad enough losing her to another man. Another woman was too much. Francis killed his wife in a jealous rage."

"Why didn't he kill her the night of the party?" Jeff said.

"Francis needed time to build up his resentment. I bet Willoughby taunted him the night of the hurricane. She'd been hanging around Tammie, who was good at that. People who've lived together know exactly which buttons to push to make their partners crazy."

"It's a good theory," Jeff said. "But it's nothing you can take to the police."

"No, but Francis bears watching, and I'm going to do it."

"Do you have his new address?" Jeff said.

"His wife gave it to me when I started looking for Barkley," Helen said. "That seems about a hundred years ago."

Helen took Francis's new address as more proof he was shrewd about money. He'd moved to a condo in Hallandale Beach, a town south of Lauderdale known as "God's waiting room." Francis was about half the age of the average resident. Many of the old people were dying off. Younger ones could pick up bargain real estate in Hallandale. Families in New York and Connecticut were anxious to sell off Mom's condo and settle her estate.

Helen called Margery from the shop. "Want to go to Hallandale?"

"Do I look that old?" Margery said.

"I'm following Francis the wife killer," Helen said. "I need backup."

"You on the outs with Phil?" Margery said.

"No, no," Helen lied. "He's checking out some names for me."

"Hmpf," Margery said. She didn't believe Helen. "Sure, I'll go. When do you want me to pick you up?"

"I get off at five," Helen said.

"Take the rest of the afternoon off," Jeff said, walking in on her call. He was still caught up in the euphoria of Barkley's return.

"You can pick me up now," Helen said.

Ten minutes later, her landlady pulled up in her white car. The inside was a haze of cigarette smoke. Helen coughed and put on her seat belt. Margery drove like a native, avoiding I-95 and U.S. 1, weaving expertly through the crazed traffic on the Dixie Highway.

Francis the self-made widower lived in a gated community off Hallandale Boulevard. They checked the condo directory at the door for his unit number—118.

"He's here," Helen said. "His car is parked in his numbered spot. Let's wait and see if he comes out."

"Why aren't we going in after him?" Margery said.

"He'll feel safer in his home, more likely to lie. I want to get him outside in public, where I can rattle him."

"It's your show," Margery said, and pulled into a guest parking spot two rows away. They sat with the windows rolled down. Helen watched flame-red flowers drift down from a canopied tree.

Margery smoked and propped her purple suede ankle-strap sandals on the dash. "Is Phil mad at you?" she said. "And don't lie to me. Sound carries on damp nights. I heard the two of you outside his place."

"But we didn't say anything," Helen said.

"Exactly," Margery said.

"I don't know what we are," Helen said. "That's all I can say about it now. Maybe you can answer this question: What is it about Florida and sex? Do we have more of it than other states? Is it weirder here? Do wives in Ohio look for sex partners for their bored husbands? Do men in Michigan drag their wives off to three-somes?"

"Of course," Margery said. "Probably more than we do. Those people have to do something during the long, cold winters. Why are you carrying on about sex like you just discovered it?"

"It seems to be the reason for Tammie's murder, and Willoughby's, too."

"It's a darn good reason," Margery said. "What are the other choices? Revenge? Money? The neat thing about sex is you can mix in the other two motives."

She was right. All three reasons were tangled up with Willoughby. There was her affair with the dead Tammie and the divorce that stripped Francis of his home and income.

If Kent killed Tammie, sex and money were in there, too. Tammie's death saved her husband a messy, expensive divorce, and he was on the prowl for a more interesting sex partner.

If Betty killed her, it was sex and money again. Only this time the money was for the animal shelter.

"I'll tell you what's weird in Florida," Margery said. "It's not sex. It's death. I got one of those coupon books in the mail. You know the kind: 'Free lunch, with the purchase of a second lunch and two beverages.' In with the coupons for lunches, dinners, and appetizers is a five-hundred-dollar coupon for a crypt. I can just see me taking a coupon to a cemetery."

"At least they don't have an early-bird special," Helen said.

Margery snorted like she'd made the Pamplona run.

"It's him!" Helen said.

Francis, pale as unbaked bread, loped down the side-walk to his silver Lexus.

"Follow that car," Helen said.

"Did you really have to say that?" Margery said.

Francis was a slow, careful driver, which earned him

the ire of everyone on the road. Old women cut him off. Young men gave him the finger as they gunned their cars to pass him. Francis seemed oblivious. He drove at a steady pace until he finally put on his left-turn signal.

"Is he going to the dog track?" Helen said.

"Not that man. He's headed for Big Irv's. It's right in front of the greyhound track."

They followed Francis into a blacktop parking lot. Irv's looked like a collection of sheds cobbled together. Francis grabbed a rusty grocery cart and rolled it past big boxes the size of playpens, filled with oranges and grapefruit.

Big Irv's was a throwback to the fruit stands of fifty years ago. There was no air-conditioning. Helen liked that. She usually carried a sweater with her. Florida buildings were kept at morgue temperatures. Irv's was warm, but pleasant. The fresh air released the smells of sweet fruit, bitter vegetables, and fresh earth.

Shopping was like hand-to-hand combat. Customers reached over and around one another for plastic bags, and used their baskets to edge their way to open bins of green beans and corn.

Irv's was the United Nations of produce. The aisles were packed with old women squeezing tomatoes, Hispanic mothers testing plantains for ripeness, Italians thumping eggplants. Tall Russian women weighed cabbages. Old men prodded spotted vegetables on the sale rack, looking for bargains.

Francis went for the most expensive items. He filled his cart with snow peas, blueberries, and raspberries. He brushed up against a shapely woman in a maid's uniform and she smiled at him. She had long black hair and a fetching overbite. Francis smiled back. She giggled. They talked for a bit by the kohlrabi, and then he gave her a business card.

Helen watched in amazement. "He picked her up. I can't believe it. What does a pretty woman like her see in him?"

"She's a smart one," Margery said. "She sized him up

the same way she checked out the broccoli. Francis
wasn't wearing a wedding ring, and he bought the most
expensive produce. She saw a rich, unattached man."

"But he's icky," Helen said.

"Ickier than mopping floors and scrubbing toilets?"

Francis carefully wheeled his basket past a staffer
opening cartons with a razor-sharp box cutter. Helen
and Margery each grabbed a cart and cornered Francis
by the strawberries.

"You!" he said. "Why are you following me?"

"To get the truth, Francis," Helen said. "We know
about Tammie and Willoughby."

Francis panicked and tried to bolt, but he was
blocked by their carts. He backed up, then leaped into
the apple bins, sending an avalanche of Red Delicious
onto the floor. They bounced and rolled with hollow
thuds.

"Hey! Get down!" yelled the staffer with the box cutter.

Francis vaulted over a mound of Golden Delicious
and slipped on a stack of strawberry boxes. They
cracked under his weight. He ran through the potatoes
and squashed the ripe avocados into guacamole.

Helen hefted a hearty two-pound sweet potato and
lobbed it at him. She missed, and it bounced into the
rutabagas. Margery started throwing tomatoes. Her
aim was better. She nailed Francis in the chest with a
swift, ripe shot, splashing his beige shirt with red color
and yellow seeds.

"What are you doing?" an old woman said.

"He killed his wife," Margery said, and hit him again.
That woman had quite an arm.

"She's a crazy old lady," Francis screamed.

It was the wrong thing to say in that crowd. The
women launched a tomato attack. The largest was
thrown by the pretty maid with the overbite.

"Coward!" she screamed. "Wimp! Here's what I
think of men who kill their wives!" Her tomato hit him
in the ear. Francis winced at her words. Her contempt
hurt worse than her well-aimed tomato. He had to jus-

tify himself to all these people. He had to explain to the pretty maid.

"I loved her." Francis's cry was ripped from his throat. His face was now as red as his shirt. "I loved her and she laughed at me. She deserved to die."

That did it. Furious women begin hurling hordes of produce and specialty foods. "You sound like my pig of a son-in-law," said a woman in a black wig, as she slung a jar of kosher pickles at the fleeing Francis. He tried to escape into the yellow onions. A young woman jogger blocked his run and beat him with a bunch of broccoli. A mother swung a bag of Idaho potatoes at his crotch.

Someone opened the refrigerator case and brought out a carton of eggs. The first one landed on his shoe with a yellow *splat!*

"She drove me to it," Francis shouted. "She left me for another woman."

There was silence, except for a juicy tomato that plopped off a counter. Francis was splashed red with juice and mashed fruit. A single blueberry stuck to his forehead like a jewel. A banana was squashed on his back, and something green and leafy sat on his head, like a Roman laurel wreath. The sharp tang of pickle juice made an eye-watering cloud. The floor around him was slippery with pasta sauce. Its red splashes looked like a crime scene.

"She was going to run off with Tammie and take our dog," Francis said.

"That's terrible," a trembling old man said. "To leave you like that and take your dog."

"Our dog is Barkley, the Davis department stores mascot," Francis said. He started to climb off the mound of onions, but Margery blocked him with her cart.

"That cute little puppy?" the jogger said.

"I've seen those TV commercials. That dog is worth some money," the old man said admiringly. His chins wobbled and he steadied his hands on his cart.

"My wife was going to live off our dog and keep her girlfriend in style," Francis said. "Our innocent puppy would support their lesbian lifestyle."

"Shouldn't happen to a dog," the old man said.

"It shouldn't happen to a man," Francis said. "I was humiliated, but I thought I could fight it in court. When I tried to talk to my wife about custody of Barkley, she said the woman she left me for was a better man than I was. I couldn't take it. I picked up a tree branch and bashed her in the head. I didn't mean to. The next thing I knew she was on the ground and she wasn't moving. I killed the woman I loved."

He was weeping now, unless the tears were caused by the yellow onions.

"I want to end it all!" he said.

"He has a box cutter," a woman shrieked.

Francis held it to his own throat. "I can't live with the shame," he said.

My God, Helen thought. One slash and he's dead. I've done this.

"Put it down, son. A jury of your peers would understand," the shaky old man said. He was clinging desperately to his shopping cart, and Helen feared the excitement would be too much for him.

"Yeah," a beefy younger man said. "Get a bunch of guys on the jury and we'll let you go."

The women glared at the men and brandished their produce in a threatening manner. Helen was afraid another food fight would erupt and Francis would kill himself before she could reach him. She looked at the horde of angry women, including the contemptuous maid. Suddenly she knew the words that might save him.

"It wasn't your fault," Helen said, stepping around several honeydew melons the size of bowling balls. "It was a crime of passion."

"Passion?" Francis said. His knobby knees and narrow shoulders were not the stuff of passion. But he said it again, more firmly this time. "Passion."

"You did what any red-blooded man would do," the beefy young guy said. The women growled, and he quickly shut up.

"You were overcome with passion," Helen said.

The pale Francis liked that. He wasn't a cuckolded

wimp. He was a man of passion. "Yes," he said. "I did it. And it was a crime of passion!" Willoughby's widower lost his hangdog look. He put down the box cutter on a pile of green-pepper cartons and squared his narrow shoulders.

The crowd applauded.

Helen was relieved to hear the police sirens.

CHAPTER 29

....

Some things were better at night. With the help of the softening shadows, Helen could have explained everything to Phil. She knew he would understand why she couldn't tell him what happened in St. Louis.

But Helen missed her chance. She and Margery had slipped away from Big Irv's as soon as they heard the wailing sirens. They came back to the Coronado, and spent a restless hour or so pacing and drinking coffee. At six o'clock they turned on the TV news. Willoughby's killer was in custody. Dozens of people had heard Francis's confession, and were eager to tell the television audience. The case was solved.

Margery and Helen proceeded to celebrate Helen's victory. Some celebration. Helen had one glass of white wine. One lousy glass. Then she fell asleep in the chaise longue by the pool.

"It's the stress," she heard Margery whisper to Phil. "She's been running on worry and adrenaline since that damn dog disappeared. Let her sleep. You can talk to her in the morning."

No! Helen wanted to say. She tried to struggle up from the sleep-numbed darkness. She felt Margery and Phil carry her home and put her to bed. They slid off her shoes and pulled cool, comforting sheets over her. She heard the clink of dry food hitting Thumbs's bowl and knew someone had fed her cat.

"Phil," Helen said. "Please stay so we can talk," she wanted to add, but she slid down the long tunnel of unconsciousness.

The next thing she knew, someone was knocking on her front door and her bedroom was flooded with harsh, hot daylight.

"Helen! Wake up! I need to talk to you," Phil said.

Damn. She didn't want Phil to see her like this, baggy-faced and dry-mouthed. She didn't want to try to explain herself now. Helen wasn't a morning person. She couldn't muster the right words until noon. She squinted at her bedside clock. Seven a.m. Five hours before she could talk sense.

"Coming," she said, and stumbled over her shoes.

Helen shrugged on a lumpy pink bathrobe. She felt frumpy, but didn't have the strength to put on something better. In the bathroom she looked in the mirror and winced. She hoped those were sleep wrinkles on her face. She brushed her teeth. An ice pick of pain hit her in the head when she bent over the sink. Her lipstick looked too dark on her washed-out face. She wiped it off. A zit shone like a beacon on her chin.

She opened the front door and threw up her hands against the sun like a vampire.

"Good morning, beautiful," Phil said.

He was so damn cheerful in the morning. Helen would have hated him, if he wasn't so good in bed. A woman would put up with a lot for a man who would—

"Hello, anyone in there?" Phil said. His chin looked freshly chiseled. He had a clean, just-shaved scent. He balanced two coffee mugs and a white pastry box on a tray. Phil kissed Helen hard and handed her the box. "Chocolate croissants."

"Yum," she said. "Come into the living room."

Helen swept the newspapers off the couch and set down the tray. Thumbs came up and rubbed against Phil, leaving a white patch of cat hair on his dark pants that would have annoyed a lesser man. Phil scratched the cat's chin until he flopped over in ecstasy.

"I wanted to catch you before you went to work this morning," Phil said.

"I don't have to go in until noon," Helen said. She sounded whiny. She managed a smile that rearranged her sleep wrinkles and sat down on the couch next to Phil. He leaned back, put both his feet on the boomerang coffee table and one arm around her. She snuggled next to him.

"Thanks for the coffee," she said, and kissed his neck. "Ummm. The croissants are warm and flaky."

"Like me," Phil said. He kissed her again, a morning kiss of toothpaste and coffee that made Helen want to go further. She felt his slight hesitation. Then Phil pulled away and said, "You need to eat. I have strict instructions from Margery to make sure you have breakfast."

Was that the reason? Helen wondered. Or was he still angry with her?

"Eat," he said, and jammed a croissant into her mouth like a groom with a piece of wedding cake. Helen bit into it and sent a shower of buttery flakes all over the couch.

"You know what I like about you?" he said. "You aren't worried about crumbs on your couch and feet on your coffee table."

"I was in another life," she said, then wished she hadn't. That was an invitation to a forbidden subject. "This furniture has been around for half a century. Nicks and scrapes give it character. Now, tell me what you've found, since you woke me up at this awful hour."

Phil finished half a croissant while Helen tried to contain her impatience. He had one flake on his upper lip. She longed to lick it off, but now she was hungry for information.

"I've found the owner of the black van, the one you saw Jeff getting out of," Phil said, and brushed off the errant flake. "It belongs to a Fort Lauderdale artist. He's quite expensive, does mostly portraits in oil. Very popular with the new rich. His name is Robard Raxley."

"Rax!" Helen said. "Tammie and Willoughby both

had Rax portraits in their homes. He's the John Singer Sargent of Fort Lauderdale. He can make any rich woman look like a grande dame."

"Jeff seems to like artistic men," Phil said. "First the decorator, then a portrait painter."

"I don't think this is an assignation," Helen said. "According to Todd, Jeff brings the man envelopes. Large, thick envelopes."

"So you're thinking blackmail?" Phil said.

"Absolutely," Helen said. "Maybe the painter saw something when he was painting Tammie and he's blackmailing Jeff. There's definitely a connection between Tammie, Willoughby, and Jeff, and the painter can connect the dots. I like it."

"But wait, there's more," Phil said like a game-show host. "I've got news about your animal-loving friend, Betty. I don't know what she was doing the afternoon that Tammie died, but she wasn't playing golf. She's not down in the club book for any tee time that day."

"I saw her leaving the Stately Palms grounds with her golf clubs in her car," Helen said.

"Right after Tammie was murdered," Phil finished. Then he finished off the croissant and licked his fingers. Helen watched him hungrily.

"Turns out our Betty has a violent streak when it comes to saving helpless creatures," Phil said. "Margery mentioned two arrests. I found those, plus two more. Betty also punched out a lawyer who tried to drown a bag of kittens in his swimming pool. She rescued the kittens and busted the guy's nose. He decided not to press charges for assault."

Phil reached for another croissant and sent another shower of crumbs over the couch.

"Betty also stole a corgi that belonged to a CPA who lived on her street. He left the dog locked up all day and it barked itself into a frenzy. Betty saw the corgi in the window, foaming at the mouth. She broke the window, rescued the dog, then decked the owner when he came home. He hit his head on the fender of his Mercedes. Those charges were dropped, too."

"Betty can afford the best lawyers," Helen said.

"Someone may also have explained to the animal abusers what the publicity would do to them," Phil said.

"That's true. Would you want a lawyer who drowned little kittens?" Helen said.

"Under certain circumstances, yes," Phil said.

Helen swatted him playfully. "We have quite a crop of suspects here," she said. "Jeff and Betty are serious possibilities. Tammie's husband looks even better, except he has that pesky alibi."

"I'd like to spend some time looking into what Mr. Kent did that afternoon," Phil said. "I want to know more about the salesman who was supposedly with him while he test-drove that car. It would be nice if someone poked around in the salesman's bank accounts, looking for recent large deposits."

"Know anyone who could do that?" Helen said.

"Possibly," Phil said, and winked.

"I don't care what the police think," Helen said. "Jonathon didn't murder Tammie. But if he goes to trial, I'll have to testify."

"So you testify." Phil chomped more croissant.

"I can't have my ex-husband find me," Helen said.

"There's more to it than that, isn't there?" Phil said.

"Yes," Helen said.

"Are you going to tell me what happened in St. Louis?"

"Someday," Helen said.

Phil got that shutdown look Helen hated. He took his arm back and began brushing off croissant crumbs.

"I'd better go," he said.

Tell him, whispered a voice. Tell him or you'll ruin everything. Where are you going to find another man like Phil?

"Stay," she said. Her finger lightly traced the crooked path of his nose. She kissed his ear, which was covered with peach fuzz. Helen longed to say more, but she couldn't. No one, not even Margery, knew her whole story. They only had pieces.

That's what you're giving Phil, pieces of yourself, but

not your whole self. He knows it. Helen could feel the chill between them. She could see their love start to die in the frost.

I can't help it, she thought. The only person I can rely on is me. I can't trust any man completely, not after what Rob did to me.

The wounds love inflicted were deep and difficult to heal. Helen thought of Francis, pelted with tomatoes, stained with strawberry juice, beaten with broccoli. The scene at Big Irv's was ridiculous, and yet it wasn't. Francis had been driven to madness by his wife's betrayal. He struck back at the woman who'd ruined his life.

That woman wasn't Willoughby. It was Tammie.

"He killed Tammie," Helen cried.

"Who did?" Phil said.

"Francis," Helen said. She was talking faster now, her words skimming and skipping along. "He killed both women, Tammie and his wife. Think about it. Francis knew the housekeeper. Lourdes didn't meet him somewhere. He went to the Grimsby house to give the dog to Lourdes. She left with the dog, and Francis went in to see Tammie. Tammie said something ugly and he stabbed her."

"With grooming scissors?" Phil said, frowning. "Where did he get those?"

"He probably had a pair. Barkley was a dog who always had to look perfect. Her owners would be trimming stray hairs all the time. Francis had those scissors with him. Can't you see it, Phil? Doesn't it make perfect sense? Tammie taunted him. Francis hated her. She cuckolded him. He lost it and stabbed her."

"How do you know that?" Phil said with the irritating male reasonableness that seemed so condescending. "Maybe he wasn't mad at Tammie at all. He blamed Willoughby for leaving him. He should have blamed himself. He dragged his wife to those threesomes in the first place."

"No! He killed Tammie first," Helen insisted. "Once you kill someone, it's easier to murder the second time. He lost it again and killed his wife. But that's the only murder that really upset him."

Phil sighed with impatience. "Helen, this doesn't work for me."

What, she wondered—our love or my theory? She loved Phil too much to lose him. She wanted him to see things her way.

"Even if it is true," he said, in a semiconciliatory tone, "how are you going to find out anything new that will convince the police?"

"I'll talk to Todd again. He was at Tammie's parties. He may have seen something I can use."

"Todd?" Phil's sarcasm was acid. "You're talking about a hustler, a blackmailer, and a gigolo. Now there's a witness with credibility."

"Phil," Helen said. "Listen to me. This is the only scenario that makes sense. Francis killed his wife's lover first, then he killed his wife. Francis has already confessed to murdering his wife. But he did them both. He can't admit that. Florida is a death-penalty state.

"Todd may be a nasty little blackmailer, but he notices things no one else does. That's why he's a good blackmailer. He saw that black van and noticed Jeff was meeting the driver and bringing him fat envelopes.

"Lucinda said Francis was moping around and drinking at those parties. She forgets half of what she says, depending on what she ingested that day. But I'll bet Francis said or did something we can use, and Todd heard it. It's certainly worth a try."

"Helen, this is really far-fetched," Phil said. "Betty is a better suspect, or even Jeff. Five minutes ago you thought Kent was the best candidate for the killer—and he was there at the shop. He could have stolen the scissors. I think I can break his alibi. You're wasting your time with Todd."

"I'm not," Helen said. She was desperate to make him see. "It's only seven thirty in the morning. We can be at Todd's condo before he leaves for work. He'll talk to me away from the shop. I'll ask him a couple of questions, and I'm out of there."

"Todd's not going to tell you anything," Phil said. Was that a flash of contempt or anger in his eyes?

"Todd will talk to me. I know he will."

"Why should he?" Phil said.

"Because I've got something on him," Helen said.

They were sitting upright on the couch, looking less like lovers and more like an insurance salesman with a difficult client. Thumbs paced at their feet, uneasy with their raised voices.

"All right," Phil said. "I'll drive you over there."

"No, Phil, you don't need to. I can handle a pretty boy like Todd."

"That's crazy, Helen," Phil said. "No cop would go there alone."

"He won't talk with you around," Helen said.

"Then I'll wait in the parking lot," he said. "If you're not down again in twenty minutes, I swear I'll come up and get you."

"I'll be fine," she said, but she was secretly pleased. Phil still cared.

"Helen," he said, "don't jump in feetfirst and start firing off accusations. You have to be careful of slander. Francis hasn't been convicted of anything yet. A smart lawyer could get him off, and then he'll be looking for revenge. You don't know if he's friends with Todd. Don't use Francis's name. This can come back and bite you. Hint around. Subtlety isn't your strong suit, but try it this time for your own protection."

"Right," she said. "I'll hit him as hard as I can with my subtlety."

CHAPTER 30

Todd opened his condo door with a surly hello, then stepped awkwardly aside, so he stood behind the door.

It's a trap, Helen thought. He's going to hit me.

She entered warily, holding her purse up for protection, prepared to use it like a bludgeon. Her keys were in her hand, ready to gouge.

Once inside she knew why Todd stood behind the door, and nearly laughed with relief. He'd stepped aside to show off his view from three walls of windows. Todd's condo seemed to float seven stories above the water, suspended in the tender morning light.

"Wow!" Helen said.

Todd had waited for that reaction. He wanted my approval, Helen thought. No, he needed it. He craved it like a junkie. He had to have other people's admiration. His own wasn't enough.

The scenery was spectacular. To the east, the ocean was an improbable turquoise dotted with white cruise ships. Straight ahead was the Intracoastal Waterway, wide and silvery gray, lined with the golden homes of the rich. A swath of silver and gold as far as Helen could see.

Straight down was a canal with boats, white as wedding cakes and as full of promise.

Infinity on three sides, Helen thought. The ocean stretched into forever. The Intracoastal was an immeasurable river of money. The boats below promised endless ease.

Todd's long living room was the perfect setting for the scenic view. The two white couches, the pair of tapestry chairs, the dark carved table with the single white orchid all glowed in the pearly morning light.

Helen looked at Todd's angelic face. She knew some of the ugly things he'd done to live high in his heaven. She could guess the rest. Yet he was flawlessly beautiful, except for the slight weakness around the mouth, and she might be imagining that.

Todd seemed different in his condo, more self-assured. He moved toward Helen with a slight, dangerous swagger that must thrill his women friends. "Why are you here at this hour?" he said.

"I need to ask you one quick question," Helen said.

"You couldn't wait until we were at work?" Todd said.

The angry edge to his voice made Helen uneasy. She decided to fight back. "You wouldn't want me to ask it at the shop. I'm doing you a favor coming here."

"I need a cigarette," Todd said. "Come on outside."

He took a cigarette from a silver box on the carved table and a silver lighter engraved with his initials. The lighter was from Tiffany's, Helen guessed. She wondered which woman gave it to him.

She followed him out onto the narrow balcony. The boats down below rocked and swayed in the water. Helen felt dizzy at first; then she was fascinated by the view. Two fishermen in a little Boston Whaler chugged along the Intracoastal. A needle-nosed speedboat roared past them, leaving a wide white wake.

Todd lit his cigarette with quick, sure movements, sucking in the smoke greedily. He said nothing. Helen waited. She wanted him to speak first.

They watched a white two-masted sailboat on the Intracoastal. It seemed to be stalled in the water. Two people ran frantically along its deck, pulling and pushing at things, but the boat didn't move.

"If you've got a question, ask it," Todd said. "I have to go to work." He blew a smoke ring.

Helen looked for some trace of the hungry country boy in his face, but she saw only the polished pretty boy with the diamond-studded Cartier watch. She remembered Phil's warning about subtlety and lawsuits. Now she understood. The people who lived here used lawyers as often as she used Kleenex.

"I wanted to ask you about a man I know," Helen said. "I can't name names yet, but he was well-known for his way with women." Helen thought that was a tactful way to describe a bottom grabber.

"He's already confessed to a serious crime. We know—and we can prove—that he's actually guilty of two crimes. The second one is the murder of Tammie." It was a small lie. She couldn't prove anything right now, but she thought she could risk the lie.

Todd looked into the distance, beyond the boats. He blew another smoke ring. Then he said, "You say 'we.' Anyone know about this person besides you?"

"A private investigator has copies of the information." Another lie, but she didn't think Todd would catch her. Once he told her what she wanted to know, she didn't care if he found out. "We're taking the information to the police whether you help us or not. But you can make it easier for everyone."

"Any way I can stop you from going to the cops?" Todd said.

"No," Helen said.

More silence. Obviously he knew about Francis. Todd seemed to be calculating something. Helen thought he might be worried that his visits to Tammie's parties would become public. That could scare off his rich widows. As Lucinda said, rich women didn't like boys who'd been around too much. They got nasty bugs. What would happen to Todd if he couldn't comfort his lonely widows and divorcées? His dog-grooming income wouldn't cover the condo maintenance fees at Sailboat House.

Todd took a deep drag on his cigarette and stared out at the water. "I knew this would happen. I was expecting the police. But I should have known you'd stick your nose where it didn't belong." Todd seemed suddenly weary and much older. For the first time Helen noticed lines around his mouth.

"I—" Helen started to say.

Todd interrupted. "I know what you're going to ask. The answer is yes. I killed Tammie."

Helen gripped the railing. The balcony seemed to rock and sway like the bobbing boats far below. She didn't expect this. She was sure Francis was the killer.

But then she remembered confronting Todd at the shop about blackmailing Jan Kurtz. "I know what you did to that woman," she'd said. Todd had dropped a case of dog food and turned deadly pale. He agreed to stop blackmailing Jan too quickly. Helen thought it was her great persuasive powers. Now she knew better: Todd was relieved that Helen didn't know about a far worse crime—Tammie's murder. Her heart was thudding. She wanted to ask a hundred questions. But she remembered Phil's caution about subtlety and suppressed them.

"I did the one thing no gigolo should ever do. I fell in love," Todd said. He was still staring ahead.

"With Tammie?" Helen said.

"Isn't that a joke? Tammie was my soul mate, if the two of us have souls. We were cut from the same cloth, and it was cheap. We both used people for money. I did well at it. Tammie did better."

The sailboat was still adrift on the Intracoastal, seven stories below. A white speedboat approached and cut its motor. Helen could see people talking to one another on the two boats, then the sailboat began tying up to the speedboat. A third boat joined them.

"So when did she drop you, Todd?" Helen said.

"Two months after we began seeing each other. It started when one of my ladies brought me to a Tammie and Kent party. I just went for grins. I wasn't expecting anything serious. But it was love at first sight."

"For you," Helen said.

"For me," he said. "Not for her." He seemed to be talking more to himself than to Helen. He watched the struggling boat and smoked thoughtfully. A breeze play-fully ruffled his golden hair. The two motorboats were towing the long, beautiful sailboat. It was bigger than both of them, but absolutely helpless.

"After that night, Tammie asked me to come to her house when Kent wasn't home. I saw Tammie in the af-ternoons, three or four times a week. She was incredible in bed. For the first time in my life I was in love. Really in love. I didn't want any money from her. I just wanted to be with her. I trusted her. I told her everything: who I was, where I came from. She knew my real name. She knew my deepest secrets."

"Pinkie," Helen said.

Todd flinched. All these years later, it still hurt.

"She laughed at me when I told her that story. I thought it meant she didn't care what I'd been. She didn't care, period. Then one afternoon she said she didn't want to see me anymore. She kicked me out. Just like that." He flipped the lighted cigarette over the rail. Helen followed its long fall. It landed on the dock, bounced once, and rolled into the canal.

Just like you treated your women, Helen thought. There was a God, and she was just. Todd was talking faster now. "I came back the next afternoon and begged to see her. I bought her presents—a diamond pendant and yellow-diamond earrings. She threw them on the lawn and told me to go away. I said I loved her. She said I bored her. She said I was as shopworn as my pawn-shop presents."

His Cartier watch glittered in the sun. His silver Tiffany lighter gleamed.

"Tammie said if I didn't leave her alone, she'd tell all my fine ladies I was the son of a murderer and a hooker. She said the Lauderdale ladies wouldn't have me in their apartments anymore. I might steal the silver and beat them up like my father. I was already a hooker like my mother. Blood will tell, Tammie said, and she'd tell if I didn't go away."

The hustler had met his match, Helen thought.

"I asked if there was another man. Tammie said she

was sick of men. She was going away with Willoughby as soon as her divorce was final and the custody battle for Barkley was complete."

Shrewd woman, Helen thought. Tammie was an aging trophy wife. Her bored husband was doing threesomes. It wouldn't be long before Kent found himself a younger blonde. Tammie knew it was unlikely she'd find another rich man at her age. Rich old men wanted younger women. But Willoughby would have enough money to keep Tammie happy, thanks to her model pup, Barkley.

"I could compete with another man," Todd said. "But not another woman. I was devastated, but I knew better than to make a fool of myself. I suppose you'd say it was justice. I'd been doing this to women for years. Now a woman did it to me."

"At least you kept your pride," Helen said. "You never saw her again."

"No. I cut her out of my life. Totally. Until the day Tammie burst into the grooming room," Todd said. "When I saw her, I fell in love with her all over again. I couldn't stand what Jonathon said to her. I wanted to protect her. But then she said that vicious thing to me."

The words had sounded so harmless to Helen. She heard Tammie say them again, and now she felt their stiletto flick: "I know what he is, just like I know what you are. Dare I say it in front of everyone? You're looking in the pink." Then she'd laughed. Now her laughter seemed brutal. "And how are your dear parents? Mummy still famous for her entertaining in Okeechobee? Daddy still in silver trading?"

Todd's mother was a prostitute. His father was a house thief who stole the family silver. Tammie had taunted him about his awful parents.

Then, for a final twist of the knife, Tammie reminded Todd of the most humiliating day of his life.

"You don't know what it's like," he said. "Being an outsider all the time. Looking in on other people's lives, people with everything. People with decent parents and real families. For a short time I belonged. I was one of them. Then she took it all away and laughed at me."

Helen couldn't tell if he was talking about Tammie or the long-ago high school vixen, Mindy.

"I wanted to kill her." Todd looked at Helen, his beautiful face twisted with rage.

"So you did," Helen said.

"I told myself I was going to say good-bye to Tammie before I left town. I wanted her to apologize, make her take it all back. Then I could go. I had the money. I'd called Jan Kurtz for one last payment. She didn't want me coming to her condo because the neighbors would talk. Jan brought the money to the store. I was never coming back here again.

"I stole Jonathon's grooming scissors, although I wouldn't admit why even to myself. I wrapped them in a dog bandanna, so my prints weren't on them, and stuck them in my belt. Then I drove to Tammie's house. Her husband and her housekeeper were both out. I walked right in on Tammie. The door was unlocked and she was sitting by the pool, naked. She was drunk. She didn't think I was any threat. Who's afraid of a boy toy?

"She said, 'Well, if it isn't Pinkie, begging for one more time.' Then she laughed. She wouldn't stop laughing. She said, 'Can I get you a drink? How about a pink ribbon?' She kept laughing and saying, 'Pinkie. Pinkie.' I wanted to make her stop. I stuck the scissors right in her chest. It was over in one quick motion."

"Except it wasn't," Helen said.

"No," Todd said.

The day was perfectly still. The two boats were still towing the stately sailboat. They'd reached a tricky turn. They were trying to steer the huge boat into a smaller canal. Helen thought the sailboat was going to crack up on the dock as it rounded the corner.

Todd was still talking. "When I killed her, part of me went dead. Now I can't run away and I can't stay. I can't sleep anymore. I keep seeing her. I miss her. I love her, even after all she did to me. I hear her laughing at me, calling me Pinkie. I'm ruined for escort work. I'm not . . . I can't . . . I can't get it up with my ladies. I'm useless. My life is over."

The sailboat slid closer to the dock, while the people on deck screamed and scrambled for ropes and poles. Helen watched, fascinated by the prospect of the elegant disaster.

When she looked back, Todd had one leg over the balcony.

"Todd, what are you doing?" Helen said. Panic made her voice shrill.

"I'm going to end it. I can't live without her."

"She's not worth dying for, Todd."

"Life is not worth living without her."

"Please, Todd, think what you're doing. If you turn yourself in, the police will work something out. You're young. You've had a hard life and a cruel beginning. A jury will be kind to you. You won't serve long, even if you are convicted."

Helen was pleading now. She'd talked Francis out of killing himself. She could stop Todd. She had to stop him. She couldn't have his death on her conscience.

"Everyone will know," Todd said. "Not just the whole school—the whole world. They'll all laugh at me, like she did."

"Todd, no!"

But he was over the balcony rail. Helen made a wild grab for him and nearly went over herself. She caught his Cartier watch by the band. Now he hung by it, seven stories above the docks. Todd looked at her, confusion on his face. He tried to claw for the railing, but he missed. The leather watchband broke, and he fell with a short, surprised shriek.

Then there was silence. The silence seemed to go on endlessly, for the rest of Helen's life.

She heard her heart pounding. Another pounding was even louder. "Helen! Are you in there? Todd! Helen! What's wrong? Open the door or I'll break it down." It was Phil.

She was still holding Todd's Cartier watch. It sparkled in the sun. She saw the minute hand move.

CHAPTER 31

....

"He jumped," Helen said.

Her words were like a bludgeon. Phil actually flinched.

He pushed his way inside Todd's condo. "Are you OK?" he said, then answered his own question. "No, you're not."

Helen felt like she was standing behind a wall of glass. There was nothing scenic about it. It was a dead place, devoid of all sensation. She could see Phil and talk to him, but she couldn't feel anything. She had trouble forming sentences. Each word was like a lead weight. She dropped her purse twice and stumbled over nothing.

"Let's get out of here," Phil said.

"Prints," Helen said. "My prints may be on the railing." She was ashamed that her mind worked that way, but she'd lived on the run too long.

"Women's prints are going to be all over this apartment," he said. "You worked with Todd. If the police mention it, you can say you dropped by last night and admired the view."

Phil hustled Helen out of Todd's apartment, stopping to wipe down the doorbell, the only part she'd touched. "With any luck," he said, "the building manager will leave his prints all over this door."

He pushed her toward the fire stairs. Helen ran down

seven flights of steps. She landed at the bottom, panting and rubber legged. Phil followed behind.

No one seemed to notice them. Helen and Phil saw a man in a suit get off the elevator, but he was busy juggling his morning coffee and his briefcase. A woman walking her beagle waved as if she knew them. They waved back. A lean jogger stared straight ahead, seeing only her goal of physical perfection.

Phil and Helen had slipped into the stream of traffic on Federal Highway by the time the first police car roared by, lights flashing, sirens screaming. Phil drove with one hand and rubbed Helen's neck with the other, then pulled her closer. She was rigid but unresisting.

"Why did he do it?" she said. "Why did Todd kill himself? He didn't have to confess to anything. He knew that. He was street-smart. Even if he said he killed Tammie, it was his word against mine. He could deny it later. Instead, he jumped. Why?"

"Because he wanted to," Phil said. "He wanted to confess and he wanted to die. He loved Tammie and he couldn't live without her. He must have been planning to kill himself for a long time. You were simply the excuse."

"But Tammie was worthless."

"Not to him," Phil said.

Helen wanted to cry, but she was sealed behind the glass wall, dry and lifeless as a museum exhibit. The only emotion that reached her was fear. Terrifying questions would suddenly jump out at her, like assassins in a dark alley.

"Phil, what if the police find my fingerprints on Todd's skin?"

"Fingerprints on skin are rare," he said. "They don't happen in real life nearly as often as they do on *CSI*. Did Todd scratch you?"

She checked her wrists and hands. "No. I'm clean."

"Then you're safe. There's no skin under his nails. The medical examiner will see there was no sign of a struggle. He probably won't look for prints on Todd's skin."

Helen felt better for about thirty seconds, until another worry leaped out at her. "What if the neighbors heard you pounding on the door and told the police?"

"What neighbors?" Phil said. "Did you check out the windows when we drove past that building? Half those condos are shuttered. Their snowbird owners won't be down until December."

A third fear attacked her. "What if they find my fingerprints on top of Todd's where he went over the railing?"

"Then we're fucked," he said.

Oddly, that answer calmed her. Phil pulled the Jeep into the Coronado parking lot. Helen said very formally, "I can never thank you enough, Phil. But I want to be alone now."

Phil, white faced and strained, seemed relieved to be away from her.

Helen didn't go to her apartment. She walked to a pay phone on Las Olas to call in sick at the Pampered Pet. Jeff answered the phone. She could tell by his voice that he hadn't heard about Todd.

"I'm so sorry you're sick," he said. His sympathy nearly brought tears to her eyes, except she couldn't cry. "There's a nasty cold going around. My Bill had it last week. Eat lots of chicken soup and call me in the morning."

Helen walked back home, still protected by her wall of glass. The life around her looked like a museum exhibit. A wise old hound sniffed the red flowers around a tree, then lifted his leg. A woman with a yellow shopping bag got out of a cab. A businessman talked importantly into his cell phone. Ordinary people. Nice people. People who never drove a young man to his death, never watched his beautiful body fall seven stories, never saw it lying broken on the ground. Helen didn't deserve to be out in the sunshine with normal humans.

Helen went home, locked her apartment door and closed the blinds. She sat in her Barcalounger, rocking back and forth. Thumbs seemed to sense her distress. The big-pawed cat jumped in her lap. The sight of his solemn round head comforted her. She dozed, but her dreams were tormented. She saw Todd reaching for the railing.

About noon Margery knocked on Helen's door and woke her up. "Phone call from your boss," her landlady said with a smile, and handed Helen her cell phone. Phil hadn't told Margery what had happened or she wouldn't be grinning like that. "Just bring it back when you're finished."

"Helen? It's Jeff." She heard his horror and distress in those three words. "Todd's dead. The police think he killed himself."

"They do? I mean, he did?" Helen said.

Jeff was too upset to notice her slip. His voice was heavy with tears. "Todd killed Tammie. That beautiful boy killed her and now he's killed himself. The police found unfinished suicide notes in his condo. They say every time he wrote, 'I killed her,' he'd put the letter down, then he'd start another. The cops said there must have been fifty of them. This morning, about eight o'clock, he jumped off his balcony. A woman walking her dog found his body."

"He wrote suicide notes?" Helen said. Why didn't she feel relieved? Those notes were her absolution.

"That's what the police say. You know why he killed Tammie? Because she laughed at him."

"Uh," Helen said. Now there was a brilliant response.

"How are you feeling?" Jeff said. "You sound terrible."

"It's just a cold," Helen said.

"Well, rest up and don't worry about coming in to work. I'm closing the store today and tomorrow. It's better that way. No reporters will be in asking awkward questions. I'm shocked about Todd, Helen. I can't believe it. But at least it's over. Jonathon will be exonerated. You were right: He's innocent. I thought that would make you feel better."

"I feel terrific," she said in a flat voice.

Helen snapped the phone shut, stuck it in her pocket, and walked over to Margery's.

"Come in," her landlady said when she heard Helen's knock. She was punching numbers on her microwave pad. Her gray pageboy brushed her brown shoulders.

Her purple top had a jaunty row of ruffles. Her purple sandals had flirty little bows.

"I'm nuking a brownie," she said without turning around. "Want one?"

"Todd killed himself. I saw him die," Helen said. She sounded like a zombie.

Now Margery turned and looked at her. "You're way too calm. You're in shock. Sit down and tell me what happened."

"He killed Tammie. I tricked him into admitting the murder. Then he jumped off his balcony. I tried to save him, but I couldn't. It's all my fault."

"What an ego you have," Margery said. "If Todd killed himself, it was his decision. He was a murderer, a blackmailer, and a hustler. His death must have been terrible to see, but we're well rid of him. Here, drink this coffee. It's loaded with milk and sugar. You need it."

Helen took a sip. She could actually taste it.

Margery put a warm square of brownie in front of her. "Eat," she commanded. "And don't argue."

Helen ate. After she got the first bite down, she was surprisingly hungry. "Do you know why he killed Tammie?" she said. "Because she laughed at him. That was all."

"All? That's everything," Margery said.

"I guess it was." Helen told her landlady about Pinkie and the ribbons. Margery listened. With her wrinkled brown face, she looked like an intelligent shar-pei.

"That woman stabbed him in the heart," Margery said. "Then he did the same thing to her."

Helen heard the opening bars of Jimmy Buffett's "Margaritaville" coming from her pants.

"That's my phone," Margery said. "I programmed it to play Florida's state song."

Helen pulled the phone out of her pocket, and Todd's watch fell out with it. Once again Helen saw Todd's confused face, heard his short shriek, and saw him falling toward the sunlit canal. It glittered like the diamonds on his watch. Helen's wall of glass shattered, and she was crying.

"It's about time," Margery said, but her voice was soft with concern. She turned off the phone and plunked down a jumbo box of tissues. Helen wept noisily, then blew her nose with airhorn honks.

"Why don't you sit in the recliner and rest?" Margery said.

"I don't want to sleep." Helen was afraid of what she might see when she closed her eyes.

"I didn't say you had to," Margery said. "Sit down."

The purple recliner seemed to enfold Helen in its pillowy depths. She was so tired. She woke up at six o'clock that evening, wrapped in a purple afghan. Margery had turned up the volume on the TV.

"Hi, bright eyes," she said. "I thought you'd want to hear this."

It was a press conference with a police spokesman.

"Is the case closed then?" a reporter asked.

"We believe that Tammie Grimsby was killed by a jealous dog groomer, who then committed suicide out of remorse. We found several partially finished suicide notes in the suspect's home."

"It's over," Helen said. "They're not going to arrest me or make me testify."

"There's that ego again. It's not about you," Margery said. "It never was."

A TV reporter interviewed Tammie's widower. Kent wore a shirt with black toucans all over it. Florida mourning. Kent tried to look solemn, but Helen thought he seemed gleefully relieved.

"This groomer guy, Todd, was, like, obsessed with my wife, Tammie, after he met her at a party," Kent said. He did not mention the party entertainment. Apparently the reporter didn't know.

"He came to the house with all these diamonds and sh—stuff. Tammie said she didn't want them. She threw them on the lawn. She was a married woman, you know."

Helen nearly choked. She was surprised that Tammie told her husband about the jewelry. Then it made perfect sense. The last piece fell into place.

Tammie had used Todd to make Kent jealous.

EPILOGUE

·····························

Helen kept Todd's watch on her dresser, and wound it every morning. She couldn't figure out if it was Todd or her own guilt she was trying to keep alive.

She'd been arrogant and overconfident. Because she'd talked Francis out of killing himself, Helen thought she could save Todd, too. She misunderstood the situation. Pale Francis didn't love or hate with Todd's intensity. Willoughby's husband had needed a reason to live, and Helen gave it to him.

Todd had wanted to die. He'd already made up his mind. He'd written those half-finished suicide notes, hoping to summon the courage to kill himself. She'd helped him over the balcony.

It was hard for Helen to walk into the Pampered Pet her first day back. It never got any easier. She saw Todd everywhere: flirting with his ladies, carrying heavy cases for customers, kissing his dogs.

A little murder and suicide didn't hurt the store. In fact, business was better than usual. Everyone made an excuse to stop by and say they knew Todd was guilty and Jonathon was innocent.

Jonathon was back as the flamboyant star of the Lauderdale grooming world. He wore gold lamé for his return, and marched into his private room like a monarch reclaiming his throne. He would tantalize his admirers with glimpses of his outrageous outfits. But Jonathon still refused to talk to anyone. His tantrums were forces of nature. Customers were thrilled when he unleashed his rage on them. In the midst of one techno-tantrum, Helen thought he winked at her.

Jonathon's secret was safe. Jeff and the Pampered Pet customers never learned he was a family man living in Davie.

Other secrets were revealed after Todd's death. Jeff finally told Helen why he was meeting Rax in the van. "He's painting a picture of my Bill," Jeff confessed. "I keep taking him candid photos of Bill for the portrait, but Rax wants more. He's such a perfectionist. I haven't told anyone but you, because I want it to be a surprise."

The animal-loving Betty told Margery where she was the day Tammie died. She really did go to play golf at the country club. The tee time was in her friend Zelda's name. But as the two women were heading for the country club, Zelda got a call. Her aging mother had taken a turn for the worse at a Boca Raton nursing home. The golf date was canceled. Zelda rushed off to see her mother. Betty stopped by Tammie's to squeeze more money out of her. Tammie insulted her and she left. Then Lourdes the housekeeper got the call from Francis and she left. Tammie was alone at home when Todd arrived.

Perhaps if Tammie had been more polite to Betty—or more generous—Betty would have stayed longer and Tammie might be alive today.

Francis admitted that he'd locked Helen in the big cage. He'd come to the shop to kill her. Willoughby had confronted him with Helen's find. She'd said that Helen had a witness who saw him pull that alibi receipt out of the trash. She also told her husband that Tammie was a better man than he was. Francis killed his wife in a red rage. He was lucky, at least for a while. Willoughby hadn't called Detective Ted Brogers with Helen's find yet.

Francis drove straight to the store to kill Helen before she went to the police with her alibi-breaking information.

He was going to wait for her in the parking lot. But then he saw Todd and Jeff leave. The shop door was unlocked. When the lights went off, Francis thought it would be easy to kill Helen in the store. He could make it look like a botched robbery. Inside the pitch-black store, he realized Helen would be the perfect suspect for Willoughby's murder. Francis left her alive and trapped in the cage.

Barkley the model pup lost her contract with the Davis Family Dollar department stores when they learned of her mistress's lesbian love affair. The dog was ruined as a family store mascot. Her only job offers were for Internet porn sites. Francis pleaded guilty and was serving eight to ten years. He couldn't keep the dog, anyway. He wasn't permitted to profit from his crime.

Willoughby's only relative, an eighty-year-old aunt with a tiny apartment, didn't want the boisterous pup. She gave Barkley to the one person who really wanted her—Tammie's housekeeper, Lourdes. Barkley lived happily ever after, frolicking in the yard in Hialeah.

A month after Todd jumped off his balcony, Helen picked his watch off her dresser. She took the bus to the Fort Lauderdale beach. It was the same endless ocean she'd seen from Todd's balcony, but up close it seemed warm and friendly. She watched a young mother and her baby laugh and slap at the waves. Then a big wave drenched the pair, and Mom snatched her child back from the wild water.

Poor Todd, Helen thought. Love took him by surprise. Men like Todd didn't fall in love with women. They were supposed to love him. Tammie was indeed his soul mate: as coldhearted as he was and just as mercenary.

The wave-slapped little boy had stopped crying. His mother gently dried his face with a blue beach towel and tickled him until he giggled.

At least Todd loved someone, Helen thought, however heartless she was. That was an achievement. It was more than Tammie had managed.

Helen looked at the sparkling Cartier watch with the broken leather band. Then she threw it into the sea. She walked to the nearest resort hotel and went in the back way to the employee entrance. She was met by a gruff guard in a beige uniform.

"Are you hiring?" she asked.

Ah, the wonders of Florida. Helen had no hotel skills. But she spoke English and she didn't have to worry about a green card. She was hired on the spot as a chambermaid.

She gave her notice to Jeff that same day.

"Why, Helen?" Jeff seemed hurt that she was leaving. "I thought you liked it here. Didn't I treat you right?"

"I love you," she said. "But I can't stay here. I keep seeing Todd everywhere. I think I need the company of strangers."

"What will you be doing?" Jeff said.

"I have a job at a hotel as a maid. I won't be tempted to get to know people. They'll stay a few days and leave. I'll like it that way."

They shook hands, and then Jeff drew her in for a hug. "Come back if you change your mind," he said.

Lulu followed Helen to the shop door, her tail wagging. Lulu's outfits were getting as outrageous as Jonathon's. Today she swanned around in a leather biker outfit embroidered with BITCH WITH A BAD ATTITUDE.

When Helen opened the door, Lulu made a mad dash for the Briny Irish Pub. "You go, girl," she said, and laughed.

It was the first time she'd laughed since Todd's death.

Helen still couldn't sleep through the night. In her dreams she was forever reaching for Todd. She'd wake up to find the sheets twisted and sweaty. The bedroom walls would close in on her, and she'd go outside in the cool night air.

Phil found her at six o'clock one morning, standing by the Coronado pool, staring at nothing. He'd just gotten up himself, and his hair had a cute little-boy cowlick.

"Still feeling bad about Todd?" he said.

She nodded.

"Come for a ride with me," he said.

Helen would have followed him anywhere with that cowlick. They climbed into his battered black Jeep. It was a chilly morning, and the plastic windows were zipped up. The sky was streaked pink and orange. A1A, the oceanside highway, was free of the tourist hordes at that hour.

At the old beach town Lauderdale by the Sea, Phil found a parking spot near the ocean. "Let's walk on the beach," he said.

The ocean was a translucent pearly gray. The morning was theirs, except for the seabirds and another pair of lovers sitting cross-legged on the beach, watching the sunrise.

Helen and Phil walked in comfortable silence, following the curve of the beach.

An old man was swimming in the cold water. A young man sat on the sand in a yoga position that made Helen's legs ache. Helen walked and watched the waves until she felt tired and peaceful.

Finally they came to Anglin's Fishing Pier. Warning signs declared the pier closed due to storm damage, but the Pier Coffee Shop was open. It was a gray building about the size of a boxcar. Tacked on the outside were battered turquoise booths overlooking the water.

Helen and Phil sat at an outside booth, the sharp morning wind driving them closer together. A waitress poured hot mugs of coffee to warm them.

"Number two," yelled the cook from the kitchen, and the waitress scurried inside to pick up an order, then came back out for theirs.

Helen and Phil watched a red tractor trundling down the beach, pulling a triangular attachment that cleaned and smoothed the sand, wiping away all traces of yesterday.

"I love you, Helen," Phil said. "But I won't live with lies and secrets. Tell me what happened to you. If you don't trust me, I understand. But then it's over between us."

Helen saw her life without Phil, stretching into lonely infinity.

"I want to, Phil," she said. "But then you'll know too

much about me. You can send me to jail. I trusted a man once and he betrayed me, and that's how I wound up on the run. What if I trust you, and you do the same thing to me? I'll lose everything: my life, my home, my new friends. I can't start over again, Phil. I won't. I can't give you that power over me."

"But I gave you that power," Phil said. "You know I do undercover investigations. You can burn me. You can kill me."

Helen felt as if he'd slapped her. "I would never do that to you," she said. "How could you even think that?"

"And I would never betray you," Phil said. "My life is in your hands, as your life will be in mine. If you tell me, we will be equals. We will both have everything to lose—and give."

Helen looked at the man she loved, and saw he was right. It wasn't a question of power anymore. They both held the same power over one another. And so she told him her story. Phil didn't offer solutions. He didn't interrupt. He seemed to listen with his whole body until she finished.

"My ex-husband, Rob, and the court are looking for me and if they find me I'll have to go back to St. Louis," she said. "Nobody but my sister, Kathy, knows where I am. I can't even trust my mother. She wants me to go back to Rob."

"What do you want to do?" he said.

"I want to stay at the Coronado," Helen said. "I want to keep on living this life. I want to love you."

"Then that's what you'll do. If you ever want to try to straighten things out in St. Louis, I will help you."

"I don't trust the law, Phil," Helen said. "I don't believe in legal justice, not anymore."

"Then we'll do it your way."

Seagulls screamed around them. They held hands and watched two shaggy dogs play in the surf.

"This place is enchanted," Helen said. "But I read somewhere they may sell the pier to developers and close the coffee shop."

Phil shrugged. "I hear that rumor every other week,

and the place is still going strong. It's true the coffee shop could close someday. A hurricane could come by next week and blow it away. Or the hurricane could blow us away. Unless we're hit by a car or run over by a bus.

"It's here now, Helen, and so are we, and that's all that matters."

Then he kissed her, and at that moment she believed him.

Read on for a sneak peek at another
Dead-End Job mystery, by Agatha and
Anthony Award–winning author
Elaine Viets. . . .

Murder with Reservations

Available now from Obsidian

The young couple looked like inept burglars sneaking through the lobby of Sybil's Full Moon Hotel in Fort Lauderdale. They were both dressed in black, which made them stand out against the white marble. At their wedding two days ago, they'd been slim, golden, and graceful, trailing ribbons and rose petals through the hotel.

Now they moved with the awkward stiffness of amateur actors trying to look natural. The bride's black crop top exposed a midsection sliding from sexy to sloppy fat. The groom's black T-shirt and Bermudas failed the test for cool. They were boxy rather than baggy. He looked like a Grand Rapids priest on vacation.

The honeymooners avoided the brown plastic grocery bag swinging between them, carefully ignoring it as it bumped and scraped their legs. That screamed, "Look at me." They stashed the bag behind a potted palm while they waited for the elevator.

"Red alert," Sondra at the front desk said into her walkie-talkie. She was calling Denise, the head housekeeper. "The honeymoon couple just passed with a suspicious grocery bag. They're getting out on the third floor."

"I'll check them out," Denise said. She was stocking

her cleaning cart with sheets and towels in the house-keeping room.

Denise turned to her coworker, Helen Hawthorne. "We've caught the honeymooners red-handed. I'm going to investigate. You stand by as a witness. I'm rolling."

Rhonda, the third hotel maid, squawked almost as loud as the walkie-talkie. "I'm coming, too. This affects my life." Rhonda, stick-thin and excitable, ran around the cart like a dog yapping at a car.

"Quiet, please," Denise said.

Rhonda shut up at this stately squashing.

A woman of substance, Denise rolled her cart down the hall with slow deliberation. Helen followed. Rhonda skittered at the rear, skinny body rigid with rage, red hair flying. She looked like an electric floor mop.

As the bridal couple stepped out of the elevator, Denise moved majestically past them, bumping the groom with her massive cart. The grocery bag slipped to the floor. Cans and bottles clattered on the carpet. The young woman flushed scarlet. The young man stuttered apologies, even though the accident was Denise's fault.

"Here, let me help," Denise said, reaching for a bouncing bottle.

"And me." Helen corralled a rolling can and stuffed it back in the grocery bag. Rhonda folded her skinny frame to pick up a brown plastic container.

Once everything was back in the bag, the young couple ran for their room. Denise waited for the slam of their dead bolt. Then her cart rumbled solemnly back to the housekeeping room. Rhonda and Helen crowded inside the room. Rhonda's pale face was set with furious determination. "If you think I'm—" she said.

"Shush," Denise said. "I have to make my report to the front desk."

The walkie-talkie squawked like an angry parrot. Denise talked through the static. "Sondra, I saw two cans of whipped cream, two squeeze bottles of Hershey's syrup, and no evidence of ice cream."

"Suspicions confirmed," Sondra said through the electric crackle.

Rhonda started wailing like a storm siren. "Oh, no. I'm not cleaning whipped cream *and* chocolate out of their Jacuzzi." Angry brown freckles stood out on her pasty face. "The whipped cream alone took me a solid hour. I had to climb inside the tub to clean it. I'm calling in sick tomorrow."

"The honey on the sheets was bad enough," Helen said. "Sticky stuff put me off my breakfast toast. How many more nights are the food lovers here?"

"A whole week," Denise said. "Maybe now that they know we know, they won't use the whipped cream and chocolate."

"They'll use it," Rhonda said. "Once a couple gets on the sauce, they won't stop."

"At least they've stayed clear of the produce," Denise said. She reminded Helen of a vegetable goddess. Her broad bosom was twin cabbages, her tight white hair was a cauliflower and her powerful arms were blue-ribbon zucchini.

"Maybe they'll have a fight," Helen said hopefully.

"Ha," Rhonda said. "Those types never do. They just bring in weirder and grosser stuff, and we have to clean it up. And they never tip."

"If you want your job, you'll be here tomorrow at eight thirty," Denise said.

The head housekeeper silenced any further discussion with a glare. Her massive arms maneuvered the cart out the door. "Helen and Rhonda, take the third floor. Cheryl will work the second floor, and I'll do one."

"I hate three," Rhonda said, when Denise had trundled out of earshot. "It's the hottest and dirtiest floor in the hotel."

"And we're the newest workers," Helen said.

"After two years, I'm entitled to some consideration," Rhonda said. She yanked their cleaning cart so hard it smacked the door frame. "Denise saves the best jobs for herself. She cleans the lobby and the free breakfast room. They're easy."

"I don't think mashed bananas in the carpet are any easier to clean up than whipped cream in the Jacuzzi,"

Helen said. "The lobby's white marble and glass shows every scuff and fingerprint, and people leave disgusting things in the fountain. They're supposed to make a wish and throw in money, not half-eaten candy bars."

"You missed the kid who threw in his baby brother and wished he'd drown. Sondra had to leap the front desk and do a lifeguard rescue in the lobby. Ruined her good blouse."

The memory of Sondra's loss cheered Rhonda. The woman ran on resentment. She was an odd creature with a round white face like a cocktail onion. Her vibrant red hair seemed to suck the color out of the rest of her. Helen thought she was plain, but she saw men stare at Rhonda. They found something about her bony body compelling.

"We're not going to get anything done standing around yammering," Rhonda said. "Might as well get started."

"What's the room count today?" Helen said.

"Full house," Rhonda said, checking her sheet. "All twenty rooms on this floor are occupied: seventeen queens, two kings, and the honeymoon suite." Thirty-seven beds and a foldout couch, twenty refrigerators, twenty-one toilets, twenty tubs, and the dreaded Jacuzzi. Sixty-five mirrors and sixty wastebaskets. Twenty carpets to vacuum and twenty-one bathroom floors to mop.

"Checkouts versus stay-overs?" Helen asked.

That was the crucial question. After the guests checked out, the rooms required a deep cleaning. Even the insides of the drawers were dusted. For stay-overs, the maids scrubbed the bathrooms, made the beds, and emptied the wastebaskets. If they were lucky, guests piled suitcases, clothes, and papers on all the furniture, and it couldn't be dusted. More stay-overs meant a shorter cleaning day.

"Six stay-overs," Rhonda said.

Fourteen checkouts. A long day. More sore muscles. Helen had worked at the hotel one week and she was just beginning to get over the back pain and muscle aches. She still winced when she had to kneel at the tub or reach for a mop. Cleaning hotel rooms required backbreaking amounts of bending, stooping, and lifting. After her first day Helen went home at three thirty in the afternoon and curled up with a heating pad and a bottle of Motrin. She woke up at seven the next morning, feeling like she'd been stomped in an alley.

Helen figured she was combining work with working out. She wouldn't have to waste time exercising when she got home. She'd have more time to sit by the pool and drink.

"Our first room is a stay-over," Rhonda said. She maneuvered the cart so it blocked the door, then knocked. "Hello? Anyone home?" Rhonda pounded and shouted until Helen thought she overdid it.

"I'm not taking any chances," Rhonda said between shouts. "Not since I surprised that naked geezer getting out of the shower. He was too deaf to hear me knock."

"Ever see any flashers?" Helen asked.

"All the time," Rhonda said. "It's always the guys with the little weenies. A man with something worth seeing never shows it."

Satisfied that the room was empty, Rhonda opened the door with her passkey. The room looked like an explosion at a rummage sale. Dirty clothes and smelly shoes littered the floor. Shirts and shorts spilled out of suitcases. Hamburger bags and drink cups cluttered the dresser. Something crunched under Helen's foot.

"What's that?" Helen asked. She was afraid to look.

"Cheerios," Rhonda said. "Usually means there's a baby in the room. People with little kids are big slobs."

"Is that a diaper on the bedspread?" Helen said.

"Yep. A dirty one. People use those spreads for diaper-changing stations, among other things." Rhonda pulled off the bedspread and piled it with the clean pillows.

"Yuck," Helen said. "Shouldn't we throw the spread in the wash?"

"No. Our bedspreads get cleaned every two weeks."

Helen's stomach lurched.

"Hey, we're better than most hotels," Rhonda said. "But I'd sooner sleep in a Dumpster than on a hotel spread."

"Why didn't they put the diaper in the wastebasket?" Helen said.

"That's on top of the TV to keep it away from the baby."

"Well, I'm glad this room is a mess," Helen said. "There's less for us to clean. We can't dust around all that junk. How do you want to divide the work?"

"I'll make the beds. You take the bathroom."

Rats. Helen hated cleaning bathrooms. Half the human race wasn't housebroken, and people shed worse than long-haired dogs. This bathtub was a hairy horror. Wet towels turned the floor into a swamp. Helen picked them up by the corners and prayed the brown stains were makeup. She didn't have much time to brood. Helen and Rhonda had exactly eighteen minutes to finish each room.

The next room was a checkout. The smell of sweat and smoke slugged them when they walked in the door. Cigarette-butt mountains overflowed the ashtrays. Helen counted eighteen beer cans tossed near the wastebasket. Two made it into the can.

"A male smoker," Rhonda said. "The worst kind of slob."

"How do you know it's a guy?" Helen said.

"Look at the john. I swear I'm going to paint targets on the toilets. Oh, man. This is so disgusting."

"What?" Helen asked.

"The guy ate peanuts and threw the shells on the floor. Peanut shells take forever to vacuum out of the carpet. You know, I can understand people thinking, 'I'm on vacation and I'm going to enjoy myself.' So they behave like total slobs and wreck the room. But if they're going to indulge, at least tip. Some women leave a couple of bucks for the privilege of throwing their towels on the floor. But men expect to be picked up after. Men are pigs."

"The men in this hotel are," Helen said. She didn't think Phil was a pig, but this was no time to praise her nearly perfect boyfriend. Rhonda wanted to rant. Helen didn't mind. A raging Rhonda cleaned faster. The two women had the room done in eighteen minutes flat, peanut shells and all.

They spent the next two hours companionably cleaning and complaining, until they were in the zone. That was when they moved through the rooms, swift and wordless, creating their own tidy ballet. Rhonda did the beds. Helen did the bathrooms. Rhonda dusted. Helen cleaned the mirrors. Rhonda vacuumed. Helen mopped. The room was done and they were on to the next one.

By two o'clock they had three rooms to go. One was a checkout. One was occupied. The last was 323, the hotel's most notorious room. Whenever anything went wrong, it was always in 323. This was the room with the loud parties. Wives caught unfaithful husbands and started bitch-slapping battles in 323. People did drugs and threesomes in that room. One man killed himself with pain pills.

Some staffers thought the room was jinxed. Others believed the problem was the location. Room 323 was near the back exit to the parking lot, so guests thought they could sneak in and out. But the security cameras caught them lugging in giant coolers or hiding little Baggies, smuggling in old hookers or underage girls. The guests in 323 were drunk, loud, rude—or all three.

Room 323 was a smoking room, and even on a quiet day it was the dirtiest of all.

"Wonder what's waiting for us today," Rhonda said.

"It can't be any worse than the dirty diaper on the bedspread," Helen said.

"Trust me, it can," Rhonda said.

Before they could find out, there was a walkie-talkie squawk from Sondra at the front desk. "The woman in two twenty-three says there's water running down her walls," she said.

"Did you say water on the walls?" Rhonda shook the walkie-talkie, in case it had garbled the words.

"You heard right," Sondra said. "She thinks it's coming from the room upstairs."

"That would be three twenty-three," Rhonda said.

"Of course it would," Sondra said.

"I'll look into it," Rhonda said, with a martyred sigh.

She knocked and pounded louder than ever on room 323, but the only response was silence. This wasn't a peaceful quiet. It felt ominous. But Helen knew the room's deadly reputation.

Rhonda snicked open the door with her key card. They heard the running water the same time as it sloshed over their shoes in an icy wave. Cold water was roaring into the bathtub full force and rushing over the tub's sides in a man-made Niagara. The bathroom floor was flooded.

Rhonda waded into the bathroom. "Look at this," she moaned as she turned off the faucet. "We'll be in here till midnight."

Helen sloshed past the disaster area into the dimly lit bedroom. At first she wondered why someone had left a pile of pillows and a Persian lamb stole on the unmade bed. Then she realized she was looking at acres of white, doughy skin. A broad back and broader bottom were carpeted with curly black hair. The hair wandered down the backs of the meaty thighs and across the upper arms. There were little hairy outbreaks on the fingers and toes.

A naked man was lying facedown on the bed.

"Not another suicide!" Rhonda shrieked like a lost soul. "I can't take it."

Rhonda's screeches jabbed at Helen like a rusty knife. The maid had turned into a creature from a horror movie. Her pale face was corpse white, and her long red hair looked like a curtain of blood.

Rhonda couldn't stop screaming, but her frantic shrieks did not wake this man. Helen didn't think anything would.

Don't miss the Dead-End Job series from national bestseller

ELAINE VIETS

Shop till You Drop

Murder Between the Covers

Dying to Call You

Just Murdered

Murder Unleashed

Murder with Reservations

Clubbed to Death

Killer Cuts

"Wickedly funny." —*Miami Herald*

"Clever." —Marilyn Stasio,
The New York Times Book Review

LOOK FOR THE BOOKS BY
ELAINE VIETS
in the Josie Marcus,
Mystery Shopper series

Dying in Style

Josie Marcus's report about Danessa Celedine's exclusive store is less than stellar, and it may cost the fashion diva fifty million dollars. But her financial future becomes moot when she's found strangled with one of her own snakeskin belts—and Josie is accused of the crime.

High Heels Are Murder

Soon after being hired to mystery-shop a shoe store, Josie finds herself immersed in St. Louis's seedy underbelly. Caught up in a web of crime, Josie hopes that she won't end up murdered in Manolos...

Accessory to Murder

Someone has killed a hot young designer of Italian silk scarves, and the police suspect the husband of Josie's best friend. Josie tries to find some clues—because now there's a lot more than a scarf at stake, even if it's to die for...

Murder with All the Trimmings

Josie Marcus is assigned to anonymously rate year-round Christmas shops—easy enough, she thinks, until she learns that shoppers at one store are finding a deadly ingredient in their holiday cake. Josie must get to the bottom of it all before someone else becomes a Christmas spirit.

The Fashion Hound Murders

Josie Marcus has been hired to check out a pet store's involvement with puppy mills. When the employee who clued her into the mills' existence shows up dead, Josie realizes that sinking her teeth into this case could mean getting bitten back...

Available wherever books are sold or at penguin.com